Dino Martini might accept his friend Seth as a lover—if they can stay alive.

Dino Martini is an old-school P.I. in a modern age. Sure, he may do most of his work on a computer, but he carries a gun, drives a convertible, and lives on the beach. Best friend and mechanic Seth Donnelly will back him in a fight, and there's not a lot more Dino could ask from life.

Until his world is turned upside down.

A dangerous case and a new apartment are just the start. His friendship with Seth has turned into a romance, only Dino has never had a boyfriend before. Can he handle this sudden twist? Just as he begins to believe it's possible, he loses Seth in more ways than one...

Books by Elle Parker

Dino Martini Mysteries
Like Coffee and Doughnuts
Like Pizza and Beer

Published by Kensington Publishing Corporation

Like Coffee and Doughnuts

A Dino Martini Mysteries Novel

Elle Parker

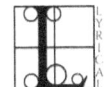

LYRICAL PRESS
Kensington Publishing Corp.
www.kensingtonbooks.com

Lyrical Press books are published by
Kensington Publishing Corp. 119 West 40th Street New York, NY 10018

Special book excerpts or customized printings can also be created to fit specific needs. For details, write or phone the office of the Kensington Special Sales Manager:
Kensington Publishing Corp.
119 West 40th Street
New York, NY 10018
Attn. Special Sales Department. Phone: 1-800-221-2647.

Kensington and the K logo Reg. U.S. Pat. & TM Off.
Lyrical Press and the L logo are trademarks of Kensington Publishing Corp.

First Electronic Edition: May 2009
eISBN-13: 978-0-98241-705-8
eISBN-10: 0-9824170-5-5

First Print Edition: May 2009
ISBN-13: 978-1-61650-900-2
ISBN-10: 1-61650-900-7

Printed in the United States of America

I had a lot of support and encouragement from a lot of people while I was writing this book, and I want to thank everyone who cheered me on. There are a few people who deserve to be thanked by name because they went above and beyond, and I want them to know how important they are. Lynda—who got me started on this, kept me going, and put me back on the right path.

Sara—who is willing to take time from whatever she's doing to dissect plot points, run scenarios and trouble shoot with me.

Ande—who'll shake her pompoms any time you ask, and who was always cheering me on. She also gives great beta.

Amberly—who gave me some great advice and a solid lesson in how to really critique my own work.

My sister Tracy—who was the first to say, "Hey...you've really got something here." And who gave one very sage piece of veterinary advice.

...

Chapter 1

When I went into Ed's Garage looking to get backup from my friend Seth, I knew immediately my job was going to be harder than I'd thought. Seth and his latest "date," a blonde with short spiky hair and pretty legs, were tangled up on top of a red Ford Torino necking like the world was coming to an end. Neither one of them had a shirt on, but she wore a black and pink polka dot bra. She also wore a pale green skirt under which Seth's hand had disappeared. My timing wasn't good, but I was glad I hadn't come any later.

She saw me first and gave me a pretty smile, apparently not too disturbed by a stranger walking in on her fun. Seth was doing something to her neck that might have been kissing, but reminded me of the way he ate.

She prodded him and said, "Hey, we've got company."

When Seth raised his head, he looked surprised, but that quickly changed to irritation when he saw who it was. He didn't need to say a word for me to know exactly what he was thinking.

I smiled. "I thought you had to have the hood *up* to do a tune up."

"Not when we start with me first," he said. "Don't you have someplace better to be?"

"I'm sorry, I had no choice. Believe me, I did not want to do this, but duty calls."

"Tell duty to call back in about an hour, Dino." He went back to what he'd been doing.

"You're Dino?" the girl asked, lighting up. "I've heard about you."

"Dino Martini, at your service," I said. "Nice...bra."

"Thanks." She grabbed a fistful of Seth's hair and pulled him up to look at her. "Don't be rude to your friend. He's obviously here for something important."

"He's here because whatever job he's got going this evening involves a high likelihood of him getting his ass kicked." He turned to look at me. "Am I wrong?"

I shrugged. "Hard to say with a case like this, but I don't like to take chances."

"What now?" Seth looked defeated already, which was good, because it meant this wouldn't be nearly as difficult as I'd thought.

"Cheating wife," I said. "You know how those can be."

"Yeah, yeah, all right."

Seth Donnelly is about five foot seven, has an unruly mop of carrot colored hair, and although he's thirty-three, he often acts like he's twelve. He's my mechanic, but he's also been a good friend for a lot of years, and there's no one I'd rather have next to me in a fight.

He slid off the hood of the car and told the girl, "I guess I'm gonna have to catch you some other time."

"That's okay," she said, climbing down and pulling her shirt on. "I have to get to work anyway. Can you look at my car tomorrow?"

"Sure, bring it by after three."

She gave him a quick kiss, got in the Ford and drove out, turning left, toward the beach. I was willing to bet she worked in one of the tourist bars down in John's Pass.

"Sorry about that," I said, turning to Seth.

"No sweat. Buy me dinner and we're square. She's cute enough, but her brother's the one I'd really like to nail."

I shook my head. "You bring a whole new meaning to the word 'sleaze', you know that?"

"Oh, come on, it's not like that. She knows. She's just in it for the fun and the free service on that wreck she drives. Did she look especially brokenhearted to you?"

"No," I admitted. "I can't say that she did."

"So tell me about the case," he said, grabbing his shirt off the workbench.

"Not that much to tell. This guy's had me following his wife for a while, and I finally caught her cheating on him with a long haul trucker. Turns out she's been meeting up with all kinds of them off a website called The Hot Trucker's Hookup."

"No shit, are you serious?"

"Yep."

"Sweet deal for the truckers, man. They can line up something everywhere they stop."

"That's pretty much the idea," I said. "They've got quite the little community on there."

I had followed Amy Ware all the way out to Florida's Interstate 75 and wound up spending an afternoon playing "Peeping Tom" through the ground floor window of a cheap hotel. On my fifth pass, I nearly swallowed my cigarette. She had her guy trussed up in a horse's harness and reins with the thing in the mouth and the whole nine yards, and she was ridin' him for all he was worth. I took easily fifty shots of that.

I'm kind of a mix between the old school P.I. and the modern "private investigator," which means I do my fair share of computer searches and background checks on top of the more traditional tailing of cheaters and mystery solving. But I drive a Mustang convertible, I carry a gun, and I live on the beach.

Well, close to the beach.

You are what you drive, they say, and I am a 1966 model of stylish sophistication with a sporty rakishness and a lot of muscle. Instead of Vintage Burgundy, though, I'm your average Italian color, and I have maybe a moderate amount of muscle. When I was a little younger, I had the classic Italian greaser look going on. Now I don't have quite enough hair on top to pull it off, but I'm told I still look pretty damn good.

I named the car Matilda because of her white ragtop, which makes her look like an old lady. She is, without a doubt, my most prized possession. I bought her eight years ago, after an especially lucrative case, and while she was in pretty good condition to begin with, Seth and I restored her to the level of perfection she exists in most of the time these days.

Outside, Seth dropped into the front seat next to me. He looked in the side view mirror and scrubbed his fingers through his hair. That's what passes for styling for him. He plucked his sunglasses out of the collar of his shirt and slid them on. It never fails to impress me how he can make slovenly look good.

"You goin' in carrying on this one?" he asked.

"I don't think so," I told him. "This guy is money. If he gives me trouble, it's going to be of the fist swinging variety, which is why I wanted you along."

"Are we gonna run it the usual way, then?"

"If you expect to be fed."

Certain people do not take bad news well, and if they can't lash out at the object of their anger, they'll often take it out on the closest thing available. I generally happen to be sitting across from them at that point, and I've learned to take precautions.

If the guy is big enough, or bad enough, I won't hesitate to slip my gun into a holster. Most of the time, I just bring Seth for backup. He may be small, but he's wiry and he likes to fight. Best of all, he'll do it for the price of a steak.

For situations like this, I prefer to arrange the meet in a nice dark bar. They're noisy, so you're not likely to get overheard, and you don't look out of place. Plus, it feeds the average Joe's romantic vision of a private eye. People seem to like it better if it goes down the way they see it on TV. And who am I to argue? I like bars.

The "usual way" is I go in first to find the client and get settled, and about five minutes later, Seth comes in and takes a seat at the bar where he can keep an eye on things. Nine times out of ten, nothing happens and he gets to enjoy a beer and flirt with the bartender, but on the rare occasion some idiot decides to take a pop at me, it's nice to know he's got my back.

I'd chosen a dive called Henry's, well outside of Ware's territory so there'd be little chance of him running into someone he knew. Not like it would be tough to explain, but I hate to put a guy in that position right after he's found out his wife is the Calamity Jane of the eighteen wheeler set.

I parked around back as usual. No sense in advertising what I drive if there's a chance there might be trouble. I grabbed my briefcase, which held the folder of photos, and climbed out of the car.

"See you in a few minutes," I said.

Seth saluted me and slouched in the seat.

Inside, Henry's was busy, but not packed. Mostly old guys with nothing better to do, or blue-collar types shaking off the workday. I spotted Ware in a back booth, clutching a glass of scotch or bourbon. He looked pretty grim. Of course, he had to know it was bad news. It doesn't take a face-to-face meeting for me to say, "Hey, your wife is pure as the driven snow and only has eyes for you, and by the way, I have some lovely shots of her shopping for Bibles."

I sat down across from him and set my briefcase on the seat. "Good evening, Mr. Ware."

A cute waitress with a ponytail and a low-cut shirt came over, and I ordered an amaretto on the rocks.

"Cut to the chase, Martini." He took a sip of his drink. "Amy's cheating on me, isn't she?"

"Yes, sir, I'm afraid so."

Seth strolled past me and plugged the jukebox, messing around with the touch screen for a minute before he took a seat at the bar. His way of letting me know he was in the room, since Ware had left me with my back to the door.

"Who is it?" Ware asked.

"Unfortunately, I wasn't able to determine that in such a short time frame," I lied. Since the guy was just one of many, I didn't see the need to share that information with Ware. "It's highly unlikely he's anyone local."

The waitress brought my drink, and I spent about half an hour explaining the deal with the truckers and the website to Ware. I also gave him instructions on how he could do a little sleuthing of his own on his wife's computer. He asked me if that was something I could be hired to do, and I told him it was, but I'd need access to her computer for a while. He said he'd hang onto my card and think about it.

When there wasn't much left to say, I brought out the folder and passed it across the table. He stuck it into his own case without looking at it. That's pretty common. Most people don't want an audience when looking at candid porn starring their beloved for the first time.

At this point, I usually like to say something sympathetic and heartening, maybe give them a bit of advice. I was just opening my mouth when a beer bottle whizzed past my face and bounced off the wall, nearly hitting Ware.

People were shouting and a couple of bar stools crashed to the floor. When I turned to look, a guy the size of a tank had Seth pinned like a bug on the bar, one meaty hand clamped around his throat. Seth gripped the guy's forearm and kicked his legs in the air, trying to score a hit or get away, I wasn't sure which. The ponytailed waitress bounced around, swatting at the tank with a bar rag and begging him to stop.

Ware looked horrified and shot up. "I think I should go. Listen, thanks for your time and trouble," he said, stuffing a check into my hand. "If I decide to have you do that computer thing, I'll get in touch."

I gave him a nod and a pat on the back and sent him on his way. Then I turned back to the scene on the bar.

"Rick, honey, come on," the waitress was saying. "He didn't mean anything. He's just a customer, babe, they say stuff like that all the time, you know that."

"I know his type," the tank roared. "All these guys think they can hit on you just because you bring 'em drinks. It's time someone taught 'em a lesson."

Seth squealed something in protest, but his throat was too constricted for anyone to make it out. He flopped like a fish out of water.

I drained the last of my drink and took a deep breath, then stepped up to the moose and tapped him on the shoulder. "Hey jack, why don't you let the little guy go, he wasn't hitting on your girl."

"Why don't you mind your own business?"

"This *is* my business," I snapped, getting up in the guy's face. I may be skinny, but I can intimidate the hell out of people when I want to. "I can personally guarantee he wasn't hitting on her, so why don't you get your fucking hands off him before I really get mad."

There was a crowd of people standing around us staring. I could see them all mentally calculating the odds of me against Rick the Caveman. The bartender hovered near the phone just in case. But see, I fight smart, and I know how to knock guys like this off their game.

"You can guarantee that?" he sneered, pausing in his attempt to strangle Seth. "And just how are you gonna do that when you weren't even here?"

"Because he's my *boyfriend*, jackass, and if you don't get your filthy paws off him, I'm gonna kick your ass."

A hush fell over the room, and Rick looked down at Seth like he was suddenly holding a rattlesnake. He yanked his hand away, and Seth immediately started wheezing air.

"You mean...you and him..." Rick tried to puzzle it out.

"That's right." I pulled Seth down off the bar and held him tight against me while he got his breath back. "And if I ever catch you trying to feel up my guy again, I'm gonna have to teach *you* a lesson. You got that, asshole?"

Rick's face turned pink and then red. He looked like I'd sucker punched him. "I was *not* feeling him up!"

"Yeah, that's what they all say." I went over to grab my briefcase, and came back pointing at him. "And yet time and time again, I got some big ox like you putting his hands all over my friend and I gotta' step in and break it up." I wrapped an arm around Seth and squeezed him. "Are you okay, baby?"

Seth sniffed. He was struggling not to laugh. "He hurt me, Dino. I was just having a nice beer and talking fashion with that girl and suddenly he was all over me."

I gave Rick a withering stare. "For shame," I said, steering Seth toward the door. "I really can't get over some people's manners. Think they can do whatever they like."

I glanced over my shoulder on the way out to see Rick dumbfounded, the bartender looking relieved, and the waitress trying not to crack up. Everyone else was already back to business as usual.

Seth fell into the car laughing his ass off. He rubbed his neck where Rick had grabbed him. "You realize half the bruisers in this town think we're dating?"

"Well, I am about to take you out and buy you dinner," I said, starting up the car and backing into the alley.

"Sure, but that's for services rendered."

I gave him a sideways glance. "Yeah, that makes it sound much better."

Seth smirked and hung his arm over the side of the car. Clearly, he wasn't traumatized by the incident.

"What did you do to set him off, anyway?" I asked.

"Oh shit, I was just flirting with the waitress a little. It was harmless. I told her those jeans must be from outer space because her ass is out of this world."

"Oh my God, did you really bring a lame line like that?"

"Sure," he said. "Us goofy little guys can get away with shit like that. People think it's cute."

"Cute and goofy are not what I'm generally going for when I approach women."

Seth rolled his eyes. "Because you're such a ladies man."

"I can be. I just have standards, is all. I'm very selective about who I choose to spend time with, whereas you'll fuck anything that moves. And several things that don't."

"Touchy, touchy," Seth said, reaching over to pet my hair. "It's all right, honey, you have a nice ass too."

I shoved his hand away. "Shut up and figure out where you want to eat."

"Aw...come on, Dino," he purred, crawling across the seat to breathe on my ear. "You chased off my sure thing for the night. The least you could do is take her place..."

A shiver ran down my spine in spite of myself, and I turned to give him the stony look I usually do when he gets this way. When I said he'd fuck anything that moved, I wasn't kidding. He's game for anything and anybody, and it doesn't matter what goodies they have on their plate.

"Dinner?" I reminded him. "Ideas?"

He sighed. "How about...the Oar House? I could eat a burger."

* * * *

After dinner, we went back to Ed's. My car was piled with the last load of boxes and suitcases from my apartment. The building was being torn down to make way for more condos, and Seth offered me his couch until I could find a new place to live.

The garage is a small red, white and blue auto shop located right next to the marina on the Intracoastal Waterway, between Madeira Beach and St. Petersburg. Seth more or less runs the place, since Ed has taken to spending all his time buying stuff at junk auctions and selling it on eBay.

When I pulled in, Ed's dogs were yapping and running around the parking lot. One is a pug with the coloring of a Siamese cat, and the other is an old mutt whose forehead is so flat she couldn't possibly have a brain inside.

I shut the engine off, and Seth got out of the car. He cast a glance over the mound of stuff in the backseat and shook his head. "Matilda looks like a pack mule, man. That is no way to treat a venerable old lady."

"Although you are absolutely correct, I would like to point out that this car is the exact same age as me, so watch it with the 'venerable old' talk. Where in the hell did you learn to use the word venerable, anyway?"

"I use words like venerable," Seth said, mildly disgruntled. "And Matilda is forty-one, that's like...ninety in car years."

"She may look like an old lady, but inside she still purrs like a kitten."

"Same as you," Seth said with a wink.

"I have never looked like an old lady." I grabbed the nearest box, shoved it into Seth's arms, and took another for myself, following him through the shop to the back room where the rest of my stuff was stashed. It took us three trips to get everything inside. The only things left in the car were my suitcase and garment bag, a box of stuff off my desk, and my laptop computer.

Seth took the box and I grabbed the bags, and we climbed the wooden stairway that ran up the outside of the garage to an apartment built over it. This was Seth's place. And mine, for the foreseeable future.

The steps creaked alarmingly and bounced more than I generally liked in my climbing apparatus. "Don't you worry about these falling off?"

"Naw," he said, pausing to lean on the railing and look back at me. "I used to, but that bugged me, so a couple of years ago, I spent about half an hour out here jumping up and down for all I was worth to see what would happen. Turns out they're more solid than they seem. Here I'll show you—"

"Do not jump on these steps right now, or I will smack the shit out of you."

Seth grinned and ran the rest of the way up.

Seth's monkey-like qualities extended to his living habits, and I never failed to be a little dismayed when I went into his apartment. Junk was littered everywhere. Magazines, pizza boxes, beer cans, laundry. Dirty dishes and open cereal boxes covered the counter in the kitchenette. The coffee table was spread with newspaper and sported a vast array of engine parts and beer cans. Behind that, against the wall, was a massive brown sofa with fat, low slung cushions. It was...pristine.

"You cleaned it?" I asked, disbelieving.

"Yup." Seth beamed. "I even pulled out the cushions and vacuumed all down in there. I knew you'd freak out about sleeping on it if I didn't."

"Since when do you own a vacuum?"

"I brought the Shop-Vac up here. Does the same job, right?"

"It would appear so," I said, putting my bags down on the one clean surface in the entire apartment. "Now all I have to worry about is what might crawl out of the darkness to get me in the night."

"Yeah, well, I think there's a box of doughnuts under the chair. You can toss those to distract it."

"You are disgusting, you know that?" I unzipped my garment bag and laid it out on the sofa. "Where can I hang my clothes up?"

Seth stared at me blankly.

"Got some space in a closet? I need to hang these up or they wrinkle."

"Um, right." Seth pivoted on his heel and kicked a path to the tiny coat closet by the door. He pulled a few computer boxes out of it and bounced them into a corner. "You need me to make some space in the bathroom for your curlers and make-up?"

"Fuck you. Normal people hang their clothes up. This is the usual way in which grown-ups do things." I bent down to look under the chair. "Are there really doughnuts under there? This is not a healthy way to live. Seriously."

Chapter 2

"There's a lot of apartments for rent in St. Pete," Seth said, reading the classifieds and taking a sip of his beer.

We were in the Blue Bottle, a dumpy place done in some kind of attempt at a beach house-sea shanty motif, which ended up looking more like an Italian crab shack. Worked for me. They had the typical seaside stuff on the walls, like starfish and life preservers, but the tables were covered in checkered red and white cloths and empty mayonnaise jars with candles in them.

"No way, I hate it over there. Hell, you couldn't get out of there fast enough, now you think I should live there? It's too bland. I came down here for the beach, and I want to stay by the beach."

"Too bland? You're worried about too bland?"

"Well, yeah. I gotta' live in a place with a little style, you know?"

"O-kay..." Seth said with a low whistle. "Dino needs a spicy apartment."

"Stylish," I corrected him. "Charismatic."

"Charismatic? You're gonna live in the place, not date it."

The bartender brought us steamed clams and chicken wings, and we shuffled the papers around, making room for the plates. I took a sip of my drink and started in on the clams. I love any kind of seafood as long as it's not in a condition to fight back, but I especially like food that requires a little effort to eat. I scooped one out of the shell and dipped it in butter.

"Mmm, man, these are good." I hummed, closing my eyes to savor it.

"Yeah, they're not too bad." Seth slurped one into his mouth and washed it down with a drink of beer. He wiped the butter from his chin with the back of his hand.

Seth will eat anything you put in front of him, regardless of the state it's in. I'm not even sure it has to be food. Let's just say I wouldn't reach in front of him to get the salt.

He bit into a chicken wing and flipped over the section of newspaper he was scanning. "Hey! Here's something," he said, marking the ad with a buffalo sauce fingerprint.

I took the paper from him and read out loud. "Madeira Beach. One bedroom apartment located in commercial neighborhood. No pets. No kids. No floozies. Call Adele."

"Got enough character for you?"

"No floozies? Are they serious?" I dunked another clam and ate it, staring at the paper. "If these are Bible nuts, I wouldn't be able to take it."

"Call the number," Seth said.

I pulled my cellphone from my pants pocket and flipped it open, checking the ad as I dialed. The phone rang several times, and I wondered if I was going to get anyone when there was finally an answer.

"Yes?" came the feeble voice of an old lady.

"Ah, hello, ma'am. Would I be speaking to Adele?"

"No. That's my sister-in-law." Her words were well formed and clipped at the end. "I'll get her."

I could hear her set the phone down and muffled voices in the background.

"Yeah, what can I do for you?" This voice was deep and gravelly, and you could just about hear the lung cancer over the line. There wasn't a doubt in my mind this woman was a heavy smoker and probably had been since prohibition.

"You have an apartment for rent?" I asked. "I'm lookin' at your ad here in yesterday's paper."

"You got pets?" she asked.

"No, ma'am. And I don't have kids, and I am most definitely not a floozy."

"You date 'em?"

"Nope, and I'm not really in the market for a roommate at the moment, if that's what you're getting at." The broad was blunt, but I kind of liked her. She sounded like she didn't take shit from anybody, and I doubted I'd have to worry about any Bible thumping going on.

"The apartment is on the second floor, six hundred a month, plus utilities. We don't put up with late payers, loud tenants, or people who mess up the place. And, you gotta' pay a three hundred dollar deposit and a month's rent up front."

"What about parking?" I asked. Seth nodded his approval.

"There's parking in the front, off the street."

"Sounds good. When can I come see it?"

"Anytime, I guess," she said. "We'll be around until tomorrow afternoon at least. You can come tonight if you don't make it too late."

"Tomorrow sounds great. What's the address? I could be there around ten if that works for you."

"That'd be fine. Nine twenty-seven First Street. Up past the Winn Dixie."

"Sure, I know the area. I'll see you tomorrow. Thanks."

She hung up the phone without saying goodbye. I put mine away and took a sip of my drink. It sounded promising. Madeira Beach is crammed into about two square miles, in the middle of a long string of other little beach towns, and the area she mentioned was convenient to everything.

"Well?" Seth asked, sucking the last bits of meat off a chicken bone.

I shrugged. "The price is right. Location might not be bad. You want to check it out with me?"

"Yeah, sure."

* * * *

"I can't believe you don't own a coffee maker," I groaned as Seth and I sat waiting for a stoplight. It was nine in the morning, and I didn't feel properly awake, since I hadn't been treated to my daily dose of caffeine for the second morning in a row.

Seth, on the other hand, was full of piss and vinegar and some neon puce colored drink that came in an industrial can. I didn't know the name of it, because I couldn't bear to watch.

"Coffee tastes like dirt," he said. "And it stinks after about the first fifteen minutes."

"It is a necessary part of life, and if you don't shut up, I'm going to kick you out of the car and run over you. Repeatedly."

Seth chuckled. "I said I would buy you a cup somewhere, just find a place and pull over."

"I know where I'm going. I refuse to drink convenience store coffee after the lousy night of sleep I just had."

* * * *

The apartment turned out to be a sweet deal, and I snapped it up. We signed the papers on the spot. Calling the First Street neighborhood a "commercial area" was a bit of a stretch. There was a plumbing outfit, the back side of a mini golf course, and the CVS at the end of the block. Everything else was apartments.

Adele's building was a plain, two-story block with a ground floor storefront and a big, faded sign over the door that read *Triggs Hardware*. The layers of dust on the plate glass windows suggested it had been closed for years, and from what I saw through them, it appeared the space was being used for storage now. The apartments, entryway and stairs were all clean and relatively well cared for.

It took a little charm, but I convinced them to let me move in right away. I used the same charm to get Seth to spend the day helping me haul furniture. I also used a lot of beer. Much as I enjoyed his company, I needed to be back in my own space as soon as possible, and I pushed to get as much done as we could in one shot.

Seth caught his end of the mattress as I slid it out of the truck, and we headed for the entryway. "You are a very surly man when you're on a mission," he said. "It's not at all attractive."

"I'll buy you dinner after we're done with this, how's that?"

"You have to buy me beer too."

"I already bought you beer."

"Yeah, but we're nearly out of that beer, and I'm going to need more beer later."

"Fine, I'll buy you dinner and beer."

"Next you'll be expecting me to put out."

Adele chose that moment to come into the hall, carrying a big, vinyl purse and a shopping bag. We were halfway up the stairs with the mattress, and she stopped and stared at us through huge, black sunglasses.

"Ah. Good evening, ma'am," I said, nodding to her. Seth grinned at me with the smug expression of someone who's not dealing with his own landlord.

"You can drop all that ma'am bullshit. Adele is fine. I thought Ruth said you weren't moving in until tomorrow." She had a sour expression that made me feel like a roach she'd discovered in her kitchen.

"Well yes, ma—Adele, she did say that, but you see there were extenuating circumstances, and when I explained them to Ruth she told me I could move in right away."

"What kind of circumstances?" she asked, all gravel.

"My friend is a pig."

Seth huffed in protest. "I'm not a pig, I just have a messy house."

"Your furniture has its own ecosystem."

"My furniture's fine, you're just a candy assed prima donna." He shoved on his end of the mattress and nearly plowed me over.

Adele shook her head. "I think this is where I came in," she said and headed down the hallway. "You won't be moving furniture around at all hours of the night, will you?"

"We're just going to do one more load this evening and get the bed set up. We won't be any trouble at all," I assured her.

"All right then, good night," she said, and left.

I scrambled the rest of the way up the stairs as Seth continued to mow me down.

An hour later I had my dining table and chairs set up by the kitchenette, and Seth was in the other room putting together my bed for me. He was clearly going for lobster and prime rib on my dime.

Chapter 3

The next morning I woke up and sighed with satisfaction. My back didn't hurt, my pillow smelled fresh and clean, and I wasn't itching any place suspicious. There are very few things as good in life as sleeping in your own bed, and I liked mine so much at that moment I rolled over and didn't get out of it until ten thirty.

That right there is one of the big reasons I decided to become a private eye. I don't like other people telling me what to do and when to do it. I'd much rather take care of business on my own schedule. If I want to sleep in, I sleep in, and if I want to work all night, then I work all night. This is also why I don't have roommates to speak of. Lovers can be as bad or worse than bosses, and I tend to like them better at a distance. Once in a while one captures my attention and I'm willing to be amused for a bit, but I meant it when I told Seth I'm selective. I haven't had a lot of success in the relationship department, and there aren't many people in the world I want to spend that much time with anyway.

Seth, on the other hand, treats sex and dating like one big party, and everyone's invited. He's deeply appalled by my loner lifestyle and is forever trying to set me up with people, both male and female. Because in his book, you never limit your options. For all I know, he's got the right idea. I've been attracted to a guy or two in my time, but never did anything about it.

When I'd finally had my fill of clean sheets and a soft mattress, I got out of bed and stretched luxuriously. I dug around in a box in the corner until I found a couple good CDs and took my player into the bathroom, where I cranked up Elvis and took a long, hot shower. That, too, was like heaven after Seth's place where I think new forms of life were breeding. Next time I use his bathroom, I'm wearing a Hazmat suit.

After a fairly obscene amount of time, even by my standards, I finally turned off the water and scrubbed myself dry with a towel—also clean, fluffy, and fresh smelling. Maybe I should have Seth stay at my place for a couple of days and see if he doesn't develop a yen for clean living himself.

The last thing missing from my perfect morning was hot brew. I wrapped the towel around my waist and went out to the kitchen, grooving to *Heartbreak Hotel*. I ground up coffee beans and measured them into the basket of the coffee maker, filled it with water, and switched it on.

I was about to go get dressed when there was a knock at my front door. Seth had left a doggie bag in my car with a hunk of prime rib, a few stuffed shrimp, and a pile of dinner rolls, and I figured he was back to get it. God forbid he should starve.

"Anything you leave in my car is fair game," I chided as I yanked the door open.

"Is that so?" said a regal looking dame with a slow Southern drawl. "In that case, you're likely to find me decorating your back seat, darlin'."

She was dressed in a flowy pantsuit kind of thing and glittered with jewelry, almost to the point of being overdone. Her perfect make-up and frosted hair suggested she was an expert at making herself pretty and never went anywhere without doing just that. I'd put her in her mid-sixties, but even so, she was unusually attractive, and back in the day she must have been quite a dish. The way she was looking at me made me feel like a main course. Cheap, and a little dirty even. Then I remembered I was half naked.

"Oh, ah...I'm sorry, I was expecting someone else," I said lamely.

"That's quite all right, honey," she said as she swept into the room. "You look just *fine* to me." She cocked her head and smiled, holding up the plate she was carrying. "I brought you some hot buns."

I clutched at my towel, because I had the distinct feeling if it fell off, I was the one who was going to get the shock of his life. This woman knew exactly what she was doing.

"You *are* Dino Martini, aren't you?" She extended a bejeweled hand over the plate of cinnamon rolls and said, "I'm Della Vinson Owen. I'm your next-door neighbor. I came to welcome you to our little family."

"That's very nice of you, ma'am," I said giving her hand a squeeze. "I'm sure I'll enjoy them very much."

She snatched the plate out of my reach and headed for the kitchen. "They're my own personal recipe, I'm sure you're going to just love them. Now, you have a seat and I'll pour us some coffee, and we can get better acquainted."

That fact that me getting dressed wasn't included in her list of instructions didn't escape my notice, and I began to get the feeling I could be in a bit of trouble. Not that I was especially worried about my virtue, but the last thing I needed was to piss off my neighbors right out of the gate.

"I was so happy when Adele told me we had a new tenant, and that he was a charming young man," she was saying as she poked around in my cupboards for plates to serve the rolls on. "I share the apartment next door with Ruth Fletcher."

"Adele said I was charming?" I raised an eyebrow.

She laughed. "Well, she didn't use that word, exactly, but she didn't use a lot of other words I've heard her call people, so I just read between the lines. And here you are, charming as anything."

She set the table with silverware and napkins, and put the rolls in the middle, then went back for coffee. Since it appeared I was going to have a brunch date whether I liked it or not, I snuck into the bedroom for some pants.

When I came back out a few minutes later, dressed in light slacks and a green silk shirt, she clapped her hands together and said, "Oh my, don't you look handsome. I do like a man who's a snappy dresser."

She took me by the arm and led me to the table, pulling out a chair for me to sit down in, and taking a seat opposite. She leaned forward, chin in hand, and said, "Now, tell me all about yourself."

"Not all that much to tell, ma'am." I tore off a hunk of my cinnamon roll and buttered it. "I grew up in New York, went to school there, then got sick of the cold weather, so I came down here. I like it, so I've stayed here ever since."

"And what do you do for a living? I bet it's very exciting."

I knew that was a standard line and it didn't matter what I said. She'd claim to be incredibly impressed even if I told her I sorted bolts, but I really hated to sound like I was playing into it. Besides, I hadn't exactly been honest with Adele about my job. If she didn't want floozies traipsing through her building, I didn't think she'd be too keen on having a P.I. there, either.

"I'm kind of a personal consultant," I said. "I help people sort out problems."

"My goodness, that sounds very interesting," she said, right on cue. "You must be a very clever man." The coy smile she gave me was right out of the Southern belle handbook, and I had to admit she wasn't at all bad to look at even if she was about twenty years out of my range.

I shrugged and took a sip of coffee. "I guess I have a knack for figuring things out. You learn to be pretty street smart when you grow up in a city like New York."

"I'll just bet."

"What about you?" I asked. "This doesn't seem like the sort of place one would find a classy belle such as yourself living. How did you end up here?"

"Oh, I used to live in a much fancier apartment when I was married, but you know how it is when you're single and living off a limited income," she said offhandedly. She deflected further questions by busying herself with fetching more coffee. "Besides, I like the ladies who live here. We've all gotten to be quite good friends over the years."

In the kitchen, she happened to glance out the front window and squealed with delight. "What a wonderful car. Is that yours? I just love Mustangs, I think it's such a *masculine* car."

I chuckled. "Her name is Matilda."

That brought peals of girlish laughter and she came back to sit down at the table. "What a quaint name for your car. I think I like that very much. You'll have to take me for a ride with the top down sometime."

The tone of her voice left me in no doubt about the thinly veiled innuendo, and I'm not sure, but I think I blushed. I must have, because she laughed out loud and said, "Oh honey, I *am* going to enjoy having you around here."

"Say, since you're here," I said, "do you know what's going to happen with the storefront downstairs? Does Adele have any plans for it?"

She looked curious. "None that I know of. We just use it for a little extra storage. Why? Are you interested in it?"

"I was thinking it might make a good office. My old one is getting torn down along with my apartment building."

"That's a shame. Well, having your office right here would be very handy, wouldn't it?" She beamed, and I could tell she was already thinking she'd be able to drop by any time she liked. I'd have to set things up so she could only do that when I wanted her to, and not when it might compromise a client. Aside from that, I wouldn't mind a dishy broad bringing me lunch once in a while.

"That's what I was thinking," I said. "I'm not in the office all the time, but having it close to home makes things easier."

The beeping of my cellphone drifted in from the bedroom, and I excused myself to go answer it. I glanced at the screen as I picked it up and saw I had a message from one of the insurance agencies I do work for. That could wait.

When I went back out, Della had cleaned up the dishes from brunch and was drying off her plate. "Well, Dino, it's been just lovely getting to chat with you, but I think I better go, now, and let you get to work. I wouldn't want to keep you from your clients. I do hope we can do this again some time."

I told her I'd like that, and I meant it too. I've got nothing against playing a little cat-and-mouse with a brassy chick who knows what she's doing. Nine times out of ten, it's just the flirting they're after anyway.

* * * *

After Della left, I got my keys and wallet and went downstairs. I remembered the message, and while I was listening to my voicemail, I took a minute to check out my new home some more. There was a small patio off the side of the building with a table, chairs, umbrella, and a teeny grill on a bench. There was also a coffee can half full of sand and cigarette butts. This was all outside the windows and side door of what I assumed was Adele's apartment. It was kind of a cute set up, if somewhat plain.

The voicemail from the insurance agent sounded like a pretty decent job, so I added them to my list of stops. I was about to get in my car when I noticed Adele walking back from the Winn Dixie with a plastic shopping bag. I waved.

"Adele," I said jovially. "Just the woman I wanted to see."

She eyed me. "Is that so?"

"It is indeed. I have a question for you."

"And what would that be?" She took a pack of cigarettes out of her pocket and shook one out, sticking it in her lips while she felt for a lighter.

"I was wondering if the storefront here might be available for rent as well? I'm in the market for an office, and I was thinking that space might work out for me."

She took a long drag while she appeared to consider it, blowing smoke up toward the sky. "Well now, I don't know exactly. We've got some things in there we're storing. I'm not sure what we'd do with that. Tell you what, let's go see what it looks like."

She had me wait while she got the keys, and we went into the shop through a side door connecting with the hall. It was essentially a large room with a couple of offices in back. The air was stale and smelled like dust. The floor was littered with scraps of paper, old price tags, and the odd cigarette butt. Brown grime covered the windows and filtered the sunlight, making it hazy.

I wandered through the room, looking at the furniture and old cardboard boxes scattered around, and turned back to Adele. "You know, I don't need all that much space. If you let me build a couple of walls in here, you could still use part of it for storage. This stuff is kind of spread out, and if it were arranged better it would fit in a much smaller area."

"Hmm," she said, thoughtfully. Streams of smoke blew out her nose. "You'd have to do the work. And the cleaning. We're not interested in getting this place all fixed up for you."

"Of course not, ma'am, I'm sure I could arrange to have all the work done." She sounded skeptical, but there wasn't more than a couple days' work involved. "You wouldn't have to be troubled with it at all, other than to approve the plans."

She nodded and flicked her ash on the floor. "I'll have to talk it over with my sister-in-law, Fern, and see what the other girls think. Don't know what we'd charge for the rent yet. Have to figure that out."

"Why don't you do that," I told her as I picked my way back over to her. "Maybe let me know in a day or two? If you think it'll work out, I'd like to get started right away."

"All right. We'll see what we can come up with."

As she walked out, I said, "Hey, Adele, can I bum a smoke off you?"

"Yeah, sure." She pulled the pack out of her sweater, shook a couple loose and held it out for me to take one. "Need a light?"

"I have one. Thanks," I told her, reaching in my pocket for a book of matches. I try to always carry one, because you never know when they might come in handy.

On my way out to the car, I flipped open my phone and dialed Seth's number. He answered with, "Talk dirty to me."

"Okay," I said. "How does an afternoon spent getting all hot and sweaty grab you?"

"Dude, that's not bad. We might just make a pervert out of you yet. What did you have in mind?" The tone of his voice was pure sex, and I think I blushed for the second time that morning.

I gave myself a shake and said, "I think Adele will rent me that storefront for an office, and I need your help cleaning it up and building a couple walls."

"*Oh*, you were so close."

"Yeah, yeah. Can I count on you?"

"Sure. I have a few accounts I could use help collecting on, you take care of that for me and we'll call it even."

* * * *

Later that evening, I returned home with a bag of actual groceries since my food supply was in dire straits and I'd been overdosing on the takeout lately.

Inside the entryway, the smell of pot roast was so strong I started to drool immediately. My stomach growled, and I was glad I had food with me. Before I could reach the stairs, Della came sweeping down them with a china bowl in her hand. "Why, sugar, what a lovely surprise! You're just in time for supper. Come with me."

"Oh, no thanks, Della. I don't want to impose."

"Nonsense, honey, we're having a little dinner party, and it just wouldn't be complete without our newest tenant." She took me by the arm and pulled me down the hall to Adele's apartment with a smooth style that didn't brook resistance. So I didn't try.

I let her lead me through the living room into the dining room and kitchen area, where there was a cozy scene. They had Glen Miller playing on the record player while Ruth and another old woman fussed around in the kitchen making salad and mashed potatoes. Adele sat at the counter with a drink and a cigarette, telling some story about her late husband and how men are. The table was set with old-fashioned china, nice silverware and a pot of flowers. I smiled and felt like I was a kid back home in New York with Ma and my grandma cooking Sunday dinner.

"Look what I found, girls," Della announced with a broad smile. "Shall we set another place at the table?"

Ruth turned around, sucking mashed potatoes off her thumb, and lit up. "Mr. Martini, what a nice surprise. Yes, please stay, we have a ton of food here."

Ruth had silver gray hair cut short in a man's style, rimless glasses, and wore jeans and a plain sweater. She looked like the type to ride her bicycle everywhere and she was probably in better shape than I was.

The other woman, a powder-faced lady older than any of them, looked fairly sour at the prospect of a strange man joining the party. I assumed she must be Fern.

Adele said, "Sure, come on in, I'll make you a drink. What's your poison?"

This was old-fashioned entertaining of the kind they just don't do anymore, and it wouldn't have taken much to make me believe I'd stepped back about forty-five years. I think I fell in love on the spot.

"You know, ladies, I would be honored to join you. Just let me go upstairs and put my groceries away."

There was a chorus of approval from all but Fern, so I took my bag up to my apartment and grabbed a bottle of wine and the last of my Disaronno. I know what's expected of men at dinner parties like these—they bring liquor and they flatter ladies. And I was in a mood to flatter ladies.

When I returned, they had Peggy Lee playing and they were putting dinner on the table. Fern was just taking a pan of white rolls out of the oven, and my stomach growled at the smell of fresh bread.

I looked at Adele. "Do you have a corkscrew?"

She nodded and crushed out her cigarette, coming around into the kitchen to get one.

"Oh, how lovely," Della said, clasping her hands.

I opened the wine while Ruth plopped butter on top of a bowl of steaming green beans, and Fern poured dressing over the salad, tossing it before passing it to Della. There was a Key Lime pie on the counter next to the sink.

Adele put out wine glasses, and I went to pour, but Della stepped into my path. She fondled the lapels of my suit jacket. "Don't you just look sharp as a tack," she purred. "You'll dress up this little party very nicely."

Adele rolled her eyes. "Wipe the drool off your chin and sit down."

Della shot a look over her shoulder. "God made men good lookin' so we could appreciate them. It would be rude not to." She turned back to me and gave my jacket a little tug. "Would you like me to hang this up for you?"

"Thanks," I said and let her slip it off me, switching hands with the wine to get my arms out of the sleeves.

I filled the glasses while Adele and Ruth went to the table, then I held a chair for Della who smiled and sat down like a queen. Fern came shuffling out of the kitchen with a big platter of sliced pot roast, which I offered to take for her. She scowled, but she let me, so I figured I was making progress. When I held a chair for her too, I'm sure I saw her flick a suspicious glance at me.

Dinner itself was a marvelous affair, with swinging music, good conversation, and amazing home cooked food. I made a silent toast to the guy who tore down my old place and thought maybe he'd done me a favor.

I learned a lot about the quartet. Adele was originally from Jersey, and Fern was her sister-in-law. Adele and her husband had moved to Florida for his health shortly after they married, and opened the hardware store. When Adele's brother Walt died, Fern came to live with them, and when Adele's Henry passed away, they closed up the shop and rented out apartments.

Ruth had been an Economics professor in Pennsylvania, but was now retired and spent a lot of her time traveling. Like the others, her husband was long gone, but she'd divorced him in her forties.

Della was born and raised in South Carolina and had also come to Florida with her husband when he retired. She didn't say so, but I gathered they had come from money, and living in an apartment above an old hardware store was most definitely not the style to which she'd become accustomed. To her credit, that didn't seem to squash her spirit in the slightest.

After dinner, Fern served pie. I got up to pour myself a glass of amaretto and offered some to the ladies.

"My, how elegant," Della said, coyly holding out a glass of ice.

Ruth looked amused. "You are an interesting man, Mr. Martini," she said, but accepted a glass as well.

"You can call me Dino," I said.

She smiled and nodded.

Adele passed in favor of bourbon and water, and we all sat down again.

Then Ruth asked the thousand dollar question. "So, Della says you're a consultant? What kind of work do you do?"

"Yeah, interesting story there." I studied the ice in my glass and figured it was time to come clean. "That is the truth, but not the whole truth. What I am is a private eye."

"Oh, *go on*," said Della waving a hand at me.

I grinned and took out my wallet to show her my P.I.'s license.

She looked it over and said, "Very sexy!"

Yeah, okay, it wouldn't be the first time I got a kick out of impressing someone with it, and I'm sure it won't be the last. Sue me.

Adele, on the other hand, looked a little ticked off, and she pointed at me with the two fingers clutching her latest cigarette. "That's what you want to use the storefront for," she said, "and have a bunch of thugs running in and out of here like a Mickey Spillane movie?"

I tried my very best placating smile on her. "It's not like that, I swear. It's mostly very run of the mill stuff," I said, and I told her about the lawyers and the insurance agents and the sweet, elderly ladies who just wanted little Jimmy from the old neighborhood to have something to remember them by.

"You can really lay the crap on thick, can't you?" she said.

"Yes, ma'am. Comes with the job. I got top marks in my crap spreading class." I grinned, because she was, and added, "But I'm serious when I tell you I have almost never had an incident at home I would call at all dangerous. Mostly it's just pissed off husbands who want to take a piece out of me for telling their wives they're cheaters."

"My goodness," said Della, fanning herself with her napkin.

"And what do you do about that?" Ruth asked.

I leaned back in my chair and smiled. "I'm a charming guy. I just explain to them how it's all better off this way, and she was gonna find out anyway, and that really I've done them a favor."

She leveled her gaze on me and said, "And if that doesn't work?"

"I knock 'em on their asses and threaten them with police action or blackmail, whichever I think will scare them the most. That usually does the trick."

Fern looked positively scandalized, but the rest of these ladies had been around the block a few times, and I got a sense that while on the one hand they were concerned about safety and the sanctity of their homes, on the other, they were all thinking that having a resident P.I. would be a kick.

"Ladies, please, you won't even know I'm here unless I get hungry and come looking for more pot roast."

Della giggled, and Adele said, "All right. You can set up shop, but you piss me off and you're out of here."

"I already assumed that was a given, ma'am."

"And cut the ma'am bullshit." She got up and poured herself another drink, and offered me one, which I accepted.

"I'll try," I said, "but where I was raised, ladies hurt you if you don't show them the proper respect."

They all laughed, and we sat around the table trading stories while Adele and I smoked and Della and Ruth polished off the wine. Fern didn't say all that much, but she sat and enjoyed her coffee and listened. Around eleven o'clock, I secured myself in their good graces by rolling up my sleeves and offering to help with the dishes. I know what side my bread is buttered on, and even Fern seemed to appreciate me as she snapped instructions on how she wanted her china washed and I followed them to the letter.

Chapter 4

I was up early the next day, feeling antsy and ready to get back into the regular swing of work. I'd been neglecting things for the past few days and needed to catch up.

Since I currently had no office, we'd set up my desk and chair in the corner of the living room, with the filing cabinets next to it. I got myself a cup of coffee, turned on the stereo, and sat down, pulling a box full of assorted desk crap to my feet. I stuck the pen cup and stapler on the desk and started to sort through the folders and paperwork I'd stuffed in there in a hurry. I spent about an hour humming along to the oldies station while I worked, setting aside a few things for billing, and filing the rest.

Next, I set up my laptop and printer, put the "In" and "Out" boxes where they belonged, and arranged file and mail sorters. It felt good to get back to normal. When I was done I had a clean desk and a stack of envelopes to mail.

I was getting up to change clothes, when my phone rang. The call was from Ernie Schmendrick of Ernie's Used Autos. I do repossessions for the guy, and he usually calls every couple of months with a new batch of cars for me to fetch.

I flipped open the phone. "Hey, Ernie, how's it goin'?"

"Not bad," Ernie said. "I got a handful of jobs for you if you want 'em. You could stop in for the paperwork this afternoon. I was hoping maybe you can run some of these down for me tonight?"

"Probably. Work's light right now. If I can get Seth, we should be able to pull in a few for you."

"Great. See you later then." Ernie hung up, and I shut my phone and headed for the bedroom.

* * * *

When I went over to Ed's to see if Seth would be free, he was on his back under a Ford Fairlane, growling a lot of extremely rude things about the placement of starter bolts. He swore loudly and whacked the underside of the car with his wrench. I have it on good authority he doesn't treat Matilda like that, and I think it's best for everyone if I just choose to believe it.

"Hey ugly," I called, leaning on the workbench with my hands in my pockets. "You wanna make some money tonight?"

"I keep telling you, Dino," he said from under the car, "I'm not that kind of boy."

"That's not what I heard."

"Come on, now...the rumor about the three sailors and the goat is lies, I tell you, all lies."

"That goat happens to be a very good friend of mine."

"You motherlovin' *whore!*" Seth snarled and his hand appeared to feel around for a different wrench.

"Strange, that's exactly what the goat called you."

"Fuck off, Dino."

Seth's sense of humor fades quick when he's frustrated, so I cut the jokes and said, "Ernie called me a while ago. He's got some repos for us, if you're interested."

"Yeah, I could probably pitch in," he said, gritting his teeth. His feet scrabbled at the floor like he was having a seizure, then he gave a loud whoop. "Got'cha, you little steel bastard."

He rolled out from under the car, holding the starter on his chest, and grinned at me. He set it aside and grabbed a rag, wiping his hands while he got up. "Easy ones or not?"

"I don't know yet. I've still gotta' get the paperwork from him and see how many I can track down. I just wanted to find out if you were free. I can give you a call later with the details."

"Sure thing, dude."

* * * *

Doing repossessions is good work and fairly easy to get. I know guys who make an entire career out of it. It's dirty work and can be dangerous, but at a hundred and fifty bucks a pop, it pays well. Seth and I can do three or four of them in a night, depending on where they are and how much trouble we have. He's invaluable to the process, and he's got the tow truck if we need it, so we split the repo fees. We also list Ed's as the actual repo agent because it looks more official that way.

Ernie's Used Autos is a decent sized dealer over in St. Pete, and he carries cars of all shapes, sizes, and price ranges. He's also willing to do a lot of the financing through his own office, and because of that, he finds himself in need of repossessing vehicles on a fairly regular basis.

I parked Matilda on the side street across from the lot and walked over, scanning the rows for Ernie. I found him showing the virtues of a Volkswagen Bug to a pair of pretty young ladies, and he was really working it. I set down my briefcase and leaned back against a Chrysler, crossing my arms over my chest. It could be a while.

Ernie's a pudgy guy with thick, black hair he wears on the long side, so it falls into his eyes a lot. He has a classic salesman personality, but possesses a ring of sincerity most of them don't have. He's an okay guy, and I like him. We meet up for beers once in a while.

After a few minutes, the girls both shook his hand, and seemed to be giving every indication of planning to come back, judging by the smile on Ernie's face as he walked up to me.

"Dino, what's with you, man? Why don't you ever park your car in the lot? It hurts me, it really does." Ernie clapped me on the shoulder and grinned.

"I don't want your clientele drooling all over my baby. Besides, she'd outclass everything you got. I'm just tryin' to be considerate here."

"You're a true gentleman, Dino. They just don't make 'em like you anymore."

I laughed. "What have you got for me?"

"Come on into the office," Ernie said, nodding toward the tiny building in the center of the lot.

"How's business?" I asked as we walked.

"Not too shabby really. We've been doing pretty brisk sales, and not having too much trouble with the loans. No more than usual, I guess, and that's about what we could hope for. It's good, real good."

"I'm glad to hear it."

Ernie held the door open and I went in, crossing the sales floor to his private office in the back corner. The place smelled like tire rubber and old coffee, and everything was covered in a thin film of the particular kind of grime that comes from being around cars. Seth's office had it in spades.

I shut the door while Ernie went behind his desk and pulled a stack of manila folders off the top of a filing cabinet. He leafed through them. "There are a couple of newer cars here that came with key codes, so that's nice, and this one I happen to have a spare key on file for. The rest of 'em you're gonna have to crack."

"Thanks, Ernie," I said, taking the files as he handed them over. I took a quick peek at them myself and slipped them into my briefcase. "I appreciate the business."

"Don't thank me," he said, holding up his hands. "You're doing me a big favor. I don't have anybody around here I could send out for this kind of thing."

"We'll pick up as many as we can tonight, and I'll stop over tomorrow to give you a report."

"Thanks, man." Ernie held the door and we left, heading for the front. "Hey," he said, "Did I hear you lost your office recently?"

"Yeah, that was a complete screw over, but I got a line on a new place, so it's all good."

"Excellent, excellent. I knew you'd land on your feet."

We said goodbye and I went out to the car, tossing my briefcase in the back seat.

Next came the work of tracking down the cars and planning how to approach each one. State laws say you have to conduct repossessions in a peaceful manner. That's all fine and dandy until someone decides to take offense to a couple of guys making off with his car minus the benefit of introductions.

The best way to avoid unnecessary bloodshed is to get the car when the owner's not around. Most of the time, this means taking the thing in the middle of the night, which is actually kind of fun. I have to admit I get a very juvenile thrill out of the whole cloak-and-dagger operation of sneaking onto someone's property and stealing their car.

That's what repo work is, a legal steal.

We swipe the cars and call it in to the cops at the first opportunity, then the cops have the fun of notifying the former owner their car's been repossessed. We send out a letter and inventory list on Ernie's letterhead the next day, telling them where they can pick up any personal effects.

Chapter 5

Back home, I spent an hour in my apartment running title searches on the files Ernie gave me, seven in all. A couple were out of state, and I'd either deal with those later or kick them back to Ernie who had someone he could call for longer range jobs. The rest, I was able to get up-to-date information for.

I packed the information into my briefcase and went to the bedroom to change into old jeans and a sweatshirt. Out on the street, I opened Matilda's trunk and made sure I had everything we'd need. There were two flashlights, which I tested, a pack of extra batteries, the slim-jim for breaking into cars we didn't have keys for, mace for dogs, and a fully charged stun gun for unpleasant human beings. I carry a gun too, but that's more for show. Waving around a Glock is actually far more peaceful than zapping the shit out of some guy on his front lawn. The State of Florida disapproves of that in most cases, so I try to avoid it.

It took me about an hour and a half to drive around town and check out the cars so I could decide which ones we'd try for first. Three of them weren't there, but I found the addresses and scoped out the terrain. The other two were parked out front, and I hoped they'd still be there later on.

When I had the legwork done, I stopped off at Hamm's Cafe and picked up two huge bacon cheeseburgers, two orders of onion rings, and a six-pack of Coke. Then I headed for Ed's Garage.

Seth was nowhere to be seen when I went inside, so I set the food on the workbench and took a look in the office. He wasn't there either. The only thing that appeared to be in the shop was the Fairlane. I figured he must have gone up to his apartment, and I headed for the side door.

I was walking alongside the car, when a hand shot out and clamped around my ankle. I just about hit the roof. When my heart started beating again, I swore loudly, and yanked my leg free. "*Get* your ass out from under that car!"

Seth rolled out, laughing like a hyena. "I've never heard anyone shriek like that." He lay on the floor clutching his sides. "Are you sure you're a badass private eye?"

"*Ass*hole. You want me to kick your scrawny little ass to prove it?"

"I am not scrawny."

"And I do not shriek."

Seth lost it all over again. After a minute, he stopped and said, "Hey, I smell onion rings."

"That would be my dinner." I wasn't really pissed at him, but I couldn't let him get away with it. I had to yank his chain at least a little. "You wanna grab me some napkins while you're upstairs scraping Cheetos off the rug or whatever you plan on eating?"

I kicked him in the ass and went to get my food and a can of Coke. There's an old bench seat from a Ford pick-up sitting on the floor in the corner of the garage, with a couple of milk crates for tables. I sat down and flipped open the lid, inhaling the scent of fried things and moaning loudly.

"You're such a jerk," Seth said as he got up and brushed off his hands and hair. "Here I'm gonna work all night for you, and you gotta' be flaunting your hamburger in front of me."

"Yeah, well, I think the burger fairy left you a surprise on your workbench."

"Oh?" Seth came around the back of the car and smiled broadly. "*Sweet.* Thanks, dude."

"You're welcome."

He took a couple of plastic cups off the beat up old refrigerator at the end of the bench and filled them with ice from the freezer, then came to join me, handing me a cup and opening up his food.

"So, what did you find out?" he asked, stuffing the cheeseburger in his mouth. He'd barely started chewing when he tried to cram an onion ring in with it.

"Were you born in a fucking barn?" I asked.

"Yefff."

I shook my head. "Okay, we've got five possibles tonight, and I have keys for three of them. I scoped out all the locations and there's nothing tricky at any of them. I've seen two. The others weren't there at the time."

Seth somehow managed to swallow and asked, "Anything fun?"

"As a matter of fact, yes," I said, grinning at him. "There is one I think you're gonna like. Seventy-eight Corvette. Sold for a pretty penny so it must be in good shape."

Seth groaned and turned huge doe eyes on me. "You're gonna let me drive that one, aren't you?"

"Sure, why not? It's your ass on the line out there too."

"Yes!" Seth pumped his fist and went back to attacking his burger like a wild animal.

"But I gotta' warn you, it's in a pretty dicey neighborhood, so we're going to have to do it carefully."

"Fine with me," he said, swallowing a mouthful of onion ring and taking a swig of Coke. "I have zero interest in getting my ass shot off."

I was starving and concentrated on eating while we sat in a comfortable silence. When Seth finished, he got up and dumped his garbage in a rusty trash barrel standing against the wall. He came back holding a newsprint Auto Trader folded open.

"Check it out," he said, dropping back onto the seat next to me and holding the magazine in front of my face.

I took it from him and ate my last onion ring. "Which one am I lookin' at?"

"That one." He tapped his finger on an ad for a 1972 Chevy Chevelle, dark orange with white stripes. It was selling for a song. Seth had been in the market for a muscle car to work on for a while, but hadn't found anything that caught his eye.

"Nice." The photos were small and grainy, but from what I could tell, it seemed to be in pretty good shape, body-wise. "What's wrong with it?"

"Doesn't run at all. The guy said the engine's seized up, and it's been sitting in storage for about four years now."

"You go look at it yet?"

"No, I just called on it today." Seth took the magazine from me and leaned back against the seat gazing at it like it was a porno mag. "Thought you might want to take a run out there with me if you're free some evening this week. Overhauling that engine would be a fuck of a lot of work, but what a blast."

I got up and threw away my garbage, brushing my hands off. "Yeah, I could do that. She's a beaut. I think you might be on to something there."

We had some time to kill before dark, so we sat around talking about the Chevelle, about Matilda, and about the schedule for the evening. It was a pleasant way to spend the time, and it left me relaxed and ready for an unpredictable night of work.

That's the thing about Seth. His antics are amusing and he's got a lot of assets that make him a useful friend, but what I like most about him is how well we get along. It's always comfortable being with him, and given the precious few people I actually like to be around, that's important to me.

* * * *

Around nine thirty, we got everything we needed out of Matilda and loaded into Seth's tow truck. I guess technically it would be Ed's tow truck, but Seth was shaping up to be owner of the place through sheer habit if nothing else. I had a feeling the old guy was planning to leave it to him when he died. If he ever did.

Seth climbed behind the wheel and we took off. We drove out to the farthest car on our list, taking a route past each of the others to check on them. We had gotten pretty good at this and had a solid routine down.

Three of the five possible cars were at home, leaving only a Trailblazer and the Corvette unaccounted for. The Corvette didn't surprise me in the least. I figured we'd have to wait until pretty damn late to get a shot at it. I really hoped we weren't going to have to stay up until dawn to bring it in.

Reconnaissance was done in half an hour and we parked up the street from a newer model Mercury Sable. This was one of the cars I'd been able to have a key made for, and I didn't expect any trouble claiming it.

Seth leaned on the steering wheel. "I'll keep watch until you're off and follow you to Ernie's. Let's hope they're all this easy tonight."

"No shit. Don't count your chickens, though. See you on the other side."

He grinned at me, and I jumped out of the truck. Walking casually across the street, I reached into my pocket and took out a penlight. I had a folded copy of the purchase agreement and used it to check the VIN number before I unlocked the car and got in. Smooth as butter, and not an ounce of trouble.

I drove it to Ernie's and parked in the back of the lot, where he'd made room for us. Seth rolled right in behind me.

"Did you call it in?" he asked as I climbed back into the truck.

"Yep, on the way over. I told her we'd have a few more, so they're expecting it."

The next one on the list was an '85 Chevy Caprice. Seth was disgusted. "Who the hell would take out a loan to buy a fuckin' Caprice?"

With no keys, we had to pop the lock and tow it back to Ernie's, but our luck was running good for the evening, and we didn't raise any eyebrows with that one either.

The third car went just as smoothly, and the next time we checked on the Trailblazer, it was finally parked in the driveway. The bedroom light of the house was still on, so we sat in the truck until it went out twenty minutes later.

"Should we go for it?" Seth asked.

"Eh, let's give it another ten. Maybe they'll fall asleep fast."

"Come on, Dino, don't be a pussy, we've got keys for this one. Just go get it and let's get the fuck out of here."

I scowled at him. "I am not being a pussy, I just don't wanna push our luck. We've had a good evening, and we still have the dangerous one to do. I think it's worth taking a few extra minutes on this one."

I've had it happen a couple times, where I'm sitting in the driver's seat of some car cranking the key while the engine hacks away, not quite catching, and watching the house light up out of the corner of my eye. That's when the thrill fades right off.

"Yeah, okay, Grandpa."

"Here's an idea," I said, holding up the slim-jim. "Why don't you shove this right up your ass? That should keep you amused for a while."

"Well, I would, except that I'll be needing it to get into the 'Vette later on."

"Speaking of that, are you gonna be able to hotwire it?"

"Sure, no sweat," he said. "Easy as pie."

"If you can't get it, you say so and we'll hoist it up on the hook. I don't want to be screwing around there any longer than necessary. I did a little checking on this Darryl Serrano, and he's not opposed to causing trouble, if you know what I mean."

Seth raised his eyebrows. "Does he have a rap sheet?"

"Nothing huge. A few arrests and a little jail time. He's an idiot, and he pulls stupid shit like speeding and reckless driving after already losing his license. He's just the type of moron to stand on his front step and blast you with a shotgun. Do not fuck around on this one."

"It'll be fine. This wouldn't be the first time everything went right, you know."

"And it wouldn't be the first time we got our asses handed to us either," I reminded him. Seth's not stupid, but he can be reckless a lot of the time, and I had a feeling the lure of driving that flashy car was going to make him take chances.

I checked my watch and figured enough time had gone by. The sooner we got this one, the sooner we could get the 'Vette out of the way and go home.

Snatching the SUV was as slick as the rest, and soon I was parking it at Ernie's while I put in a call to the front desk of the cop shop. I gave her the scoop and let her know we had one more to go for the night. She wished me luck and hung up.

I walked up to the truck as Seth came to a stop for me and got in. "Should we go find you a Corvette?" I asked.

"I have to use the can first," he said. "And we could stand to get more gas before we finish. It would really suck if the truck died right in the middle of this dude's street."

"Yeah, you could say that."

We drove across the street to the Hess station to fill up and use the bathroom, and I got a cup of coffee. I refused to let Seth get one of his caffeine bomb, battery acid drinks. The last thing in the world I needed was for him to slam twenty-seven grams of sugar before taking off in a hot Corvette.

When we got back in the truck, I took the driver's side so Seth could be ready to jump out and hit the car running. Before I started it up, I went over the file with him again so he was sure of the details and had the VIN number.

"All right," I said, pulling out of the gas station. "Let's get this done. You be careful."

Seth smiled broadly at me. He's actually got a Cheshire grin when he smiles like that, and a couple of his teeth are pointy, so the whole effect is a little feral. It's weirdly charming, but it often spells trouble.

"I am not shittin' you, Seth," I said, pointing at him. "We do this quick no matter how we have to, and we get the hell out of there."

He nodded. "I hear you, Dino."

We got to Monroe Street and circled the lot of Serrano's tiny apartment building. The car wasn't hard to spot. It was cherry red, sitting low on the ground and gleaming in the parking lot lights. I heard Seth moan quietly, and I turned to stare at him.

"Fuck, Dino, I know, all right?" He held up his hands like an exasperated teenager. "I swear, if it doesn't start right off I'll give you the sign and we'll tow it."

I nodded and moved the truck to where I'd be able to back straight in if we needed. We decided since this was the last one, and because it was so flashy, we'd park it behind Ed's for the night and throw a cover over it. I wasn't comfortable with leaving it at Ernie's, because when this guy found it missing, he would certainly come looking for it.

Seth got out of the truck and shut the door quietly, taking the slim-jim, a screwdriver, and his pocket knife with him. I watched him crouch low and trot over to the car. He checked the VIN number against the paperwork, and went to work on the lock. Less than two minutes later, he climbed in the car, half the battle won.

I had the truck idling and gave it a soft rev so if I had to move fast, it wouldn't stall out. I kept my eyes glued to the back window of the 'Vette, where I could just make out Seth moving around inside. I waited a few more minutes and checked my watch. Nothing happened.

"Come on," I muttered through clenched teeth.

I was about to make my move when the car finally roared to life. It was loud as hell. If we hadn't been noticed before, we certainly would be now. Seth clearly understood the same thing, because he didn't bother backing out slow and quiet, he just whipped it out of the parking space and wheeled smoothly around to the parking lot entrance.

I turned and stepped on the clutch to pull out after him, when a blurred figure exploded out the door of the apartment building and streaked past me. It was a young guy, mid-twenties or so, with short blond hair and a button-down shirt only half on, flapping around him as he ran. I guessed this was Darryl Serrano. He hollered after the Corvette, using quite a lot of colorful words, but his hands were empty, which was a relief. If he had a gun on him, he'd have pulled it by now.

What he did next surprised me more than a gun would have. He was really moving and started to chase down the car. I pulled out on the street in time to see him catch Seth at the intersection when Seth slowed to make the turn.

Darryl launched himself into the air and landed on the hood of the 'Vette in a flying tackle, screaming and pounding on the glass. Seth snapped the front of the car toward the curb and stomped on the breaks, rolling the guy off onto the grass, then streaked away with a squeal of tires. I imagined he enjoyed the hell out of that, and I didn't expect him to sleep for two days.

With Seth out of danger, and long gone, I drove along slowly as if I was a mere passerby. I kept an eye on Serrano while he picked himself up and limped back toward the apartment building, swearing and waving his arms. He picked up a beer can and hurled it at the block of mailboxes on the lawn.

Once he was inside, there wasn't any reason for me to hang around, so I stepped on the gas and drove back to the garage. I wasn't the least bit surprised I was the first one to get there, and I already had the car cover out and ready when Seth finally pulled in, some kind of heavy bass beat making the windows throb.

He didn't get out of the car right away, and I could see him inside thrashing around to the music, so I supposed we were going to wait out the end of the song. I leaned against the door frame and folded my arms over my chest, grateful I was on this side of the glass.

When the song ended, he drove the car around back where we'd decided to stash it. I followed him and met him climbing out of it.

"Fuck, Dino, is that a sweet ride," Seth said. He grabbed an edge of the cover and helped me drape it over the car. He was practically bouncing. "Are you absolutely sure we have to give it back?"

"Ah, that would be a definite yes," I said, grinning. "We have to give it back. Trust me when I tell you you're going to like the Chevelle a whole lot better. Personally, I think it completely outclasses this thing even with a fried engine."

"Yeah?"

"No question."

We got the Corvette stowed away, and Seth was still crashing around as if he *had* downed a can full of sugar. I was extremely grateful I'd pulled rank on that one.

"Driving that car really got you wired, didn't it?" I asked, watching him shadowbox a Firestone Tire sign and then kick it right over.

"Are you kidding? I've had a boner for half an hour. I'm completely jazzed right now."

I had to ask.

Since it was only one thirty and the paperwork could wait until morning, I said, "Well, you're gonna have to handle the hard-on yourself, but I'd be happy to take you down to the Oar House and buy you a few beers to settle you down."

He gave me an absolutely predatory smile. It made me a little weak in the knees, and I was prepared for one of his offhanded come-ons, but instead he just said, "You're on," and jogged halfway down the sidewalk before coming back to walk with me.

Chapter 6

I woke up the next morning feeling moderately hung over, and pissed when I realized I'd left Matilda at the garage and was going to have to walk to Seth's in that state. My new place was only eight blocks or so from him, but there's no amount of walking I want to do on a bright and sunny morning with a hangover.

Turns out, it had taken quite a lot of beer to calm Seth down, and not only had we closed out the Oar House, but we'd walked over to the Backroom Bar which tends to do a lively after hours business. Seth and the bartender dug out a pile of bartending guides she'd printed off the internet, and amused themselves by making every drink that had a dirty name. I wasn't allowed to leave until I'd thoroughly discussed the merits of Sex on the Beach versus a Screaming O. Since I chose to be a good sport about the whole thing, they rewarded me with an amaretto Sweet Pussy, which was actually pretty good.

My cellphone was on the nightstand next to me, so I grabbed it, figuring I could call Seth and make him bring the car to me, but it went straight to voicemail. Irritating little shit.

I crawled out of bed and into the shower where I washed off the bar smell and cigarette smoke. Then I went to the kitchen and brewed coffee while I dug out the biggest mug I could find. If I had to take the walk of shame, I was doing it armed with caffeine.

Unfortunately, I ran out three-quarters of the way there, and there's no decent coffee to be had in that part of town, so my mood hadn't lifted any by the time I climbed the wooden steps and beat on Seth's door.

He wasn't answering that, either.

We had a long Saturday ahead of us, which included inventories of the repossessions and cleaning out the storefront, and I was in no mood to piss around. I pounded on the door until I heard crashing and groaning inside, and Seth pulled it open, staring blearily at me. He had on jeans and nothing else.

"Fuck, is it morning already?"

"It is, and I have no coffee, and we have a lot of work to do, Red, so wake up. You've got only yourself to thank for the state you're in."

"Well, aren't you Mr. Sunshine this morning," he deadpanned, holding the door open for me.

"You can thank yourself for that too. I would have been perfectly happy with beer."

"Hey, I don't remember anyone pourin' the stuff down your throat, man." Seth grabbed a T-shirt out of a pile, sniffed it, and pulled it on.

"I think there's probably a lot of things you don't remember, because that is exactly what you tried to do. My damn shirt was sticky when I got home."

He grinned obscenely and said, "Oh yeah, that must have been the Blow Job."

I rolled my eyes. "Don't start. It was cute last night, but now? Not so much."

"Yeah, yeah, yeah." Seth took me by the arm and dragged me into the kitchenette, pointing over my shoulder. "Look...coffee. How much do you love me now?"

"You don't have a coffee maker," I said, even as I was staring at a shiny white KitchenAid with a pot of decent smelling coffee steaming away on it.

"It's new. It has a timer and everything. I don't know shit about grinding up beans or whatever the hell you do with them, so you have to suffer with canned coffee, but it's better than nothing, right?"

"Yeah, this is great," I said, pouring some into my cup. "This is remarkably thoughtful for you, I'm impressed."

"Ouch, asshole, why don't you twist the knife a little more." Seth hopped up on the counter and peeled open a pack of Pop-Tarts, taking a big bite before continuing. "So, what the hell was up with that Serrano dude? I've never had anyone try to tackle the fucking car before. Did you see that?"

"Yeah." I blew on the coffee and took a sip. "I was going to talk to you about that last night, but you didn't give me chance. Anyway, I told you I thought that guy was going to be trouble, and I was right. There's no way he's going to let this drop. I'm gonna give Ernie a call and warn him as soon as the lot opens, and I think we should be careful when we take the car over there."

"Think Ernie's going to have trouble with him?" Seth asked.

"Maybe a little, but Ernie's got insurance for that, and he knows a guy on the police force who's usually willing to do a few extra drive-bys for anyone who'll drink beer and watch football with him."

"Can I drive it over there?"

"As long as you promise not to try to jump Ernie afterward. His wife is the jealous kind, and she could totally kick your ass."

* * * *

We went outside to check on the Corvette, which was right where we'd left it, and I called Ernie to give him a report of the previous night's work. He was thrilled to hear we'd gotten the 'Vette back and said he'd give his pal a call just to be on the safe side.

When I got off the phone, I found Seth already in it having some kind of religious experience. I rapped on the window. He rolled it down and I said, "Let's do the inventory and condition report here and then take it over. That'll be less time we have to hang out at Ernie's while we do the others. I'd rather not be there if Serrano is gonna come and make trouble."

Seth agreed and I went to my car to get the forms out of my briefcase. I gave him a clipboard and the Condition Report form, and took an Inventory Report for myself. I also carried a small cardboard box to collect whatever was inside.

While I got in and started to go through the glove compartment, Seth moved around the car making note of any damage or modifications. I noted the usual stuff, owner's manual, tire gauge, registration, spare fuses. Serrano also had a Florida map, Miami map, two Snickers bars and a bunch of matchbooks from a place called The Shark Pond in South Beach. There was a cheap paperback fuck book wedged between the passenger seat and the console, and a silver lighter on the dash.

"Hey," said Seth, poking his face in the window. "What's the odometer reading?"

I peered at it and read the numbers off.

"Thanks."

In the interest of being thorough, I climbed out of the car so I could check underneath the seats. There was nothing under the passenger seat, but under the driver's seat I found a small padded envelope, folded in half and wrapped with rubber bands.

"What the fuck is that?" Seth asked when I stood up, turning it over in my hands.

"I have no idea," I said. It was dirty, presumably from riding around on the floor of the car, and contained something fairly bulky.

I pulled off the rubber bands and unfolded it. There was a return address label from one of those mail order porn places, and a mailing label that was addressed to Serrano, but had a Miami address.

Seth said, "Oh-ho, have we found Serrano's sex toy stash? My money's on leopard print lovecuffs, what do you think?"

"Lovecuffs?" I asked, casting a sidelong glance at him.

He shrugged. "I read the catalogs. There's all kinds of crazy shit in there."

"Yeah, 'cause you need that."

"Just biding my time, baby..."

I lifted the envelope flap and looked inside. What I saw was curious in how unremarkable it was.

"Well?" prodded Seth, trying to see for himself.

I tipped the contents into my hand. There was a small notebook, also wrapped with a rubber band, a key card, and a set of keys. Just two keys on a plain ring with a green rubber fob advertising Chico's Car Wash. One was a car key, and the other a small gold one.

"Well...that's interesting," Seth said, picking up the keys and examining them.

I tucked the envelope under my arm and looked at the notebook. There wasn't anything special about it I could see. I took the rubber band off and started to flip through it with Seth looking over my shoulder. Most of the pages were blank, but a few had notes on them, and several pages had lists of numbers written in groups.

"What the fuck?" Seth muttered. "Obviously this stuff means something or he wouldn't have stashed it under the seat like that."

"Yeah, but what?" I mused on it for a few minutes, trying to come up with a plausible explanation. Most of the information looked like it might be in code, which certainly piqued my curiosity.

"I'll tell you one thing," Seth said, "these keys aren't for the 'Vette. This one's new, and it fits a BMW."

"I wonder where that car is then."

"Good question."

"Listen," I said, ignoring the protest my conscience was making. "Let's not list this on the inventory, all right? I'd like to have a closer look at it. We can always drop it off with Ernie later, say it fell out of the box on the way over or whatever."

"You smelling a mystery here, Nero Wolfe?" Seth joked, elbowing me in the ribs.

"I'm not Wolfe," I said. "I'm Archie Goodwin."

"Well I'm sure as hell not Wolfe." Seth looked horrified.

"No, you're Fred Durkin."

"Who the fuck is Fred Durkin?"

I rolled my eyes. "You need to read more."

"So who is he? Is he hot like me?"

"Yes. He's hot like you."

"You're doing that thing with sarcasm again, aren't you?"

I smirked and wrapped up the notebook and keys the way we'd found them. Yeah, I know—keeping it was very unprofessional, not to mention stupid, but I was curious as all hell, and I was itching for something a little more intriguing than skip tracing and tracking cheaters.

* * * *

Later at Ernie's, I had already completely inventoried the Caprice, and done the Condition Report before Seth finally rolled in with the hotwired Corvette. It's a damn fine thing Ernie is a good sport. When Seth still hadn't shown up fifteen minutes after I arrived, and Ernie was looking a little concerned, I told him I thought Seth might be taking the 'Vette for a test drive. I don't think I've ever seen Ernie laugh so hard.

When Seth did show up, he pulled up next to us and climbed out, giving me a wicked leer and a shit-eating grin. I was shocked to realize I knew damn well he had a hard-on. Ernie tried to give him a sales pitch on the car.

"Seth!" I yelled. "We have three more to do, and a pile of paperwork for this. Get your ass in gear."

Seth flipped me off. "Hey, Ernie," he said, "have you read the Nero Wolfe books?"

"Sure," Ernie said, nodding. "Those are pretty good reads."

"Who is Fred Durkin?"

I steered Seth away and shoved him in the direction of the three vehicles we had left to do. Behind us, Ernie yawned and trudged into his office. He'd been dragging all morning, and I wondered what was up. Ernie is usually a pretty perky guy.

Twenty minutes was all it took for us to get done. I tucked the paperwork into my briefcase and went to tell Ernie we'd have the finished reports for him as soon as possible.

"Thanks," he said choking back another yawn. "Sandra will have your check ready, and you can come get it anytime you want, unless you'd rather have her just mail it."

"Great. I'll come and get it, I don't trust the mail at the new place yet. What's up with you, don't you sleep at night?"

"Nothing serious. The alarm went off in the wee hours of the morning, that's all. It's not a big deal, happens every couple of months, short in the system or bird hitting the window or whatever. But it's a pain in the ass, because I have to get out of bed and come down here to meet with the police to make sure everything's all right."

"And was it?" I asked, because I didn't think this was any short in the system.

Seth had just stepped in the door and gave me a dubious look.

"Yep, everything's accounted for and nothing's broken. You know, the only time I've ever actually been robbed was in broad daylight when some punk took a Firebird out for a test drive and just kept on going."

"Yeah..." I said, rubbing the back of my neck. "I think this was more than a bird hitting the window. I wouldn't be the least bit surprised if it was that crackpot I told you about who jumped the 'Vette."

"You think?" Ernie looked completely dumbfounded. "I suppose anything's possible. I'm glad he didn't tear the place up when he didn't find the car. That was good thinking, you guys. Anyway, my buddy's going to keep an eye on the place for a few days."

"Good plan," I told him. "Get some sleep tonight."

It was time for lunch when we got out of there, so I offered to buy Seth a quick sandwich if he'd help me do the paperwork before we started cleaning the storefront.

There's a lot of paperwork involved in doing repossessions. I don't mind it so much. I happen to be one of those rare people who doesn't hate paperwork with a passion. I love to sit down with a full "In" box around lunch time and end up with an empty one just in time to go out and get some dinner. Seth, however, hates paperwork and complains like a baby, so he ended up in a mood similar to mine of that morning.

Chapter 7

"That's my *foot* you dropped a credenza on, motherfucker!" Seth yelled as he squeezed out from behind it, limping.

"Well, I just told you I was gonna put it down, get your damn toes out of the way!" I said.

"What the fuck is a credenza anyway?"

"It's one of those things," I said, wiping sweat off my brow with the back of my hand.

Mother Nature seems to have a sick sense of humor about these things, and it was at least ten degrees hotter than usual and twice as humid. Seth and I were both tired, drenched in sweat and getting pissy. We'd worked all afternoon, moving boxes and furniture, sometimes twice, until we had everything arranged in the least amount of space, but in a way you could still get to most of it. The credenza was the last thing we had to move.

Seth stripped off his shirt, scrubbed the sweat off his face and flung it across the room. "If I had any idea what a bitch of a day this was gonna be, I never would have agreed to it. I hope you know you're gonna buy dinner and beer all night."

"I'm doing collections for you," I reminded him, sitting in a chair we had parked in front of the fan. "And I bought beer all last night."

"Not enough. That is just not enough for this kind of torture. And you still owe me for helping you move too." Danny Williams's *White on White* came on the radio, and Seth made a gagging noise. "And this…" he said, heading for the radio. "You have a really twisted sense of what constitutes decent tunes, I swear to God."

"You touch that dial and I start snappin' fingers," I said, pointing at him.

"Asshole." He spun around and planted his hands on his hips, staring at me. "Now what?"

"Now we clean." I got up, grabbed a broom out of the corner, and started to sweep the floor.

Seth took over my spot in front of the fan and bent forward to let it blow across his head. He sat up and leaned on the back of the chair, propping his head in his hand, and watched me.

After a while, he shook a finger at me and said, "You know, this is a good look for you, with the old jeans and the wife-beater and your arms all glistening with sweat, workin' the broom. You look all tough and blue-collar."

"Flattery will not excuse you from working. Get off your ass and grab that dustpan."

He did, but with a lot of overblown bitching and moaning. His contribution was to sit down on the floor and hold it half-heartedly while I swept. We got the first pile of crap cleaned up and dumped in the garbage can, when Della came in carrying a tray with a pitcher of lemonade and large glasses of ice on it. I could have kissed her.

"You boys are just working so hard in this terrible heat, I thought you could use a little refreshment." She smiled at us and cocked her head.

Seth flopped onto his back and waved a hand in her general direction. "Look, Dino. Angels! We died of heat stroke, and angels have come to take us away."

Della set the tray down and poured him a glass of lemonade. She knelt down to hand it to him. "Poor baby," she said, brushing the hair out of his eyes and patting his cheek. "You look just plum tuckered out."

"Yeah, don't encourage him, Della," I said, pouring myself some lemonade. I drank the whole thing in one shot and filled my glass again, while Seth pouted and held out his glass for Della to refill. It was sad, it really was, and I told him so.

"Oh, don't be silly," she said. "Who could refuse an adorable face like that?"

When she turned to pour him another glass, Seth stuck his tongue out at me, so I flipped him off.

I'll say something for Southern hospitality, being fawned over and downing three big glasses of ice cold lemonade will do wonders for anyone's disposition, and within a few minutes, I was feeling a hell of a lot better than I had all day. Judging from the blissed-out smile on Seth's face as he leaned against the credenza, he was feeling better too.

Della checked out our work and was remarking on what a fine job we'd done when Dean Martin came on the radio singing *Sway*. She clapped a hand to her chest and sighed, looking dreamy, and I wondered what she was remembering.

Feeling inspired, I set down my glass and held a hand out to her. "May I have this dance? I know I'm not exactly dressed for the occasion, but what are you gonna do?"

Both she *and* Seth looked at me like I was crazy at first, but then a slow smile spread across her face and she took my hand. "Why, yes, I think I will, Dino. There's nothing I like better than a sweaty, handsome man."

I took her waist and led her into a swishy rumba she didn't have the slightest difficulty keeping up with. I happen to love to dance, and *Sway* is one of my all time favorites. There is a moment with a dance partner, sometimes, when you both realize you know what you're doing and you can really cut loose. When Della figured out I could actually dance, she lit right up. She was good too, and we sailed around on that old wood floor, twisting and spinning and turning. At the end of the song, I dipped her, and when she stood up, she beamed at me and clapped gleefully.

"Oh, darlin', you are a *marvelous* dancer!"

Seth was staring at me in that main course kind of way Della had when she met me, and he arched an eyebrow. "Where in the hell did you learn how to dance like that, man?"

His open appraisal of me was a little different than his usual teasing, but the tone of voice was all Seth, if maybe deeper than I was used to. I shrugged and sat down, pouring myself the last of the lemonade. "My grandma lived with us, you know, and she loved to dance. So when I got tall enough, she made me be her partner every Sunday afternoon when they did the ballroom dancing show on the radio."

"Oh, that is so sweet," Della said, playing with a string of pearls she wore. "You are a rare breed, Dino Martini."

Seth chuckled. "She's right dude, you were clearly born in the wrong era."

I grinned at them. "What can I say? I'm a classy guy."

* * * *

After we finished cleaning up, Seth assured me he'd been completely serious when he said I was buying him dinner, and went home to shower and change clothes. We ate at an especially nice restaurant, and it was clear from Seth's meal he'd decided money was no object. I figured I owed it to him, so I didn't argue. He was more than paid back for his hard work.

We were both in great spirits that evening, feeling comfortably full of crab legs and sweet potato french fries, and enjoying the satisfaction of a job well done. Neither of us had any inclination to turn in early, so we decided to hit the bars again for beer and pool, ending up at one we'd never tried before.

It was a smallish place and kind of seedy, but in the way that gives a bar character. The room was long and narrow, with the bar running nearly all the way down one side of it and a row of booths and video games on the opposite wall. No pool table at this one, so we took stools at the bar.

I hailed the bartender. "Couple of Landsharks down here."

Seth sat backward on his stool, leaning against the bar while he checked out the crowd, which was pretty healthy even for a Saturday night. He reached over to poke me in the ribs with his elbow and gave me a conspiratorial look. "So, you got something going on with Della? That was pretty hot stuff today, man."

"Ah, no, I don't," I told him. "That's just Della. You hang around enough and she's gonna be puttin' the moves on you too. I think she just likes the chase."

I told him about the impromptu dinner party and everything I'd learned about the ladies. "And you know, I actually had a pretty good time. They're a lot different when they aren't standing on manners and they'll act normal around you."

"Boy, I don't know..." Seth said with a slow shake of his head. I could tell he wanted to take my word for it, but couldn't wrap his mind around the idea that a person could have a good time with a group of old women.

The bartender delivered the beers, and I slid a ten dollar bill across to him. Seth spun around and took his, squeezing a lime into the beer and shoving the rind down the neck of the bottle. He licked his fingers off and took a drink. When he saw me watching him, he grinned and licked his lips. I rolled my eyes.

"So, I started thinking about the office after you left," I said.

"That's great. You're going to be so much more fun to be around when you're not going completely anal about the whole relocation thing. I like you better when you're settled."

"Ah, yeah, fuck you. Okay, I've got to figure out the right way to do this, because I've been thinkin' it would be good to have kind of a two part office, so there's a place I can meet with clients, but they won't be able to see everything on my desk, you know?"

"You're getting pretty high class on me here, I don't know. Better be careful, Dino. Next you'll be wanting a secretary, and then it's gonna be all about playing slap-and-tickle at the office, and you won't get any work done. The money stops coming in, you lose all your clients, then you wind up as a homeless wino and you die in a gutter in Poughkeepsie." He took a swallow of beer.

I stared at him for a moment. "Right. So, anyway, here's what I was thinking…"

I took a notepad out of my pants pocket, flipped it open to a clean page and started to sketch out what I had in mind. Seth stuffed a couple of pretzels in his mouth and looked over my arm at the paper.

That's when all hell broke loose. One second he was watching me draw, and the next he squeaked with surprise and slammed face forward into the bar with a sickening crack. I turned to see what was going on and found Rick, the big ox from the other night, towering over us with the meanest look on his face I've ever seen.

"What the *fuck*?" I was on my feet in a flash, shoving myself between him and Seth, who slid to the floor with dazed groan. A chill raced through me when I saw that his face and the front of his shirt were covered in blood. At least he was conscious.

White hot anger seethed through me as I turned to face the huge bastard. "Rick," I said, going ice cold, "you just made a big mistake, my friend."

"Don't give me that boyfriend bullshit," he said, taking a pop at me, which I managed to duck. "You two made a fool out of me, and nobody makes a fool of me and gets away with it."

He swung a second time, catching me square across the jaw. Then he shoved me against the bar and kicked Seth in the ribs making him cough and double over, inhaling blood from his nose and spitting it onto the floor. Without even thinking about it, I reached into the waistband of my pants and pulled out my gun, shoving it under the guy's chin and pushing him back away from Seth. The room went silent, other than the dinging of the video games and the drone of the TV behind the bar. He was furious, and barely in check, but the gun in his face gave him enough pause for me to get the upper hand.

"You guys ain't a couple," he said, glaring daggers at me. "You were just shittin' me."

"Don't think that doesn't mean I won't fucking take you apart, you son of a bitch," I growled, advancing on him slowly. "You and me are gonna have a little talk outside, Ricky, and if you're lucky, you'll be able to crawl away from it."

The bartender came rushing around the end of the bar, waving his hands. "Hey, hey, none of that shit in here. We don't want any trouble. Why don't you boys just calm down now and put that away?"

"We were just leaving." I looked up at Rick and jerked my head toward the door. "You heard the man, out. Let's go."

Behind me, Seth was struggling to his feet. Someone handed him a napkin, which he stuffed up under his nose, groaning like he wasn't completely with the program. I felt like I should probably help him, but there was still Rick to deal with, and my own burning need to kick the shit out of this guy. Testosterone won out, and I herded Rick toward the door before he got any ideas about taking a parting shot at Seth.

At the front door, I spun him around and held the gun to his back, shoving him down the sidewalk. "Around back, slimeball," I said. "We're goin' in the alley, and I'm gonna kick your ass."

"You're dead, motherfucker," he shot back over his shoulder.

"I'm what? I'm dead? Is that what you said?" I jabbed him in the back. "You just attacked a very good friend of mine, and you think I'm the one who's gonna be dead? You are not very bright, Ricky boy."

We got to the edge of the alley, and he stopped and turned to face me. "You're not gonna shoot me," he sneered, and hauled off and punched me right in the eye.

I went down, but I was able to control it so I could roll over and plant a hard kick right below his knee. He dropped to the ground swearing, and I was already on my feet in a crouch when he looked at me. I held his gaze long enough for him to see me flip the gun over in my hand, and then I smashed the butt of it into the side of his head. He bellowed like an elephant and held up his hands to try to deflect the next one, but I planted a knee on his chest and shoved them out of the way, hitting him again.

"You pissed off the wrong guy, jack!" I yelled, backhanding him with it this time.

I was going for another solid blow to the head when Seth appeared at my side, catching my arm. "Dino," he said. "Come on, Dino, that's enough, man."

Adrenaline was running high and I tried to jerk free of him, but he was prepared and wouldn't let me. I relented and took a deep breath, eyes locked on Rick as I stood up and backed away, letting my arms go limp.

"That's good, real good," Seth said patting my chest. "Excuse me just a minute."

He eyed me for a second to make sure I was going to stay put, then turned to Rick, who was on his knees and trying to pull himself up using the corner of a dumpster.

"Okay, asshole, that is the second time you've pinned me to a bar and I'm starting to take it personally," Seth said, kneeling down to look at the guy, "So I'd really appreciate it if you'd leave me the fuck alone from now on, all right?" Then he punched old Rick in the gut hard enough to give him dry heaves.

We left him like that and got into my car, pulling out of the alley and turning to head for my place. Once I calmed down, my head started to throb and I could only imagine how much Seth hurt.

Seth leaned the seat back and said, "Correct me if I'm wrong here, but did we just get beat up for *not* being fags?"

* * * *

Up in my apartment, I yanked open my kitchen cupboard, took out a bottle of whiskey and set two glasses on the counter. Seth closed the front door and wandered over while I poured a couple of shots in each one.

"Whiskey?" he asked.

"Dulls the pain, gets the taste of blood out of your mouth, and makes you feel better about the whole situation. What more could you ask?" I pushed a glass at him.

My attempt at humor fell flat because I was still pissed as hell, and it came out sounding grim and dark. I looked at Seth and winced. He was a mess. Blood stained the front of his shirt and his face, as well as his hands and arms from trying to stop the flow of his bloody nose. He had a cut on his forehead and bruises forming down the side of his cheek and jaw where he'd hit the bar the hardest. On top of all of that, he was standing in a guarded way that told me his ribs were hurting pretty bad.

"Let's get you cleaned up," I said, tipping back half my whiskey in one swallow. "I'll grab you one of my shirts. You drink some of that, it'll help."

When I came out of the bedroom holding a T-shirt for him, he was clutching the glass and wheezing. "How in the hell do you drink this shit, man?"

"You thinkin' about your pain right now?" I asked.

He shook his head and grinned wryly.

I turned on the hot water, then switched on the radio and got a couple of beers out of the fridge which I gave to Seth to open. I put the stopper in the sink and put a little soap and two clean dishrags in the water. Then I went to the bathroom and came back with my first-aid kit.

"Come here and take your shirt off," I told him, shutting off the water and swishing the rags around to soak them. I pulled a stool over and pointed to it.

Seth came around the end of the counter, setting his beer down, and grabbed the hem of his shirt. He got it about halfway up before he stopped with a sharp gasp and some vile language. I went to help him take it off, which he seemed to appreciate judging by the expression on his face.

"Are you all right?" I tossed the shirt on the floor by the garbage can.

He arched an eyebrow at me, but didn't look upset. "Now you ask?"

"I've been watching."

"Yeah, I think I'm okay."

There was a large bruise starting to darken the left side of his chest, and I ran my fingers along it as gingerly as I could, feeling each rib. He barely made a sound, but when I was done, he reached for his whiskey and drained the rest of it.

"Sorry 'bout that," I said, "but I don't think any of them are broken. Cracked maybe. But I'm no expert."

"Can't do much about it either way," Seth wheezed. I took the glass out of his hand before he dropped it.

He sat on the stool, and I wrung out a dishrag to clean him up. When I turned to him, I noticed the blood had soaked through his shirt and was streaked all over his chest. "Stand up," I said.

"You just told me to sit."

"Now I'm telling you to stand. You got blood on your chest."

I handed him the rag and he took a couple of half hearted swipes at himself and thrust it back at me, leaning against the counter. "It hurts too much, you do it."

"Oh, now you're just bein' a baby."

"Sue me." He tried to smirk, but it was weak.

I laughed and started to wipe the blood off his chest, while he sipped his beer. His cheeks were flushed pink where they weren't bruised or bloody, and I thought the whiskey was hitting him. He never took his eyes off me once.

Finally, he spoke. "Can I ask you a question?"

"Shoot." I dipped the rag in the water and squeezed it out again.

"Why in the hell were you carrying your gun?"

I shrugged and thought for a minute, because I wasn't sure myself. "I don't know, I just sort of had a feeling that I might need it tonight, I guess. Like I knew something might happen, but I didn't know what."

Seth considered that and nodded. "Well, next time you wanna share that feeling with me, please?"

"Now you can sit," I told him. I spent a few minutes cleaning up his face and sticking a bandage over his cut, for which he was remarkably cooperative, then I held his head steady and felt along his nose with my thumbs.

"Ow," he said finally, struggling out of my grasp and poking at it himself.

"That's not broken, either," I said, picking up my whiskey glass and finishing it. "You're lucky."

"Yes, I feel very lucky right now." He stood up and I helped him put on the clean shirt, then he said, "Your turn."

"My turn, what? I'm fine."

"You're bleeding. He put a gash right above your eye. Didn't you notice?"

"I haven't been thinking about that."

He gave me a warm look and said, "Sit."

I took a seat and let Seth dab at my eye with a fresh rag. He took his time about it, and I wasn't sure if he was drunk or tired, but it didn't matter. The slow pace helped me calm down and finally relax. I think maybe he knew that, because he said, "You know, you kind of scared me out there."

I made a face. "I scared you? What do you mean? You've seen me in a fight before. Hell, you're worse than me when you've got your head on straight."

He paused and cocked his head. "Dino—you just pistol whipped a guy in an alley on my behalf. No, I have never seen you do that before."

"Well...maybe you're just not usually lookin' in the right direction."

He gazed at me flatly while he peeled open a bandage.

"Fine," I said with a sigh. "I don't know. I don't know what got into me. I was just so incredibly pissed off, and I really, really wanted to hurt that guy. It was just... You know, things have actually started to turn out good lately, and I was having a great time, and then this huge schmuck had to come and fuck it all up. I saw you on the floor, and all the blood, and I just...snapped."

"Don't get me wrong," Seth said, "I think the guy was totally asking for it. I've just never seen you quite that over the top before. Personally, I thought it was hot, but I wanna make sure you're not flipping out or anything." He stuck the bandage to my forehead and smoothed it flat with his fingers, still moving in slow motion. I wondered if he was dragging it out on purpose. Another one of his teases, only maybe more serious this time.

"No, I'm not flipping out." I took a sip of beer. "I just got a little out of control is all. And, ah, you thought that was hot?"

Seth grinned. He touched a finger to my lower lip. "Looks like he got you here too, I think there's a cut. You should put some ice on it."

"Seth?"

"Yes, Dino, I thought it was hot. Really, really hot. Like you're hot when you're all sweaty in your undershirt, and you're hot when you dance the tango." He was still touching my lip.

"Rumba...actually."

Okay, so I had a bead on what was going on, but I wasn't sure where it was coming from. It's no real mystery that Seth could be into me, if he wanted. He's pretty much into anything that seems like it would be a good time, but he's never once acted genuinely serious about it, so I've never brought it up. Besides, I never have figured out what I would say, anyway.

"Whatever it was, dude, you looked *good*." He smiled real slow and put his hands on my shoulders, moving closer.

I caught him gently by the arms and said, "Seth, I think the whiskey's getting to you. You're drunk."

"I'm not that drunk."

"You've never honestly hit on me before," I pointed out. Taking a shot at your best friend is a move you shouldn't make when you've had your bell rung and you're half in the bag. I didn't believe he really knew what he was doing.

"Don't think that hasn't taken some work, either," he told me.

"Oh, really," I said, giving him a look.

"Yeah, really. You find that so hard to buy?"

"Ah, yes, I do, actually."

Seth snorted. "I'm trying to figure out which one of us you're selling short."

"I'm not doing either, I'm just sayin' you've had a hell of a long day, and you're saying things you don't really mean."

He turned serious and said, "Yeah, Dino, I mean what I'm saying."

I didn't have a reply to that. I still thought I was right, of course, but he was sure he was right and we were just going to go around in circles on that point. I was about to suggest we call it a night, when he put a hand under my chin and kissed me. He moved slow and careful, like everything else, which I finally realized was one big seduction. He knew damn well what he was doing.

My pulse shot right up, which I took to be panic, and I froze. I could taste beer on his lips, and the coppery scent of blood still lingered under the soap. When he backed away looking like the cat who swallowed the canary, I blurted out, "I'm too old for you."

He laughed. "An eight year age difference is not exactly stretching the bounds of math."

"You're too young for me, then."

"I'm thirty-three years old, Dino. I'm not some horny teenager grasping at straws, here. I know what I'm doing."

"Yeah, I know what you are. Not too many people left who don't." He narrowed his eyes so I let that drop. "Why now, then?"

"Shit, Dino, I don't know. Because you're hot and I like you, because this seems like a good time? Because you almost killed a guy for me tonight?"

I rolled my eyes. "I didn't almost kill him. I just gave him a very good reason not to mess with you again."

"And I'm just sayin' that's a hell of a thing."

"You would have done the same for me."

"Doesn't that tell you something?" He gave me a shit-eating grin. Then he pressed up against me, standing between my legs so his body brushed my thighs. It felt absurdly intimate, given who he was. My pulse raced again, and this time I knew it wasn't panic. Damn if he wasn't getting under my skin.

Seth smirked. "How's this? I just got my face bashed in because we jerked a guy around by acting like a couple, and I think I should get to do what I got beat up for."

"Yes, that's an excellent reason to jump into bed."

"Dino, shut the hell up."

His hands were resting lightly on my neck and he slid them up to hold me captive while he kissed me again, longer and more insistent. This time he was not going to take no for an answer. He moaned softly and ran his tongue along my lower lip. His fingers tensed on my skin and he pulled me deeper into it, like he was either going to convince me by sheer will or get his money's worth while he could.

The whiskey left me warm and mellow, and the heat of his mouth on mine made my head spin, weakening my resolve that this was a bad idea. The rest of me was right on board with Seth, because it had been a long time since I'd had a warm body pressed up against me, and I wrapped my arms around him in spite of myself. There are some urges you just can't resist, and pulling someone close once they're in your arms is one of them. It felt good to be holding someone like that again, even if it was one person I knew damn well I shouldn't.

It also scared the shit out of me, because friends like Seth don't come along often, and I didn't want to mess up a good thing. Seth apparently wasn't worried, because he had one hand cupped around the back of my head and was starting to fumble at my shirt buttons with the other. I knew where that led.

We had to slow things down, and fast. My own lack of a recent date was no excuse for me to abandon reason at just the point when Seth clearly had none at all.

I broke the kiss and said, "Let me try the practical approach with you, then. Have you ever tried doin' it with banged up ribs?"

He lifted his head to look at me quizzically, and I gave him an extra firm squeeze. He groaned with pain and slumped over my shoulder. "God, you're an asshole."

"I'm just tellin' it like it is, kid. You're out of commission with me or anyone else for a couple of days at least. You're also tired, drunk, and in for a lot worse pain than you have now, so I think you should try to get some sleep before it sets in."

"Here?" he said with a slow smile.

"Sure," I told him, untangling myself and standing up. "You can crash on my sofa."

He scowled and backed away from me, snatching up his beer and drinking the rest of it. All the way down the hall, I could feel his glare on my back while I went to get him a pillow and a couple of blankets. I spread them out while he sulked against the counter with his arms folded over his chest. The ice didn't thaw much when I held out a hand to him, and he came over slowly, broadcasting loud and clear what he thought of this plan.

"Trust me, Seth, if this all has just been the whiskey talkin', you'll thank me in the morning."

"It's not."

"Then we'll talk about that tomorrow." I nudged him down on the sofa. "Get some sleep, all right?"

"Yeah, all right. Goodnight."

I put away the whiskey bottle and drained the sink, then snapped off the lights and went down the hall to fall into my own bed, mind reeling and body aching. It felt like a million years since we were sitting in Paradiso eating crab and talking about football. I had to figure out what I thought about it all, because there was no way I could pretend nothing had happened.

I was drifting off when I heard feet padding across the floor outside my bedroom. Seth appeared and climbed into bed, peering down at me. I opened one eye and he said, "You didn't really think I was going to sleep on the couch, did you?"

"You can stay, but we're *sleeping*, got that?"

"Fine by me. I have a splitting headache," he said, easing down onto his back.

Chapter 8

I woke up the next morning with an immediate awareness that I wasn't alone. Everything from the night before came back to me in a rush, and I opened my eyes to find Seth sitting up, staring at me.

He blinked at me with a bewildered expression and glanced around at the bed and us in it. "Dino? You wanna tell me what's going on here?"

For about three seconds, I was gripped by an ice cold chill, then I caught the tiniest flicker of mischief in his eye. I sat bolt upright and grabbed him by the collar, pulling him to within an inch of my face. "Do *not* yank my chain over this, you hear me?"

He snickered. "You were so askin' for it, with all your worrying last night." He leaned forward and kissed me. It was lazy and relaxed, and I was stunned at how easily he could switch gears. He pushed me down on my back and rolled onto me, stretching out gingerly.

I, however, do not adapt so easily, and I was trying to struggle out from under him without hurting his ribs, when Seth caught a look at the clock radio and said, "Shit, is that the time?"

"You in a hurry, here? I think we have a few things we need to go over, don't you?"

He had already scrambled off the bed and disappeared into the bathroom. When I turned over and saw the clock, I discovered it was only eight in the morning. "Oh, what the fuck are you doing?" I groaned. I hollered out to him, "It's Sunday, we don't need to be getting up at the crack of dawn!"

Seth appeared in the doorway, buttoning up his jeans. "I have a very sick little Chevy in my shop whose owner thinks I actually work during the week instead of chasing you around, and is expecting to be able to get her car tomorrow." He turned and darted back down the hall.

"What do you mean chasing me around?" I said, throwing back the blankets and getting up. "You spent one day helping me move."

"And a whole afternoon cleaning out your new office, and the better part of a day doing inventories and paperwork."

"Hey, I could have taken the 'Vette to Ernie's and left you to your work, you know. You're the one who made that call."

"My point is, I've gotta' make a living. And you need pants because you have to take me home."

I'd gone into the kitchen while he flailed around getting dressed, and was filling a pot of water. "I haven't had my coffee yet."

"Then give me your car keys," he said, sitting on the arm of my sofa to put his shoes on. He winced and sucked in breath when he bent over to grab them, and came up slowly, clutching his side.

A pang of sympathy gripped me, and I went to the bathroom to get him some ibuprofen. I brought it to him with a glass of water. "You look like hell, you know, and you're not movin' too good. How are you gonna work on cars?"

"I'll be all right. If I pour enough caffeine and pain killers down my throat, I'll be too wired to know if I hurt."

"That's a terrific plan."

"It's not the first time I've been beat up. I can handle it." He came up to me and kissed my neck, cupping the side of my face with his hand. He whispered, "Now give me your keys."

"Over my dead body."

* * * *

I dropped him off at the garage no more than twenty minutes later, in spite of what he tried to say about sloths, the progression of time, and hell freezing over. He was moving pretty slowly himself, but more out of necessity than laziness. I felt sorry for him, so I offered to go get him anything he liked for breakfast. Predictably, he chose doughnuts, but I think he sensed I was feeling guilty because he plastered on an especially pathetic face and requested doughnuts from a bakery which happens to be halfway across St. Pete. It was a nice enough day, and I didn't have any pressing plans, so I agreed, pathetic face or not.

He gave me a saucy smile and was about to get out when I grabbed his arm. "When are we gonna talk?" I asked.

"Tonight? Your place? I'll bring some pizza."

"Yeah, all right," I said, letting him go. "Take it easy today."

"You too." This time his smile was genuine.

I watched him head inside and wondered what in the fuck I'd gotten myself into. See, the thing is, I don't do flings. I don't mess around, I don't have affairs, I don't usually go out on a *date* with a person unless they're someone I think I could get serious about. I just don't operate that way, because I'm not very casual about my love life. Or my sex life. Those aren't separate things for me.

Seth is the exact opposite. He runs around, dates more than one person at a time, and has one night stands. He's always out there having fun. It's rare that I've ever seen him get serious about anyone.

So, I didn't know what this was to Seth, and I didn't know what letting myself get dragged into it meant for me. It had huge potential to end badly, which is what bothered me the most. I sighed and ran my hands over my face. Somewhere in the back of my brain, I realized it also had the potential to turn out pretty good, and I think maybe that worried me too.

With these happy thoughts in mind, I set off, first to get coffee, then to fetch Seth's doughnuts.

* * * *

I'd gotten maybe two blocks from Ed's when my cellphone rang. It was Seth.

"Think of something else you want?" I answered, reaching over to turn down the radio.

"You need to get back here," he said, sounding edgy. "Someone broke into my apartment."

"How can you tell?"

"Oh, that's rich. Har, har. Get your ass back here."

He was not amused, and he hung up on me. I tossed the phone on the dash and whipped a fast U-turn. It was highly unlikely whoever broke in was still there, but the image of Seth hunched on the floor, covered in his own blood, was still fresh in my mind, and I had no desire to see that again anytime soon.

When I pulled into the garage lot, Seth's door was wide open. I could hear Seth up in his apartment swearing a blue streak, and I was no longer worried about intruders hurting him. In fact, I really hoped for their sake they were long gone.

I reached the top of the stairs and poked my head in to see a mess about twice the size it normally was. And that's saying something. The place was trashed. All the kitchen drawers had been pulled out and dumped on the floor. The cupboards hung open, most of the contents swept out over the counter. The living room furniture had been upended and the undersides slashed, cushions ripped and flung on the floor.

I followed the streak of violent swearing into the bedroom, where Seth stood in the midst of more of the same devastation. The bed had been tossed, but the mattress looked like it was still intact, which was something. CDs were all over the floor. In fact, they were scattered like someone had flung them across the room, which was the first real sign of purposeless destruction I'd seen. Seth was so angry, I wondered if he'd done it.

"It was that fucking *asshole*," he seethed. "I know it. That fucking rat bastard didn't think beating the shit out of me was enough, he had to come and fuck up my place too. I should have let you beat the cocksucker's brains out, Dino."

"We don't know that." I picked my way along the wall to have a look in the bathroom. It was the same in there, cupboards open and drawers dumped on the floor. The shower curtain hung only from two rings. Some of the other rings had snapped from the pressure of being yanked, and lay in pieces at the bottom of the tub with the soap and shampoo. Another sign of loss of control.

"What do you mean, we don't know that? Who the fuck else would come in here and do this? Of course it was that fucker, it's obvious. He's not gonna lay off until we really have a showdown, and I tell you what, I'm gonna give him one. If that fucker thinks he can scare me by tearing the shit out of my place, he's as dumb as he is ugly. We're going out tonight, and we're gonna hunt that prick down and settle this once and for all." He picked up an empty beer bottle and threw it at the wall as hard as he could. It exploded with a heavy crash that sent pieces of glass flying everywhere.

"Hey, stop that," I said. "Get a hold of yourself. We're not doing any such thing."

He turned on me with fury in his eyes, and friend or not, I took a fight stance, just in case.

"The hell we're not, Dino. You saw what that cocksucker did to me last night, and I'm not letting him get away with it."

"We didn't let him get away with it. We took care of that."

"Does this look like it's taken care of to you?" He gave the bed a ferocious kick and then wheezed with pain, clutching at his side.

"All right," I said, going over to help him get steady on his feet and prevent any further violence. "If you're done playing twelve pounds of fury, here, I'd like to point out a couple things to you."

"Fuck off, Dino," he snapped, giving me a dirty look. "This isn't funny. He raided the shop too, you know."

"I know it's not funny. You want to listen to me now?"

"What?"

"Okay, first of all, if this was someone lookin' to get even with you over a fight, they would have done a hell of a lot more damage."

He got indignant and gave me a shove. "You don't think they did enough?"

"Get a grip!" I snapped, glaring at him. He locked eyes with me and silently panted with rage. After a few seconds I saw him get control over his anger and ease off. "You gonna behave yourself now?"

He scowled, but nodded and looked at me expectantly.

"What I mean," I told him, "is this place hasn't been vandalized, it's been ransacked. If this was revenge, he'd have smashed your TV and your stereo, broken some windows, maybe spray painted threats on the wall. He'd make damn sure you knew who was here, and why. But this mess? This was made by someone looking for something. You got robbed, Seth, and the only connection it has to last night is that you weren't here, so they could."

"Well, if I got robbed, wouldn't they have *taken* my TV and stereo?"

"Not necessarily. Some guys don't deal in stuff like that. They take cash, jewelry, and anything they can use for identity theft. Small, portable stuff."

Truthfully, that didn't seem too likely either, because those thieves don't hit crappy garage apartments, they work the expensive high-end homes in the suburbs. But I've seen enough search jobs to know what one looks like.

Seth looked around slowly, taking in what I'd said, but he was shaking his head. "I don't know, Dino, I don't believe in coincidence. That bastard was in here last night, I'm sure of it."

"No, you just want someone you can kick the shit out of for this, and he's convenient. I can pretty much guarantee he wasn't in any shape to do much of anything last night."

That finally got him to calm down and climb off the Kill Rick the Rat Bastard platform. He knew damn well I was right because his own parting shot would have been enough to put the guy out of commission for the night.

"Well, then who in the hell was it?" he asked, grim faced and still boiling just under the surface.

"I don't know, but I'm gonna find out, okay?" I put a hand on his shoulder. "I think we oughta' report this, though."

"Yeah, fine, whatever."

"Listen, why don't you try to figure out what's missing. Don't dick with stuff too much, just have a look around so you know what to tell the cops when they get here."

"Where are you gonna be?"

"My phone is down in the car, and I want to take a look at the shop. I'll call it in while I do that. Are you calm now? Can I do this and not worry about you goin' all vigilante on me?"

He flipped me off, but nodded. "Yeah. I'm good. I think. Shit... What am I gonna do, Dino? I don't have time for this crap. I have work to do."

I looked around. "Don't worry about it. We'll talk to the cops, and then you fix the Chevy and I'll start cleaning up the mess here. You wouldn't know how to do it right anyway."

"You can't do this all yourself."

"Oh, I don't plan to," I said. "But I can get a good head start while you catch up downstairs, then you can help me finish."

"Shit, we'll be up all night..." With his anger wearing off, he sounded weary and annoyed over the whole situation.

"No, no. We can start in here, and do the kitchen so it's livable, and tackle the rest later. It'll be good, you'll see."

He nodded, but didn't look entirely convinced as he started to poke around. I gave him a pat on the back and went outside to get my phone.

Chapter 9

I have a couple of good friends on the force, and we help each other out from time to time. They occasionally have situations where their need to follow the letter of the law hampers them in getting the job done, so I come work the edges for them. Then there's times when I find a more official approach makes my job run smoother. Generally, it's a win-win situation, as long as we don't step on each other's toes.

I flipped open my phone and dialed while I crossed the parking lot to have a look in the shop. It was actually in much better shape than I'd been expecting, based on the mess upstairs. Obviously, someone had gone through the whole place, digging in drawers and shoving stuff around on shelves, but it wasn't the wholesale sacking the apartment got. My impression was they'd started downstairs and gotten sloppier and more destructive as they'd moved on.

The phone rang several times, and I was about to hang up and try someone else, when a breathless voice came on the line. "Hello?"

"Teresa, hi," I said brightly.

"Dino? Wow, it's been a while."

"Yeah. Say, did I catch you at a bad time?"

"I was in the back yard playing football with the boys. I think you did me a favor actually," she said with a smile in her voice. "I was getting my ass kicked. How are you?"

"Well, you know, I've been better, but I'm getting things straightened out. Listen, I need a favor. Someone broke into Seth's place last night and I want to report it, but I'd like to keep it low key. Can you come and take the report?"

Teresa Clyne and I had been friends for almost fifteen years. I met her when she was working as a Service Aide for the police department in the early days of her career, and I could always get her to do a little digging in the police records on the sly for me. If she hadn't already been married to a construction worker, with two little kids, I might have asked her out.

"I see," she said. "And why do we want to keep this low key? What did you do, Dino?"

"Ah, I can't really get into specifics, you know how it is, but let's just say there may be some circumstances involved. I don't know."

She sighed heavily. "Are you asking me to bend the rules, here, or toss the manual right out the window? I do have limits, you know."

"Hey, come on, you know me. You know I don't operate that way. I'd never ask you to do anything seriously illegal."

There was a long pause. "Yeah, all right. I can't promise you carte blanche, though. You know that, right?"

"I know that," I said. "You're a sweetheart. We're at Ed's Garage just off the causeway. By the marina."

"Sure, I know the area. I'll be there in about half an hour."

I thanked her and we hung up. Then I spent a few more minutes checking out the shop. The Chevy was there waiting, an old green thing with rust around the wheel wells. The other slot was empty. In the office, it was clear someone had gone through all the drawers, but these ones hadn't been dumped. I went over to the filing cabinet where Seth kept the cash box and opened the drawer. The cash box was there and undamaged, but I couldn't tell from looking at it if it'd been opened.

Seth appeared in the doorway and ran a hand through his hair. "I can't come up with anything that's missing, Dino. I mean, I don't have a lot of shit anyone would want to steal. Granddad's pocket watch is still there. It's really not worth much, but it's an antique. Petty thieves wouldn't know any better."

"Did you look in here?" I asked, nodding toward the file drawer.

He looked startled. "Shit, no. I was in too big a hurry to see if they'd been upstairs."

I reached in and flicked open the latch as gingerly as I could, but decided either there were prints all over the place or there weren't any. I lifted the lid. Inside was a small stack of bills, mostly fives and tens, a cup of assorted change and a roll of quarters. I looked at Seth.

He shook his head. "I just did a deposit on Thursday. I left about a hundred bucks total for petty cash, including the change. I could count it if you want, but it looks like it's all there."

"Yeah, so robbery's not looking so good anymore."

Seth's expression turned dark again. "You want to take a run down to Henry's tonight and bust that fucker up?"

"Jesus, will you cool it, already? When did you start channeling Joe Pesci?"

"Damn it, Dino, I don't get why you're not with me on this."

"Because it doesn't fit, that's why."

I was saved from further argument by the sound of a car pulling into the lot and shutting off. Seth and I walked through the garage and reached the door in time to see Teresa climb out of her SUV. Teresa is a reasonably attractive woman in her late thirties with shoulder length brown hair and practical cop clothes. She's down to earth and has a warm smile I like.

"Hey, Dino," she said, giving me that exact smile as she came up to us, opening a small notebook and taking out a pen. "Aside from the circumstances, it's good to see you."

"Good to see you too. You know Seth, right?"

"We've met a couple of times." She looked Seth over, then me, then crossed her arms and stared pointedly at the bruise around my eye. "Okay, what happened to you two?"

"I fell down the stairs."

"I ran into a wall."

"Uh-huh," she said, sucking her teeth. "That's how you're playing this?"

"Dino told you about the break-in, right?" Seth asked, hedging toward the stairs. "That is what you're here for?"

"Yep, it is, lead the way," she said, giving us both a dubious look.

Teresa followed Seth up to the apartment and I went after her. She did the usual, checking the door for signs of forced entry, which there were, and making notes about the events of the last twelve hours as she questioned Seth.

She stood in the middle of the living room, looking around, and asked, "Have you been able to come up with a list of what's missing?"

"That's the thing," Seth said, studiously ignoring me "There's nothing missing. I think this was a personal attack. They didn't even take the cash box. This was just to scare me or get revenge or something."

"Someone was getting even with you?" Teresa asked, raising an eyebrow.

I groaned inwardly.

"Well, look around at this mess," Seth said, getting testy. "They didn't take anything, so what do you think?"

She poked a pizza box with her toe and flipped it up to reveal a handful of crusts and two slices of pizza dried into stiff curls. "And these vengeful thugs brought rotting pizza and dirty socks with them to really do the job right?"

Seth gaped at her and then looked to me. "This is your idea of help?"

Teresa looked at me too, grinning. "How much of this mess is vandals?"

"Half," I told her. "Maybe a third."

"That's great," said Seth, stomping around. "Make jokes. That's real nice. Both of you can just suck my left—"

"Hey!" I barked, glaring a warning at him. I turned to Teresa. "You saw the door. Someone was definitely here."

"Oh yeah, I can see that," she said with a nod. "They did a hell of a job too. Lucky thing you weren't here at the time."

"Exactly," said Seth, "and what's to say he's not going to come back and finish the job?"

"Ah, now we're getting somewhere," Teresa said, looking smug. "Who's *he*?"

It finally occurred to Seth to shut his mouth, but of course it was a little too late for that. It didn't matter much anyway, the idea Rick the Rat might come back to finish the job was exactly why I wanted to file a report in the first place. I still wasn't convinced it was him, but if it was and he was going to keep going after Seth, I wanted something on record. I just had to be careful about it.

"Come on, boys," she said in the exact same tone I'd heard her use with her sons. "Who wants to go first? Red? What happened to your face? That's not even a day old."

Seth sighed and gave her a brief account of our tangles with Rick, starting with hitting on the girlfriend, and ending with Rick taking a swing at me in the bar. In his version, that's where it ended. I didn't say anything.

"Sounds pretty cut and dried," Teresa said. She narrowed her eyes at me. "Dino?"

"Yes?" I tried to look innocent, but she wasn't buying it and continued to regard us both suspiciously.

"What? That attack in the bar was totally unprovoked," Seth said. "There were about thirty witnesses who saw him jump me."

I gave up. "Yeah, and those same thirty witnesses saw me herd the guy out the door at gunpoint, Seth."

"No, I am not hearing this..." Teresa said, holding up her hands. "I'm not hearing this, don't say another word."

"Now you understand why I wanted to keep it low key?"

"You didn't shoot him, did you?" she asked.

"I did not shoot him, I swear," I told her. She seemed significantly relieved and I said, "What kind of a thug do you think I am?"

"It's only because I actually do know what kind of a thug you are, and are not, that I'm not hearing any of this." She stuffed her notebook in the back pocket of her jeans. "I'll file a very carefully worded report which will get conveniently lost on my desk. If you have any more trouble with this guy, it'll be on record. But I am telling you both...do *not* have any more trouble with this guy, you hear me?"

"Yeah, yeah," I said. "Trust me, we don't plan to. Personally, I don't think it was the guy."

"What makes you say that?" she asked.

Seth looked mutinous, but I could worry about that later. "It's not right for a revenge or a scare tactic. The place was methodically searched, not outright vandalized. Don't you think?"

"Yeah, I can see that," Teresa said thoughtfully as she studied the scene again.

"But what in the hell would anyone be looking for?" Seth said, throwing his hands in the air.

Then it hit me. Of course. I knew exactly what someone might be looking for, and I had a pretty good idea who it probably was. Mentally, I gave myself a good, swift kick in the ass. How could I have been so stupid?

"Ah, yeah, you're probably right," I told Seth, patting him on the back. I turned to Teresa and said, "Well, we've kept you away from the kids long enough. Thanks for stopping by. If you need a favor just give me a call."

I ushered her toward the door, but she resisted, looking highly skeptical. "You sure changed your tune in a hell of a hurry."

"Yeah, you didn't hear that either."

"Dino..." she said reproachfully.

"It's probably nothing," I said, pushing her outside. "If it turns into something, I'll let you know."

"You'd better," she said as she went down the stairs. "I'll be keeping an eye on you."

I went back in to find Seth crouched on the floor carefully lining up engine parts on the coffee table. He looked up me with a smug expression, which I took great delight in squashing with the words, "Darryl Serrano."

"What?" he asked, screwing up his face.

"Darryl Serrano. That's who was in here, I'd bet you a hundred bucks."

"What the hell are you—" Seth stopped as understanding dawned on his face. "The shit from the 'Vette. You mean fuckin' Ernie ratted us out?"

"No, no, remember how tired he was? He was havin' a bad day because the alarm went off the night before. We thought it was Serrano then too, but I never figured he'd go any farther. Ed's Garage is listed all over the paperwork as the repo agent."

Seth stood up and rubbed his hands on the front of his jeans. "Then he's got your name too."

"But no address. I never gave Ernie the new address, and it's too early for anyone to be able to trace where I'm at. It's not like he can just look me up in the phone book right now."

"Well, I guess that weird-ass little notebook is worth something after all," Seth said.

"Yeah, and I bet he wants his car keys too. You and I both know he didn't find what he was looking for."

Seth looked around at the trashed apartment. "That is very true. I think for my own personal safety, and yours, I'm going to have to sleep at your place again tonight."

"Yeah, but who's gonna keep me safe from *you*?"

He flashed a wicked grin, which was pretty convincing in spite of the bruises on his face.

"I'm serious, Seth, we need to talk."

"Hey, if I can walk and chew gum at the same, I sure as hell can talk and fu—"

"All right, all *right*!" I said, cutting him off. "Just go downstairs and get to work. I'll start in on this mess, see how far I can get."

"Yeah, yeah, okay," he said, clearly relieved to be getting out of cleaning duty.

"Seth," I said, catching him on the threshold. He turned to look. "You're buyin' the beer this time."

He gave me a thumbs up and was gone.

Chapter 10

I spent most of the day cleaning Seth's apartment, and although I'd made pretty good headway, the place was still a wreck. That meant it was more or less back to normal, but I figured since he'd helped me move, I could probably put in some extra time and get the place really fixed up. That wasn't going to happen in a day, though.

The problem with working there alone was it gave me too much time to think, and I wound up more confused than ever. When Seth hollered up to say he was going to work through lunch, I was relieved, but at the same time, it was driving me nuts to keep putting off the talk we needed to have. I wanted to know what in the hell was going on in his head.

I certainly wasn't having much luck figuring out what was going on in my *own* head. I knew damn well the whole thing was a very, very bad idea, and I was reasonably certain it was mostly Seth's own impulsive nature at work, rather than anything serious. But I couldn't deny that in some small way he'd gotten to me. If I tried, I could almost feel his mouth, and his body under my hands. Part of me wanted to feel that again. If nothing else, I was curious to see if I responded to him the same way.

Sometime in the early evening, someone knocked at the door, and I went through the living room to answer it. To my surprise, there stood Seth. He was wearing his sunglasses and leaning against the door frame with a pizza in one hand and a six-pack of Coke dangling from the other. "You ever played that game with the pizza delivery boy and the lonely housewife?" he asked.

"As a matter of fact I have, and I left both of them begging for more."

"*Oh*, big talker." He came in and put everything on the kitchen counter.

I shut the door and followed him, pulling out some plates and napkins and putting them next to the box. It was from Spinelli's, my favorite pizza place, and I wondered if that was an intentional gesture on his part. I went to the fridge and took out a beer, twisting the cap off and tossing it at the garbage can. It hit the wall and bounced in.

"You want a beer?" I asked, taking a sip.

"Nope, I'm good." He snapped a can of Coke out of the six-pack and held it up.

Having pizza without beer is damn near a crime in our book, and I raised my eyebrows at him.

"You're not going to have to wonder if anything I say or do tonight is the result of impaired judgment," he explained.

"Yeah, all right, I guess that's fair." I felt a little clammy because this was it, and I wasn't sure I was ready.

Seth sat down across from me, piled several slices of pizza on his plate, and opened his Coke. "So what's it gonna be, Dino? You think you can handle me?"

"You think you can be serious for ten minutes?"

He blinked at me, mouth stuffed full of cheese and pepperoni, and nodded. His eyes met mine and held my gaze as if he could prove it to me. It had the effect of making him look extremely earnest, even with tomato sauce on his lip.

"So, you want to tell me where in the hell this came from?" I asked. "We've been hanging out for a lot of years and never once have I gotten the idea that you were actually interested in me. It was all just kidding around."

He swallowed. "Yeah, well, it's not like you'd notice, man."

"What's that supposed to mean?"

Seth wiped his mouth and took a drink of Coke. "You're not really the most...romantically attuned person I've ever met."

I frowned. "I can be very romantic when I want to be, what the hell would you know about it?"

"That's just it—when you want to be, which as far as I can tell is pretty few and far between. I don't know how the fuck you maintain sanity. You get laid like, what? Twice a year?"

"So what am I, a charity case for you?"

"No. You wanted to know why you had no clue that I've checked you out from time to time, and I'm just saying it's because you're never looking for that."

"Then why, what is this?"

He finished gnawing on a pizza crust and dropped it on his plate. He wiped off his hands and said, "I don't know, Dino, I really don't. I've always thought you were hot, and you're great to hang out with. This past week has been kind of cool. And when you tried to beat a guy to death for me last night, I got to thinkin' maybe you'd go for it."

"You know I've never dated a guy," I said, drinking beer.

Seth coughed into his fist and smirked at me. "Right, you're the poster boy for Straight America."

"Excuse me?"

"Sorry, you just don't scream hetero he-man, dude. I wouldn't call you flaming or anything, but let's just say your toes are singed. Hell, I read straighter than you do."

"You know, having a little class and style doesn't have anything to do with—"

"That's not my point, Dino," Seth said, cutting me off. "Look, I may never have seen you *date* a guy, but I sure as hell have caught you checking them out, and as far as I'm concerned everyone is at least a little bit bi given the right circumstances. I just thought I might have found yours."

Yeah, well, given my reaction, maybe he had. I could see that. But I could also see where this was a dicey proposition for what was currently a great friendship. "So what does all that mean?" I asked. "What's in it for you?"

"Are you always this uptight about relationships?"

"Yeah. Yes, I am. That's me in a nutshell, right there," I said, challenging him. "That's why we're sitting here having this discussion. It's also why you think I only get laid twice a year."

Seth leaned across the table with a hopeful expression. "Oh, please tell me it's more than that?"

I rolled my eyes and got up from the table, collecting the plates and putting them in the sink. I dropped the napkins in the garbage, then closed up the pizza box and shoved it in the fridge.

Seth was right behind me when I turned around, giving me a very calculating look. He pushed me gently back against the fridge and leaned into me. My brain simultaneously spit out the fact that he felt pretty good, and a reminder of everything I knew about his dating habits.

"I don't do flings, Seth," I blurted out. "I don't mess around much at all, and I'm really not sure I'm your type. Or speed."

"You need to relax," he said evenly.

"That's easy for you to say, you do this kind of thing all the time."

He smirked. "Then you know you're in expert hands."

"I'm tryin' to be serious, here," I said, pushing him a few steps back.

"Dude, I know that, I'm being serious when I say you have to relax, at least a little. Get messy, go with the flow. Ease up, man."

"You sound like a hippie."

"You were into it, Dino. You wanted me last night." He leaned back against the counter and slouched into a pose he had to have perfected years ago, given how naturally he slipped into it. "Tell me you don't like what you see."

I took a drink of beer and considered him. He's very good looking when it comes down to it, minus the bruising and black eye. He'd raked his thick hair in place with his fingers, and it curled up at the back of his neck. He had a day's worth of razor stubble, and I realized he had the damnedest bedroom eyes. I'm pretty sure I was meant to notice, and it made me want to touch him again, which unnerved me and excited me at the same time.

I moved closer, trying to negotiate the strange tension between us that was half flirtation and half challenge. I licked my lips and nodded. "Yeah, I like what I see."

"You're pretty good lookin' yourself, you know." His eyes gleamed, and he reached out to pluck at my shirt. "Come on, take a chance. Please?"

I did want him. I couldn't deny that after the way I'd reacted. I had a lot of reservations about it, but I still wanted him. So, I tried kissing him. Yeah, I know I'd kissed him a few times in the last twenty-four hours, but those were all him hitting on me. This time, I was the one doing the kissing and I meant to take my time about it, find out if this was something I really wanted to jump into.

I kissed him softly a couple of times, brushing over his lips. Getting acquainted, so to speak. Then I pressed my mouth to his, kissing deeper and longer, learning the taste and the feel of him. He moaned and melted against me, clutching at my waist. It was *good*. My pulse raced, and I felt drunk. Before I knew it, I was holding him back against the counter, pressed hip to hip, while I completely dominated a kiss I wasn't willing to end.

After a few minutes, Seth's hands clamped over my wrists, and he broke away to take a deep breath and pant, "Jesus...you are fucking intense when you finally figure out what you want."

"I don't have anything figured out," I said. "But once a thing like this is out of the bag, you can't stuff it back in and pretend it never happened."

For better or worse, it was out there, and the fact remained that he was right, for whatever reason, he'd gotten to me.

"Not too easily," he said. He kissed me again, nipping at my lip and mouthing a hot trail down the side of my neck. Then he slipped out from between me and the counter and started walking backward toward his bedroom, eyeing me with a shit-eating grin.

My heart was pounding and my breathing heavy. I could feel an electric buzz on my skin everywhere we'd touched. I watched him in the dim light, and his grin widened.

When I didn't follow, he peeled his T-shirt off and dropped it to the floor. I know he was trying to be sexy and maybe tempt me to do the same, but I didn't miss the fact that it hurt him, and my eye was instinctively drawn to the dark, menacing bruise stretching across his ribs. A flash of anger shot through me, and I went over to him, kneeling to check the damage.

Seth gave an exasperated sigh. "For fuck's sake, Dino, I'm *fine* already. If you're so concerned about my health, let's talk about the monumental case of blue balls I'm gonna have when I finally get you into bed."

I smirked, but couldn't help running a hand down his side, feeling for anything that seemed out of place. He was right, of course, there was nothing wrong that time wouldn't fix. Although, I did think a couple of Ace bandages might help.

"If you want to have the serious talks," he said, "how 'bout you tell me where *this* came from. When did you develop such a mother hen complex?"

I stood up and sighed. "I don't know, I just don't like seeing you hurt, especially when I was sitting right there. I do care what happens to you, you know. Friends care about each other."

"Well, Mom, you can relax. Now do me."

He started to flick open the buttons of my shirt with surprising dexterity, and I watched with impressed interest for a moment before I caught his hands. "Seth...you're still not in any shape to be doing this."

"I can personally guarantee that getting a blow job will not in any way affect the healing of my ribs."

I grinned, but said, "Well, I'm still getting used to this idea. I told you I wasn't your speed."

He scrunched his fingers in my shirt slowly. "This isn't as completely out of the blue as you think it is, Dino."

"It is for me," I said. "You're gonna have to give me a little more time."

He relented, and managed not to look terribly put out. "Yeah, all right, I hear ya. But you can't expect me to like it."

"I wouldn't dream of it."

"And you said I should stay at your place tonight." He licked his lips and glanced up at me from under his eyelashes.

"I still think you should. But I do expect you to behave yourself."

He nodded and turned to head toward the bedroom. "I'll be ready to go in about ten minutes. I'm just gonna go take a cold shower and stab myself in the heart with my toothbrush a few times."

"Okay," I said. "You need me to lock up downstairs?"

Half an hour later, I parked Matilda outside my apartment building. Seth's caffeine had worn off, and his injuries were taking their toll. He was exhausted and had fallen asleep in the seat on the way over. I nudged him until he sat up with a startled expression.

I smirked. "Yeah, and you thought you were gonna make time with me like some big shot Casanova..."

"Shh," he said, putting a finger to his lips. "Don't tell anybody, I have a reputation to maintain."

Chapter 11

Seth had managed to flip my world right on its ear, and I don't think he even knew it.

I tried to spend the next afternoon skip tracing for a bond agent who's a regular client of mine, but I couldn't concentrate. My mind kept drifting back to Seth. His sudden interest had me at a total loss. I had no frame of reference for turning a friend into a lover, male or female, and I didn't know what the rules were. I wasn't even sure it was such a hot idea.

But, I couldn't deny I wanted him, and I'd made the choice to kiss him. Right or wrong, I was knee deep in it, and I had to figure out where I stood. The best solution I could see was to approach the situation the only way I knew how.

At two o'clock, I gave him a call.

"Hey," he said, sounding pleased to hear from me. He managed to put one hell of a seductive lilt into that single word.

"Listen," I said, "how'd you like to have dinner at my place? I'll cook."

"You wanna cook dinner for me? You mean like a date?" He sounded dubious.

"Yes, like a date. You know, it's that thing people do when they're into each other and want to spend time together. If you had a normal love life, you would know this."

Seth made a rude noise. "I know what dating is, asshole."

"Really? Tell me about your last date."

"You met her," he said, "you tell me."

"The girl in the garage?" I rolled my eyes. "That wasn't a date, that was combat." His response to me was pointed silence. "Did you buy her dinner first? Talk to her? Do you even know her last name?"

"Yes, I know her last name."

"Well, that's a start. See, the thing is...I date. I'm an old fashioned kind of guy and there's just a certain order things are supposed to happen in. This is how it's done where I come from."

"Ah, I got news for you, Dino," he said with a chuckle. "New York is hooker central. Fifty bucks gets it done where you come from."

I sighed. "First of all, I was referring to the way I was raised, and second, New York is a very romantic city."

"Don't get your panties in a wad, I'm in, I would love to have dinner with you. Should I bring the beer?"

"Yeah. Come early, you can help me cook."

"Shit, you're gonna make for work for everything, aren't you?" he groused, and hung up.

I put the phone away feeling a kind of anticipation I hadn't felt for a while. I was also nervous as hell, because this was still Seth I was thinking about, and part of my brain kept telling me it was flat-out wrong. Seth was for football games and fist fights, not dating and sex.

I was committed to my plan, though. I wanted to find out if my reaction to Seth was real, and if there was anything behind it. There was no question that I cared about him, but I was curious to see how far that went.

I walked to the grocery store to pick up the ingredients for Cioppino— fish stew my mother used to cook. It's easy to make, but you look impressive as hell when you're chopping fresh herbs, slinging around white wine, and have six different kinds of seafood sitting on the counter.

While I was out shopping, I began to get into the spirit of getting ready for a date. I was planning to wine and dine Seth whether he liked it or not. He would just have to deal with me. If it felt right, that would be a sign we were headed in the right direction. If it didn't, well...it was still food and beer.

After I got the herbs, tomato sauce, and other ingredients at the grocery store, I stopped off at a small fish market I like. Looking at what was fresh, I picked two kinds of fish, mussels, shrimp, scallops and a big lobster tail to chunk up. I got white wine for cooking, red wine for serving, and a fresh loaf of bread from the bakery. Then I headed for home.

First, I had to get the fish stock for the Cioppino going. I cleaned the two fish, throwing the heads and bones into a stock pot, then did the same with the shrimp and lobster, adding the shells and putting the meat away for later. I put onion and celery into the pot, ground some pepper on top, and covered it all with water. Then I put it on the stove to simmer. The rest could wait until Seth got there to help.

Once the stock was well under way, and the kitchen cleaned up, I took a shower and got dressed. I combed my hair, brushed my teeth, even shaved and slapped on a little cologne. I put on black slacks and a thin, gray sweater I think sits on me pretty good.

As I dressed, it occurred to me that I got a charge out of the vast difference between my style and Seth's. Something about the contrast between us appealed to me. I didn't know what, exactly, but I would have been disappointed if he showed up in anything other than a ratty T-shirt and old jeans.

I went into the living room, turned on the stereo, and put on my favorite Dean Martin CD. I played *That's Amore* twice, because I don't care what anyone says, that's a hell of a good song. After that, I programmed the player to skip it, because it would more than likely send Seth screaming from the building.

Around five-thirty, he let himself in through the front door, shoving his sunglasses up on his head and carrying a six-pack of beer. It wasn't cheap beer this time, it was Corona and he had a lime jammed in among the necks of the bottles. He didn't disappoint me in his choice of wardrobe, either. His jeans were soft and faded, and his T-shirt had a cartoon bunny with the caption "Hi. Eat me."

He paused in the middle of the room and looked me over, then glanced at the stereo, gnawing his lip the way people do when they're trying not to laugh. I flashed him a smug smile.

Seth gave me one of his own, which made his eyes sparkle with wicked glee. Without saying a word, he set the beer on the counter and put his sunglasses with it. He came into the kitchen, slammed me up against the refrigerator and kissed me hard and dirty, shoving a thigh between my legs. I returned the favor by grabbing a fist full of T-shirt and wrapping an arm around his waist to pull him closer.

When we had to break it up for air, he said, "Just checking."

"Checking what?"

"That you haven't gone completely Martha Stewart on me."

"Not completely," I said.

He took two beers out of the box and tossed me the lime before putting the rest in the fridge. I took down the cutting board and sliced it into wedges, while Seth hopped up to sit on the counter.

"Have a good day?" I asked, stuffing a lime into my beer and taking a sip.

"Fuck," he said with a disgusted tone. "Ed got it into his skull that he should see how the shop is doing, so I came home to find him crashing around in there rearranging everything. For some reason, he thought the garbage cans should be on the other side of the workbench, then we had to resort all the tools. And on top of that, he made me haul a bunch of shit in from the truck."

I couldn't help but chuckle.

"It's not funny, Dino. I have the shop set up just how I want it, and he gets in there and fucks it all up. Drives me crazy, I swear. I think he's getting senile." Seth shook his head and took a long drink of his beer.

I got the herbs and vegetables from the fridge, and set them by the cutting board, then took a knife and minced garlic while Seth talked.

"After all that, he wanted to piss around in the office and look at the books and everything. I mean, that's fine, it's his business and all, but he gets crotchety about it and the whole thing is just one giant pain in the ass."

"That is why I work for myself. I don't think I *could* work for anyone else again." I scraped diced celery off the cutting board into my hand and put it in a bowl, then took a drink of beer and started on the onion.

"Yeah, well, that's my goal," said Seth. "Someday, that old fart is going to realize he's old, and then he'll let me have the place. Problem is, I think I get the fuckin' dogs too."

"I like the flat headed one," I said. "She's a sweet dog."

"Yeah, she's cool. But Edgar is an irritating lump of shit, and I'd give my left nut to be allowed to drop-kick him over the fence just once." Seth finished his beer and tossed it in a neat arc, landing it squarely in the wastebasket.

"You gonna help me out here?" I asked, gesturing to the food on the counter.

"No, you seem to have it covered pretty well," he said, leaning back on the palms of his hands. "I'm just here to look pretty."

"Fuck that. You'll look just as pretty opening cans of tomato sauce and getting out a skillet."

Seth jumped down and pulled open the drawer underneath the oven. "Which one is a skillet?"

"A fry pan. Sauté pan." I turned to look. "The flat one, moron."

"Hey, don't get shitty with me, I'm not the cook around here." He set the skillet on a front burner and dug through drawers until he found the can opener. I pointed to the cans of sauce, and he started to open them.

When the onion was chopped, I threw it in with the celery and did the peppers. Seth opened a second beer for himself and sat on the counter near the stove while I cooked.

I put both butter and olive oil in the pan like my mother used to. When it started to sizzle, I dumped all the vegetables in and gave them a quick stir.

I handed Seth the wooden spatula and said, "Keep an eye on that."

"What's it gonna do?"

"It's gonna cook down a little. Just push it around a few times so it doesn't burn."

"Where are you going?"

"Ah, two feet away. I think you can handle this." I smirked to myself as I went to chop up the basil, oregano and parsley.

"Hey, bitch, get in here and cook my damn dinner!" he barked.

I flipped him off.

After I threw the herbs in the pan, I added the garlic and a few other seasonings and gave the whole thing another stir with the spatula Seth gratefully handed over. Delicious smelling steam rose out of it and combined with the scent of the fish stock still simmering. Took me right back to my childhood.

Seth sat there with his beer in his hands, watching with interest. More than once, I could feel his gaze squarely on me, rather than the cooking, and I got a rush from the attention.

"I don't suppose you know how to open a bottle of wine?" I asked him.

"Nope," he said, taking a swig of beer.

I turned down the heat under the skillet and got out the wine opener, then put the white wine on the counter in front of me, peeled off the cover, and dealt with pulling the cork.

Seth grinned. "You know, all this skill in the kitchen, it's really hot, Dino."

"This gets you hot?" I asked, holding up the wine opener and the cork I'd just twisted off it.

"Yup," he said, giving me one of those smoky looks of his. "It's very sexy. I like it."

As I said, Cioppino is impressive stuff to make. I poured some wine in the pan with the onions and celery, and added Tabasco and Worcestershire. I mixed everything together and took out another soup pot to put it in. The final step was to add the tomato sauce and let it simmer alongside the fish stock.

"There," I said, wiping down the counter and rinsing my hands. "In about an hour we can eat."

"Gee, what should we do until then?"

I moved to stand between his knees, sliding him to the edge of the counter so we fit together nice and cozy. It was awkward and bizarre to be coming on to him, but I wanted to do the evening right, and I already knew I liked what came next. "I imagine we can come up with something."

He draped his arms around my neck, and I leaned in to kiss his throat. He was warm and smelled spicy and clean. I ran the tip of my tongue over his skin, lapping at him as I kissed my way up to his ear. He moaned, and the sound went right to my cock, making me half hard. I'd barely touched him.

I wrapped my arms around his waist and held him tight, not just because I liked the feel of his body against mine, but because I was overwhelmed by how much I actually wanted him there. I wasn't expecting that. He hooked a leg around me and moved so he could kiss me on the mouth, lips moving seductively over mine until we were both breathless. I felt light-headed.

"Dino?" he asked softly, dipping down to lick at my throat.

"Yeah?"

"Are you going to make me listen to Dean Martin all night?"

"I might."

"You are such a prick."

I grinned. "You got something else you want to listen to?"

He gave me an enthusiastically sloppy kiss and slid down off the counter. While he ran out to his truck to get some CDs, I stirred both the soup and the stock and drank some of my beer. What I was feeling had moved away from my initial panic and was starting to feel like something I could maybe get used to.

When Seth came back, he was clutching a stack of CD cases that looked like they had seen better days. He headed straight to the stereo. I went and looked over his shoulder while he took out Dean Martin and replaced it with some band I'd never heard of, that had a name I couldn't pronounce. The music, if you could call it that, sounded like someone knocked over all the garbage cans and stepped on a cat.

"This is your idea of something good to listen to?" I asked, staring at him.

"Yeah. This is raw and powerful. It kicks ass and gets me pumped up. Can't you feel that?"

"I can feel it making my fillings throb."

He shook his head sadly. "We have got to expand your horizons, man."

He spent the next hour trying, with limited success. After a while, I checked my watch and said, "You know, I think we could finish the Cioppino just about any time."

"Great, I'm starving. It smells amazing in here." Seth snapped a CD into its case. "I'll pick some music for dinner."

"Ah, no, you will not," I said, catching his hands and moving him back away from the stereo. "We're not listening to anything that's going to ruin my digestion."

"You don't trust me."

"Not on this I don't."

I put Dean Martin back in, and this time I didn't skip *That's Amore*. Seth rolled his eyes and muttered something I couldn't make out, but assumed wasn't complimentary. I smirked.

"When you do the cooking, you can pick the music," I told him.

"It's a damn good thing you're as hot as you are."

I went back into the kitchen and took the fish stock off the stove so I could strain it. Seth came up behind me and made a face at the bones and fish heads in the strainer. He said, "Dude. Maybe there's part of this process I didn't need to know about."

"I throw away the fish heads, you know," I said.

"Oh, thank God."

I laughed at him, and tossed the fish bits in the garbage, washed the strainer and put it away.

"That's nothing," I said. "Wait until I put it all together."

I washed the pot from the fish stock and set it on the stove, then combined the stock and the tomato base. The final step, when you add the seafood and pour in a healthy splash of white wine, is the really showy part, and I was pleased when Seth made appropriately admiring remarks.

"All we have to do now is wait about ten minutes for the fish to cook," I said.

We talked about the storefront project while I ripped up the loaf of bread and put it in a bowl. Seth had some ideas about how we could build the walls, and we discussed the layout of the offices. The subject hadn't come up since the incident in the bar, and I found myself glancing at the bruises on Seth's face.

Before long the stew was steaming, and the whole apartment smelled warmly of tomato, herbs, and fish. I got out bowls and ladled the right mix of fish and seafood into them, topping each with a couple of open mussels.

Seth carried the bowls to the table and came back for the bread. I followed with the red wine and glasses, which I filled. I also put a candle in the middle of the table and lit it.

Seth shook his head and glanced at me out of the corner of his eye. "You must really be hoping I'll put out, man."

"Shut up and eat your dinner," I said, grinning at him.

I passed the bread, and we had exactly the kind of pleasant meal I'd been hoping for, with me doing most of the talking and Seth doing most of the eating.

Afterward, we cleaned up, and I poured more wine for each of us. It was getting dark outside, about the time you'd turn on a light if you had anything to be doing that wasn't romantic in nature. As things stood, however, I was pretty sure that's exactly what was next on the menu, banged up ribs or not, so I didn't bother with any.

I went into the living room where Seth was flipping through CDs, and set his glass down for him. He was reading song titles written on a homemade disk, and showed it to me when I came up behind him. Most of it was decent stuff, songs I've heard on the radio. He slipped it into the player and turned to me. Any lingering concerns I might have had about his well being vanished when he ran his warm hands up my chest under the sweater. He tugged on it, and I let him take it off.

At first I felt ridiculous, standing half naked in the dark with my best friend, but I forgot all that when he mouthed a path along my collar bone, breath hot on my skin. He bit me firmly, then smoothed it over with his tongue. I shivered, and swallowed hard, going hot wherever he touched me. It took me a while to remember I should return the favor. I pulled his T-shirt over his head, dropping it on the couch, and began to slide my hands over his body. He kissed me, and I met his tongue with mine, teasing. I could taste the wine on his lips.

Pushing me forcefully, he steered me backward to a wide, low armchair and shoved me down into it. He climbed in my lap, and we settled into a tangle of warm bare skin and roaming hands, necking like a couple of teenagers. Before long, I was hard as a rock, and so was Seth. I knew this because he grabbed my hand and shoved it into his crotch, thrusting against me with an eager moan.

"Shit," he panted, pressing his face against my neck as I obligingly rubbed his cock through his jeans. "How in the hell do you go so long without this?"

"I have a very talented right hand."

"Yeah?" he said with a grin. He scrambled to his knees, wedging one leg down beside me and resting the other on my thigh. Sitting back on his heels, he popped open the buttons of his fly. "Show me."

That was a hell of a sight. Seth Donnelly perched in my lap, half naked, fingers lightly teasing his own cock. He stared at me with unvarnished hunger. I swallowed hard and reached out to touch him, trailing my fingers down the length of his erection. I'd never touched a man like that before and it shocked me as much as it thrilled me. I circled my hand around him lightly, trying to get the feel of doing it for someone else.

Seth looked down, breathing hard and trying to keep still. He was stroking my wrist and arm like he wanted to make me go faster, but knew he probably shouldn't. Either way, he was screwed on that score, because not only did I need to figure out a whole new set of bedroom skills, I was also getting seriously turned on by his desperate desire, and I had no intention of giving him any kind of quick release.

"Christ, Dino," he said, clutching my arm and rocking his hips into my hand.

"Did I lie?" I asked, amused.

"No, you sure as hell didn't."

He leaned forward to brace his free hand on the back of the chair, bringing him close enough for me to kiss his neck. He tilted his head for me, then moved so he could reach my mouth. His kiss was rough, fueled by need and his attempts to restrain himself. That was a whole new level of hot, especially when I had his bare cock in my hand.

I did my best to draw it out as long as I could, ignoring his moaning and swearing. This was a side of him I'd never seen before, and I liked it. Eventually, Seth reached the do-or-die point and he wrapped his hand around mine, setting the pace he needed to finally get off.

"Oh, *fuck*..." he moaned loudly, burying his face in my shoulder.

I held him tight against me and squeezed his cock, making him shudder and jerk his hips. He came, wet and warm, over our hands, thrusting forcefully until he was spent. When he was done, he sat down in my lap and leaned against me with closed eyes, breathing hard. I wiped my fingers off on his jeans, and rubbed his arm and his back slowly, earning me a contented smile.

"Holy shit, man," he said. "If that's how you treat a simple hand job, then I can't wait to try you out on bigger and better things."

"Yeah, well, we'll see about that," I told him, running my hand over his chest. We'd reached the limits of my practical experience of things you can do with a guy, so I wasn't entirely sure I'd be able to measure up.

After a few minutes, he slid out of my lap and onto the floor.

"Hey, where are you going?" I asked.

"Just right here," he said, kneeling between my legs and resting his hands on my thighs.

"Ah. You look good there."

He smirked. "This is nothing, wait and see."

He tugged me forward in the chair, making me slouch, and reached for my belt buckle. He's got nice hands and watching them yank it open was hot as hell. That was nothing compared to the first touch of his fingers on my bare cock, though. His grip was warm and solid, and desire curled in the pit of my stomach. I felt my skin flush.

"Oh my God," I moaned as he worked me with expert strokes.

Then to my surprise, he bent down and ran his tongue up the length of my hard-on. I nearly lost it then and there. My mouth went dry, and all I could do was stare. He looked up at me with those blue eyes of his, then took my cock in his mouth. He was as good at that as he was with his hands, and it didn't take long before I was gripping the chair arms, breath ragged and short.

I took one look at him, actually sucking me off, and knew what he'd meant when he said "wait and see." I reached down to thread my fingers through his thick hair, and he moaned around my cock, leaning into my touch.

"Damn, Seth. You are somethin' else."

His response was to put his all into it, so I wouldn't ever forget that, apparently. He was a marvel of hot mouth and clever tongue and strong hands, and I could barely remember my own name. My whole body shook, and when I finally came, I came hard, thrusting involuntarily and groaning with pleasure. He kept at it until I sat weak and breathless in the chair.

I opened my mouth to say something, anything, but my mind was blank.

"Like that better than your own right hand?" he asked, looking smug.

"What you do you think?"

"I think that's the best blow job you've ever had."

I rolled my eyes and gave him a look, because I wasn't about to tell him it probably was. Not yet anyway. I sat up and slid off the edge of the chair, settling down on the floor with Seth between my legs. He fit himself against me and let me kiss him thoroughly.

When I stroked his hair, he moaned again and I said, "You like that..."

"Yep." He nodded. "I like it a lot."

"Kinda'...romantic for you, isn't it?"

"Shut up."

We stayed there half naked, pants undone, necking for half an hour. The mood was lazy and comfortable, but it was late, and Seth eventually yawned, reminding us both there was a world beyond our sexual desires and we were expected to be a part of it when morning came.

"I suppose we should think about heading to bed," Seth mumbled, hanging his head over my shoulder.

"You can stay for the news if you like," I told him, reaching for the remote and turning on the TV.

He grumbled his disappointment. "I could stay a lot longer. I need a bodyguard anyway."

"I don't know. I'd like you to stay, but I'm thinking it might be a good idea for both of us if you didn't. Nothing's happened since the break-in, I think you're safe."

Seth chuckled softly. "You need me to get out of your hair so you can freak out about doin' it with a guy."

"No, it's not the guy part that freaks me out, it's the friend part. I don't want to lose a good friendship."

He shook his head slowly and leaned in for a remarkably sensual kiss, which I imagine he meant to be reassuring, but came across to me like he didn't want to make any promises he couldn't keep. I slid my arms around him and pulled him close, not exactly sure what I should be feeling.

On the one hand, there was no question I was intrigued, and it seemed stupid to walk away from a good thing just in case it turned bad. On the other, I still wasn't sure this was the right idea, because if things went wrong, I stood to lose my best friend. I couldn't really see us going back to being buddies. Even if everything worked out, I really didn't think I was Seth's speed. Sooner or later, he was likely to wonder how in the hell he got himself mixed up with an old-fashioned dinosaur like me.

The whole thing gave me a headache. I sighed and put my head back on the cushion of the chair, squeezing my eyes shut and wishing for answers.

"Dino?"

"Yeah?"

"You're not supposed to start freaking out until after I go home."

"I'm not freaking out," I lied. "I'm fine."

He made a rude noise and said, "Yeah, and I'm six feet tall and have a dick the size of a Buick."

"Good thing I have big hands then."

He laughed and climbed over me to head to the bathroom. While he was in there, I fastened my pants and went to find our shirts. Wandering around in the TV flicker, with the stereo playing in the background, reminded me of being in high school. I half expected Seth's dad to barge in and threaten to beat the shit out of me.

When Seth came out, I gave him his shirt and helped him put it on because his ribs were hurting him again.

Seth said, "I've got a full load tomorrow. I'll be busting my nuts at the shop all day. You want to swing by after work?"

"Yeah, I could do that." I was about to say something else, but the picture on the news report caught my eye and I reached over to turn it up.

The anchorwoman had finished with the world news and was moving on to local headlines. "A tragic boating accident claimed the life of a young man in Clearwater early this morning. Police were called on the scene when bystanders noticed an overturned boat abandoned in the water. The body of the man police have identified as that of Darryl Serrano, was discovered nearby. It is believed that he drowned when his boat capsized. Serrano, aged twenty-four, was formerly of Miami and recently residing in St. Petersburg."

Seth raised his eyebrows and looked at me curiously. "You buy that?"

"I don't know," I said. "It's possible, I guess, but I don't like the coincidence."

"Me neither. At least I don't have to worry about him breaking into my apartment again."

"Yeah, well, watch your back anyway."

"I always do." He stepped backward away from me, reaching for the doorknob with a loopy smile. That damn near undid me, and I felt a pang of something a lot more than ordinary friendship.

Then he was gone, and for the second night in a row, I was left wondering what in the hell I'd gotten myself into.

* * * *

After Seth left, I pulled out the package we'd found in the Corvette and set it on my desk. With everything that had happened in the past couple days, I'd been too busy to look at it. Serrano's death coming right on the heels of the break-in, gave it a whole new importance.

I took the rubber bands off and unfolded the envelope. It was obviously recycled, pulled out of the trash or whatever, and used to keep the stuff together. Nothing remarkable about it, aside from providing an address for Serrano in Miami, and confirming the guy was interested in sex. Aren't we all?

Next, I looked at the contents. A notebook, two keys and a swipe card. What the hell was so special about them they needed to be wrapped and hidden? It was certainly reason enough to trash someone's place over, and maybe enough to kill.

The car key was one of those new electronic keys, and thanks to Seth, I knew it fit a BMW. I had no idea what model, other than a car with electronic keys would be new, and probably expensive. The small gold key on the ring was more mysterious. It could fit any number of things.

The key card was plain white, nothing on it all except for the magnetic strip. It wasn't likely to be a hotel room key, since those all have the name and logo on them. I tried to think what other places I knew used them, but came up blank.

The last item was the notebook, and that was the oddest thing of all. I took the rubber band off, turned it upside down, and fanned the pages to see if anything fell out. Nothing did. The notebook itself was unremarkable. Just a spiral bound notebook smaller than an index card, with a dark green cover sporting the Mead logo. The edges of it were worn, like it got carried around a lot, but it wasn't in bad shape.

I opened it to the first page, which had a phone number scribbled down the side of the paper, the way you do when you need to write something down quick. I made a note of it and kept going. I came to one of the pages that looked like it was written in code. There were sets of numbers listed down the middle, with a random letter thrown in here and there. It made zero sense to me. All together, I counted twelve pages like that, and two of them had the corners folded down.

Aside from those, there was a page that had two nicknames with phone numbers to go with each. The first was Snake, very original, and the other was Tango. It was like a bad Eighties movie. There were a couple of shopping lists, which might have been part of the code, but I didn't think so. Nothing on the back cover, nothing inside the covers.

I spread everything on the desk in front of me and leaned back in my chair staring at the strange assortment. It hardly looked like anything someone would go to that much trouble for, but without knowing what the codes meant, I had no idea.

Unfortunately, my mind wasn't really on the job. My thoughts kept drifting back to Seth. How he felt, how he kissed...and what he had in mind for us.

I put everything back in the package the way I'd found it and stashed in my desk, then snapped the light off and took my drink into my bedroom. Sleep was a long time coming.

Chapter 12

Tuesday at five thirty, I was done for the day and driving toward Seth's with the top down, the radio on loud, and my suit jacket on the seat next to me. I was looking forward to seeing him again, but nervous too. I didn't know what to expect. I kept thinking maybe it was all a fluke.

Only one way to find out. I pulled into the lot, hopped out of the car, and went into the garage to look for Seth. He wasn't immediately visible, but that's not unusual. "Seth?"

"Out back!" His voice drifted in through the side door, and I followed it to a spot behind the garage where he and Ed have a bunch of chairs set up in the shade of some palm trees.

It was the ugliest collection of plastic loungers and makeshift tables you've ever seen, but it was a hell of a place to hang out in the afternoon drinking beer and listening to a baseball game on the radio. Especially with Ed and a bunch of old codgers who were there in the days when baseball really was the American Pastime.

I turned the corner to find Seth alone, stretched out in a tacky green and white lounger he'd claimed for his own. He wore a T-shirt and jeans, and a pair of amber sunglasses. There was a six-pack of cheap beer on the table next to him, one of which he was already drinking.

"Hiya, sexy," he said with a smile. "Got a beer here with your name on it."

"Thanks," I said, walking over and taking one. I twisted it open and tossed the cap into an old garbage can. "I talked to Teresa today. Got her to do a little digging on that Serrano thing for us."

"Yeah? What did she say?" Seth took a drink.

"They've officially ruled it an accident. Police say there was alcohol involved, no signs of foul play, the whole nine yards. Notify the family, and case closed."

He shook his head. "Still seems weird if you ask me."

"Yeah, I know what you mean. Maybe someone was gonna repossess the boat, and he tried to tackle that too, but missed."

I put my hand in my pocket and stood there sipping my beer, wondering what to say next. It was a whole new experience to be bullshitting like usual when I could vividly remember Seth going down on me.

"So, you done freaking out yet?" he asked.

I shrugged and studied the dirt around my feet. "Yeah. I don't know. I'm not exactly sure what it's supposed to feel like when I do."

Seth drew his knees up and pointed at me. "We need to get you to stop thinking of me as a friend, and start thinking of me as that incredibly hot mechanic you're sleeping with."

"You are a friend, why do we need to do that?"

"Because you're stiff as a board and not in the way I want you to be."

I chuckled and shook my head. "I'm just sayin' that I'd rather have you be both."

"I still am, Dino, but you seem to be lagging behind in the viewing me as an incredibly hot mechanic department. Which, you know..." He stretched out on the lawn chair, posing for me. "You're totally missing out, dude."

"Is that so?" I asked, rocking back on my heels.

He nodded gamely. "I think you need a lesson in the old Donnelly sex appeal."

I raised my eyebrows at him, and he smirked. He set down his beer and rubbed a hand down his chest to his groin, palming it lewdly. I rolled my eyes.

He seemed to take that as a challenge, because the smirk faded, and what I could see of his eyes through the amber glasses appeared to be fixed on me in the most mesmerizing way.

He popped open the button of his jeans and unzipped them, then dipped his hand inside, rolling his hips and sighing in a soft hum. When he seemed sure he had my attention, he licked his lips and started to rub his cock through his underwear.

I glanced around to see if there was anyone nearby who might notice what was going on. "Yeah, okay, Seth, you're very sexy, point taken."

He just smiled and pushed the underwear out of the way, exposing himself to me. Without a trace of self-consciousness, he ran his fingers lazily along the length of his prominent erection.

"I am not fooling around with you out here," I told him. "Where's Ed?"

"Ed is out junk hunting for the rest of the week, and you don't have to fool around with me. Just watch."

I got warm under the collar and short of breath when he wrapped his hand around his cock and started to stroke it slowly, settling back on the lounge chair and spreading his knees to give me a better view.

"You're gonna jerk off right there?" I asked him. Which was a pretty stupid question, because that's exactly what he was doing. Guys get like that when you put sex in front of us. Our brains go straight south.

"Oh yes," he said, but the tone left me wondering if that was an answer, or a moan. The fact that he was biting his lip suggested the latter.

I felt conspicuous standing around while my friend—make that my hot mechanic friend—whacked off right there in broad daylight. Drinking my beer did nothing to alleviate that. Neither did loosening my tie.

"Oh man," Seth panted. "Do that again."

"Do what, drink beer or mess with my tie?"

"Both. Mostly the tie."

I reached up and tugged on my tie for him. He rewarded me with a throaty moan and a roll of his hips. His hand worked steadily over his cock, and I found myself staring and thinking about putting my hands on his thighs. I had a raging hard-on.

"You're crazy, you know that?" I said.

He gazed up at me, cheeks and neck flushed, free hand thrust under his shirt to rub his chest. "You have any idea how hot you've got me right now?"

"I don't know," I said, taking a deliberate sip of beer. "I think you better show me."

"God," Seth groaned, reaching up to grab the top of the chair behind him. The effect was stunning, and I noticed things about him I never had before, like the way the muscles in his neck moved when he swallowed, and the freckles on his forearms.

I almost lost it myself when he started rocking his hips and thrusting up into his own hand. He let his head roll back, muttering, "Oh please, oh please, oh please..."

"Please what?" I asked, captivated by what I saw. "I hope you're not asking me for anything, because you told me I just had to watch. I'm not touchin' you."

"Fuck, fuck, *fuck*," he cried out, and came with his back arched and his knees drawn up so he could brace his feet on the chair. His hips jerked reflexively a few times and come ran down his fingers, then he went slack, panting hard.

I was completely breathless, and stared at him helplessly. I wanted to come so bad I could taste it.

"Damn," he said, reaching out for his beer. He looked down at himself and grinned. "I'm kind of a mess, eh?"

When I finally found my voice, I said, "I can't believe you just did that." I pulled my handkerchief out of my back pocket and held it out for him.

He stared at it and blinked. "Are you for real? What era were you born in?"

"You want it or not?" I asked, finishing my beer and throwing the bottle in the garbage can.

Seth took it and mopped himself up, then stuck it in his own jeans pocket. He looked up at me and laced his fingers behind his head. "Your turn."

"Ah, no, I don't think so." I still had a desperate need to get off, but performing like a sideshow act really wasn't my thing. Seth could sure as hell make it work, but I'd look like an ass.

He sat up and leaned forward, arms on knees, cocking his head at me. "Oh, yes, you are..."

I shook my head and scowled at him. "What are you gonna do, make me?"

"That's not a half bad idea," he said, and leapt out of the chair.

He was on me before I had time to react, grabbing hold of my tie and pushing me up against the back of the garage. I could feel the concrete window ledge digging into my shoulders and smell the faint hint of gasoline. I could also smell the heat of Seth's body, pressed up against me, emanating sweat and the spicy deodorant he wore.

"If you won't do it, I'll have to," he said in a low voice, wrapping my tie around his fist, and yanking open my belt buckle.

If I'd thought my need to come was bad before, it was nothing compared to what I was facing now. I wasn't going to last long at all. The power he had to turn me on was unnerving, and I wondered why I'd never known about it before.

Then Seth's hand was in my pants, and I felt his fingers close around my dick, warm and strong. He didn't give me any time to catch a breath, starting right in with long, firm strokes that had my knees weak in seconds.

"Jesus," I gasped, bracing myself against the wall. I let my head fall back and closed my eyes, completely caught up in what he was doing to me.

"Oh, no, Dino." He gave the tie a jerk, snapping me to attention. "You look at me. We're workin' on changing the way you see me, remember?"

I opened my eyes, took one look at the fierce, wicked determination on his face, and came almost immediately. I know it was more than watching him jerk off, and more than having him do me. The situation was so bizarre, what with being outside where anyone could see us, and Seth still wearing his sunglasses...hell, just the fact that it *was* Seth. Maybe it was the illicit thrill of the whole thing, but I don't think I've come so fast in my whole life.

Maybe his idea worked, because when he got out the handkerchief and cleaned me up, it wasn't nearly so weird. And when he took my tie off and opened up two more beers, that wasn't very weird at all. Best of all, when we sat down in the lawn chairs and talked about the same shit we always did...that felt pretty normal. Maybe better.

Eventually, the conversation turned to Darryl Serrano and what the hell we thought was going on surrounding him and the strange string of events over the past few days. Although I was pretty sure he'd been responsible for both the break-in at Seth's and the disturbance at Ernie's, I had no proof whatsoever, and even if I did, that still didn't explain the man's death. I don't like coincidences very much, and this one was about as fishy as it gets.

"That reminds me," I said, pulling out my cellphone. "I've been meaning to check in on Ernie."

"Good idea," Seth said. "While you do that, I'll order dinner. How do gyros sound? My treat."

"Hey, did hell just freeze over?"

"Yeah, fuck you," he said, getting up and tossing his beer bottle. "I buy plenty and you know it."

I grinned and told him gyros were fine, then dialed Ernie's number. He sounded perfectly healthy when he answered, and I said, "Hey, how's it going?"

"Can't complain. We've had a pretty quiet couple of days here, which is nice for a change."

"That's good to hear. I wanted to find out if you've had any more trouble since the alarm went off."

"Nope. Everything's been fine," Ernie said. "Hey, did you hear about that guy, though? Talk about having a bad week."

"Yeah, I caught it on the news last night."

"The guy's brother-in-law called today, wants to stop in and pick up the personal effects we got out of the car. He's in town helping the family deal with everything as quickly as possible. I guess it hit them pretty hard and they don't want to drag it out any longer than necessary."

"I can see that," I said. What I was thinking was it seemed pretty unlikely to me that in the wake of a sudden death, anyone would be hot to retrieve a porn novel, some matches and a tire gauge. "Did he say when he was going to drop by?"

"Some time tomorrow, I guess. Sounded like early afternoon most likely. Why?"

"I might try to be there, check the guy out. You know me, always curious."

"You know what they say about curiosity, Dino," he said with a grin in his voice.

"Yeah, yeah. That's why I don't have a cat."

Ernie laughed. "Well, feel free to stop in. You're welcome anytime."

"Thanks, man, have a good night."

I stuck my phone in my pocket and opened another beer as Seth was coming back from ordering dinner. He looked as skeptical as I was when I told him about Serrano's brother-in-law, but he was in favor of blowing it off for more pleasant conversation, such as his campaign to change my view of him. So, I let it drop and spent the evening playing hard to get just for the fun of making him try.

Chapter 13

After a morning's worth of fairly fruitless cold calling, I picked up a sandwich and coffee for lunch and headed in the direction of Ernie's. I wanted to see this guy who claimed to be Serrano's brother-in-law. For one thing, I didn't buy the story as told, and for another, I had a pretty good idea why he really wanted the stuff from Serrano's car.

I had the package with me in my briefcase, and I planned to slip it into the box when I got a chance. We'd already had a taste of what happened when someone went looking for that notebook and came up empty, and I didn't want to provoke any more violence. I was also interested to see what he'd do when he had it, but beyond that I didn't have a plan.

I parked in my usual spot across the street and wandered over, eating the last corner of my sandwich.

Ernie was just shaking hands on a deal and sent the guy toward the office so he could come talk to me. He shook his head. "You never fail to amuse me, Dino. I knew you'd show up."

"What can I say?" I shrugged. "It's what I do."

"Well, your timing is good. He just called, he's on his way over right now."

"Great," I said. "Let me take a look at the stuff before he gets here."

"Sure. What are you looking for, anyway?"

"If I knew, it wouldn't be a mystery."

Ernie rolled his eyes and led the way into the office. I know I was being cagey with him, but it was mostly the truth. What I really needed was a chance to put the package back so it could be found.

Inside, Ernie pointed to a stack of boxes in the hall closet. "They're right where you guys left them. Well, except for a couple the owners already came to get. I haven't had time to deal with them."

That was all to the good as far as I was concerned. I didn't think Ernie would have been too terribly bent out of shape, but I preferred not to tell him that I'd been withholding items from the cars, since I don't actually make a habit of that. I stalled until his back was turned, and did a little sleight of hand. When I carried the box over to the sales desk, everything was as it should've been.

I took out the book and thumbed through it several times to see if there was anything stuck between the pages. There wasn't. I even checked all the matchbooks for phone numbers or messages, but they were blank too. Whatever Serrano's weird gig was, it centered on that package.

We had a few minutes, so I poured myself a cup of coffee and talked shop with Ernie and his receptionist, who's cute, but kind of a severe gal. She keeps the paperwork in line, but I wouldn't want to deal with her every day.

A gleaming black SUV pulled into the lot and parked smack in the middle of everything, like he owned the place. The door opened and a slick looking suit with mirrored sunglasses got out. He had short, sandy blond hair, and a bored expression. He looked like money.

When he came in, he sized us up and decided Ernie was the guy he needed to talk to. "Ira McCann," he said, extending a hand. "I believe we spoke on the phone earlier."

Ernie shook hands with him and said, "Yes, sir. I'm very sorry for your loss. We have your brother-in-law's effects right here."

He led McCann over to the box and McCann peered in, noting the contents with efficient disinterest. He placed both palms on the edges of the box and said, "Now, this *is* everything that was in the car?"

"Absolutely," Ernie said, falling all over himself to impress the guy. "We're very meticulous about that. This is the guy right here, Dino Martini." He clapped me on the shoulder. "He does all our repo work, he's a licensed private investigator, bonded and everything. You can't ask for anyone more reliable."

I cringed. Why didn't he tell him my address and dick size while he was at it? I bit my tongue and nodded. McCann raised an eyebrow, but only nodded back.

"Well then," he said, scooping up the box, "it seems that everything is in order. Do you need me to sign a receipt?"

"Yeah, right here." Ernie slid the paperwork across the table and handed him a pen.

McCann scrawled a hasty signature on it and left. I was faced with a decision—let it go and swallow the nagging itch of an unsolved mystery, or follow him. And do what? Peek in his windows? Eavesdrop on his phone calls? I didn't think so.

Ernie was hotfooting it out to the lot to check on some prospective customers, so I gave him a wave and went back to my car. I felt a strange mix of relief and dissatisfaction. It annoyed the crap out of me to leave something unsolved, but in this case, it wasn't mine to solve anyway. I opted, instead, to focus on something I could finish. My office.

With that decision made, I turned in the direction of home and planned to spend some time in the store taking measurements.

I was about halfway there when my cellphone rang. "Dino Martini."

"Ah, Mr. Martini." It was the slick from Ernie's place, with his bizarrely cultured speech. He sounded very East Coast. "We met earlier, at the car dealership. The gentleman was kind enough to give me your number when I called him. If I remember correctly, he said you were a private investigator?"

"That's right. Something I can do for you?"

"As a matter of fact there is. There are some unusual items in Darryl's effects, and I'm wondering if you might be able to shed some light on them. The whole family is just terribly broken up over his death, and I have some concerns."

"Unusual items," I said, "really? Boy, I sure don't remember anything out of the ordinary."

"No, you might not. I didn't notice it at first, either. Not until I pulled over for lunch and got curious."

Didn't notice it, my ass. "I'd be glad to take a look at anything you got. When would you like to meet?"

"I don't suppose you're free at the moment?" he asked. "You see, I need to be getting back to Miami, and I'd like to have all this unpleasant business wrapped up."

I was already making a U-turn. "Works fine for me. Where are you now?"

"A restaurant called the Longhorn Steakhouse. It's not very far from the dealership."

"I know the place," I said. It was one of Ernie's favorites, and I'd bought more than my fair share of steak there, for both him and Seth. "I can be there in about fifteen minutes."

"I appreciate you taking the time, Mr. Martini."

We hung up and I spent the drive trying to figure out this guy's angle. When I heard he was coming, I'd been pretty damn sure he knew exactly what he was looking for. So, why did he need me? I tossed out the idea that he was legit, because I just couldn't buy it. More likely, he hadn't bargained on the notebook being in code.

I spotted his SUV as soon as I pulled into the parking lot, but went around the side to keep Matilda out of sight. I prefer to put her in the shade, anyway.

Inside, the crowd was light and he wasn't hard to spot. He stood and shook my hand when I came up to his table, then invited me to sit. I ordered a beer, and we got down to business.

Not surprisingly, McCann pulled the package out of his coat pocket and laid it on the table. I feigned polite interest as he slid it over to me. "Is this the unusual item?" I asked, reaching for it.

"Yes, I'm concerned due to some of the contents." He paused and took a sip of his wine. "Darryl was quite a black sheep, you might say, and I would hate to see some of his indiscretions come back to haunt the family."

I opened the envelope and tipped the familiar items onto the table. Everything was there, just as I'd left it. I made like I was examining the keys and the card, but I was paying more attention to McCann out of the corner of my eye. "And you don't know what or who these belong to?" I asked.

He shrugged and shook his head. "I have no idea. He didn't drive a new car. I suppose you know that, of course."

I smiled and opened the notebook, flipping through the pages slowly. "I certainly can see why you thought this was unusual," I said, laying it open to one of the coded pages.

"Do you think you can figure out what it means?" he asked, overplaying the concerned innocence. "Find out if he was in some kind of trouble?"

I thought it over for a minute, weighing my options. Yeah, it could be kind of dangerous, but my decision seemed pretty clear. I'd get to continue investigating the package and get *paid* for it. Hard to see the downside there.

"Three hundred a day, plus expenses," I said, accepting the job. "First day up front."

The guy took out his wallet and gave me three-fifty in large bills. Clearly, affording my services was not going to be an issue. "I hope that's sufficient to cover your expenses for now," he said smoothly. "If not, please let me know."

He pulled out a business card also, and handed that over. I glanced at it before shoving it in my suit pocket with the money. It had nothing more than his name and contact numbers, no business information.

As I packed up the envelope, I said, "It'll probably take me a couple of days to get a lead on this and figure out where to go from there. I'll give you a call with a report, but if you have any questions, you've got my number. Are you heading back to Miami today?"

"I believe so. There's not much left for me to do here." He watched my hands intently as I worked, and I wondered if it bothered him to give it up so soon. He'd just gotten a hold of it. Still, it probably wasn't much use to him if he didn't know what it meant. I was curious as to what he *did* know about all this, but of course, I couldn't ask him.

* * * *

That evening, I sat at my desk with the package in front of me yet again. I was right back where I'd started, only three hundred dollars richer. I tried to call Seth to let him know what was going on, but only got his voicemail. That wasn't unusual. If he was hip deep in someone's engine, he rarely bothered to answer.

In the meantime, I got to work. I was already familiar with everything, so I started with the notebook, turning to the first page. The lone phone number. It was easy to figure that out. My laptop was on, so I pulled up the Miami White Pages and plugged the number in. No hits. I tried the Yellow Pages. Bingo. The number was for Sammy Chan's Seafood & Chinese Takeout.

I flipped open my cellphone and dialed the number, looking at my watch. Right in the middle of dinner rush. That was good, they'd be too busy to think real hard.

"Chan's," came the answer. "Can I take your order?"

"Uh, yeah, ah...I gotta' order dinner for my boss," I said with a nasal tone, trying to sound as dumb as possible. "But he didn't say what he wanted. I thought maybe you guys keep regulars on file or something?"

"Get real, man." A female voice with way too much attitude. I could hear a ton of noise in the background. "We don't keep anything like that. You'll have to figure it out on your own. You want to order now or call back?"

I toyed with the idea of yanking her chain for a while to teach her a lesson about manners, but decided against it. She was the type who'd just hang up on me, anyway.

"No, I'll have to call you back," I said. And then she did hang up.

I hadn't honestly expected to gain much, and even if I had, what would knowing Serrano's preference in Chinese cuisine get me? If the restaurant had any significance at all, I would have to be able to drop Serrano's name, and that would only work if it was to the right person, under the right circumstances.

I pulled out a pad of paper and jotted down what I knew so far. That was a hell of a short list. After that, I reached for my file on the latest batch of repossessions, which I still had on my desk because it held the rap sheet for Serrano. I made copies of all the paperwork for the Corvette and started a new folder.

My phone rang, and I saw it was Seth, which hit me in a completely different way than it used to. Now, instead of thinking immediately of food and beer, I started thinking about the weight of his body, and sex.

"Talk to me," I said.

"What are you wearing, Dino?" he asked in a sultry voice.

"Little Bo Peep costume, how 'bout you?"

"Oh, dear God, so many sheep fucking jokes, so little time. We may actually have to try that one of these days."

"I am not fucking you wearing a pinafore."

"Come on, dude, loosen up," he said. "This might be a good time to tell you about my secret life as a furry."

"A what?"

"Oops, that's right, you're a dinosaur. Never mind."

"Did you call for a reason?"

"Of course I did. I want to see you, man."

"You didn't get enough of me last night?"

"Nope."

"Or the night before?"

"Nope."

I smirked. He may be in his thirties, but he sure doesn't act it. I said, "What are you, insatiable? You'll give me a heart attack."

"Do you know what I'm doing right now, Dino?"

"Ah, talking on the phone?"

"That only takes one hand..." I could hear the grin in his voice.

"Okay," I said, "I'll bite. Where's the other one?"

"Down the front of my boxers, stroking my cock while I listen to your voice."

"You're not serious."

"Yes, I am," he said, sounding a little breathless, which got me thinking maybe he really was. "I'm sitting here with my coveralls open, and my jeans unzipped, and my hand in my underwear."

"And when did you start doing this?" I asked, leaning back in the chair. I put my feet up on the desk, and took a sip of my drink. Things were about to get entertaining.

"About ten minutes ago."

"You can last ten minutes?"

"Fuck you, Dino," he snapped.

"Where are you?"

"I'm sitting in the front seat of Mrs. Beasley's Oldsmobile, with the seat back."

"You're whacking off in some old lady's car? You really are a sick little shit."

"You know I am," he said. "Come on, I want to hear you too."

"You want me to jerk off on the phone with you?"

"Hell yeah, Dino, whip it out. Guys rack up huge credit card bills for the experience you're about to have."

He moaned, probably louder than necessary, but it was enough to get me hard, and I could picture him leaning back in a car seat with his eyes closed and his mouth open, running his hand over his cock. I felt my skin go hot.

"Yeah, okay," I said, putting down my glass and unbuckling my belt.

"Ooh, yes..." he moaned. "I knew you wouldn't let me down."

I got my pants unzipped and was pushing my shorts out of the way, when the memory of Seth stretched out on that lawn chair came back to me, and I could see him arching his back and rocking his hips into his own hand. "Jesus," I gasped as I grabbed my dick.

Seth's breath was ragged in my ear, so close I expected him to lick me at any moment. "Mmm...that's good, Dino. Tell me you're doing it."

"I am," I said. "I was just thinking about you in the yard yesterday, behind the garage."

"Oh yeah?"

"Yeah."

"You liked that." Seth was panting now.

I fisted myself steadily to get as close to the edge as I could. "That was one of the hottest things I've ever seen. You should always wear sunglasses when you jerk off."

"As a matter of fact, I'm wearing sunglasses right now."

"You are not," I said, but I groaned anyway. I could vividly remember the way he smelled. That scent of hot sunshine and motor oil, slightly sweaty. Like he probably was at that very moment, sitting in the garage in someone else's car. "Oh shit, Seth, I'm right there."

"Me too. Go for it, I wanna hear you."

I let go and stroked myself hard and fast, giving voice to a lot more groaning and swearing than I would have done on my own, playing it up for Seth's benefit.

Before I could even catch my breath, Seth was swearing, and I could hear him writhing in the car seat. "Fuck, yes. God, Dino, do you have any idea how good you sound when you come?"

"I think I do now," I said, feeling incredibly relaxed and mellow after all that. "You're not so bad yourself, kid."

"My God," he moaned. "I'm totally wasted. You did me in without even touching me."

"You're spreading it a little thick, don't you think?"

Seth snickered. "Fine, but this seriously was hot as hell."

"Yeah, I'll give you that," I said. "Were you really already playing with yourself when you called me?"

"Yep, I really was."

"What got you goin'?" I stood up and went to the kitchen to clean myself off.

"The usual stuff," Seth said, starting to sound like his regular self again. "Thinkin' about the other night, and what else we could do with that chair. So, you want to get some dinner?"

"I think I'm gonna beg off tonight. I'm beat, and I could use some extra sleep. I'll just have something here and turn in early."

"Eh, all right," he said, sounding a little disappointed, which I have to admit pleased me. "I suppose it wouldn't kill me to catch up on invoicing. Did you meet Serrano's supposed brother-in-law?"

I tucked the phone against my shoulder so I could zip up my pants. "I did, and I have some news about that."

"Yeah?"

"The guy *hired* me to check out that notebook."

"You're shitting me."

"Paid the first day up front and everything. I have his card in my pocket. Listen, I want to swing by there tomorrow and have you take another look at this stuff. You might see something I don't."

"Sure, anytime," he said.

"Thanks. I'll see you tomorrow then."

"G'night, Dino."

Chapter 14

A good night's sleep never fails to do wonders for my outlook, even when my outlook was pretty good to begin with. Which it had been. Yeah, life had thrown me a few curveballs lately, but overall, things were pretty damn good.

I cranked up the tunes, took a long, hot shower, and dressed a little better than I normally would for going to hang out with Seth. It's not that I actually dressed up, so much as I dressed to look good. I put on my watch, pocketed my phone and wallet, and was out the door by nine.

Since I was in a Seth impressing mood, I drove down to the bakery at the corner of John's Pass and picked up a dozen doughnuts. Sharp clothes may or may not attract his attention, but a box of concentrated sugar sure as hell would.

When I walked into the garage, Seth was bent over the engine of some Chevy, rapping along with the radio about whores in fast cars. He didn't hear me come in, so I took a minute to admire his ass. I'd seen it that way lots of times, but now I had a whole new appreciation of it. I set the box of doughnuts on a shelf and put my briefcase down so I could sneak up and cop a feel before he realized I was there.

He squeaked and said, "You better watch it, jack. My boyfriend is one tough motherfucker, and he'll tear you limb from limb if he catches you with your grubby mitts all over my ass."

"Maybe he'll think you're messin' around on him and tear *you* limb from limb, did you ever think of that?"

"No way," he said, still working on the car. "He worships the ground I walk on and would never harm a hair on my head."

I scoffed. "Yeah, I wouldn't go bettin' the farm on that if I were you."

Seth finally stood up and graced me with that Cheshire smile of his. Then he caught me off guard by throwing his arms around me and kissing me in an especially dirty fashion. I kissed him back, but then struggled to get free.

"Okay, okay," I said. "The doors are wide open, and you're gonna get grease all over my clothes."

He gave me an arch look and said, "Nice to see you too, asshole."

"Well, come on, you're dressed for this kind of thing. I'm not."

"Yeah, fine, I'll give you that. I'll pay a little more attention. But you can kiss my ass on the doors being open. I don't give a flying fuck who sees us."

"That's easy for you to say," I muttered, checking out my slacks and shirt.

"Wait a minute," Seth said, turning to face me with his hands planted on his hips, clutching a wrench. "You mean you can tell a bar full of thugs I'm your 'baby' if we're *not* dating, but when we really are, no one should see?"

I laid on every inch of New York sarcasm I had and reached out to stroke his cheek with the back of my fingers. "That bruise of yours is healing up real nice. It oughta' be gone in a few more days."

He slapped my hand away. "That happened because we jerked that guy around and made an ass out of him, not because he thought we were gay."

"You think so? I don't."

"It doesn't matter, because I don't give a shit anyway." He challenged me with a look and went back to work under the hood of the Chevy.

I let it drop because the truth was, I hadn't given it a whole lot of thought. Somehow, I just figured it was going to be business as usual, with the addition of a physical side that went on more or less behind closed doors. I hadn't considered anything else. I filed away the issue for consideration later.

For a while, I leaned against the corner of the car and watched Seth change out a cracked gas line. Finally, I said, "I brought doughnuts."

He stood up and took a rag out of his pocket to wipe his hands, not looking at me. "I made coffee," he said nodding toward the back workbench. I turned to look and saw he'd brought down the new coffee maker and set it up.

"So, you want to take a look at that package we found in the 'Vette?" I asked.

"Yeah, you said you started in on it yesterday?"

Just like that, the ice was melted. Seth sniffed out the doughnut box and tucked in, and I got myself a cup of coffee and perched on the stool at the end of the workbench with my briefcase.

"Hey, could I have one of those before you inhale them all?" I asked, not willing to risk loss of limb by simply reaching for one.

He handed the box over, and I fished the package out of my briefcase. I took an apple fritter and bit into it while Seth turned the package over in his hands, examining it with interest. He went through the same routine I had, pulling off the rubber hands, reading the mailing labels, and dumping out the contents.

He picked up the keys first, tossing them in the air and catching them. "So, somewhere there's a car that's not going anywhere," he said. "And it's no wonder the dude defaulted on his loan if he was footin' the bill for a big ticket car like this."

"Maybe he didn't bother to pay for this one."

"No doubt," Seth said with a nod. "But that's assuming it's his. He could have these for whole lot of reasons. Say his girl was cheating on him and he kicked her to the curb. Snagging her car keys on the way out the door would be pretty sweet revenge."

"You're a vindictive little shit," I said, taking a sip of coffee.

Seth flashed an evil grin. "You know, if he stole it, it would be too hot to drive around for a while. So, he could have stashed it to pick up later, and he keeps the keys tucked away safe until it's time to go back. Personally, I'd rather have the 'Vette, but these Miami boys like everything cutting edge."

"Yeah," I said. "It could also be his mother's for all we know."

Seth pulled the key card from the pile and held it up. "Ten to one says this gets us into wherever he's got the car stashed."

"That's got potential. Look at the notebook, see what you think."

Seth put down the keys and grabbed the notebook, sliding off the band and flipping it open. He thumbed through the pages fast a couple of times, and then again slowly, stopping to look at one that was written on. Finally, he shook his head, looking perfectly bewildered.

"Well...the first one's a phone number. But I'm guessing you probably already worked that out."

I swallowed my last bite of fritter. "Goes to a Chinese takeout place in Miami. I didn't get anything there."

"Snake and Tango," Seth read off the last page, laughing. "That's rich."

"Yeah. My money says they have a combined IQ of nine. They do sound like the kind of guys who would hang out at a place called The Shark Pond, though."

"The what?"

"The Shark Pond. It's a place in South Beach. Serrano had a bunch of matchbooks from there in the glove box. Maybe there's a connection."

"Did you check it out?"

"I just thought of it."

"Well, work some of your cyber hocus-pocus and see what you get."

"I'll do that tonight." I took the notebook out of his hand and turned it to one of the pages of codes. "That leaves these to consider, and that's gonna take some work. I didn't get to that part last night."

I showed him the twelve pages of seemingly random characters, each one looking more or less like this:

1417
1269227
1FTDR11T5GTA01050
R9-17
132209

Seth looked them over and said, "Well, I guess the dog eared ones are important, since they're marked."

"If you'd gone to the trouble of putting something important into code, would you go and stick big red flags on them that said, 'Get Your Answers Right Here?'"

"I might if I was the kind of guy who had friends named Snake and Tango," Seth said with a grin. "Maybe they're decoys and one of the other pages is the real deal."

I considered that while I flipped back and forth through the coded pages. Seth stood at my shoulder so he could read them at the same time.

"VIN numbers!" he blurted out, smacking me upside the head. "You and I both should have picked that up without even thinking about it." He looked disgusted.

"Then why am I the only one who got hit?" I asked, smoothing my hair back into place.

"Because I *did* see it."

I looked, and sure enough, each page had a set of characters that fit the pattern. "Not only are you pretty, but you're smart too," I told him, patting him on the stomach.

"Hot."

"What?"

"Hot. I'm hot, not pretty," he said.

I gave him a quick appraisal and said, "Yeah, I guess hot works too."

"You *guess*? Clearly, I need to step up efforts to change the way you see me."

"I liked phase one," I said. "What do you have in mind for the next step?"

Seth pressed against me and reached down to run a hand over my thigh. "Hey, I know," he said, breathing on my ear while he spoke. "Let's go to Miami."

"What?" I asked, looking at him like he was nuts. "I hate Miami."

"You've got to check out this Shark Pond place anyway, right? Let's go do it in person, instead of you looking it up on the net. We could hit a couple clubs, get a hotel room... You following me?"

I thought about that for a minute. "Yeah, I could see that. I was figuring I'd probably end up going there for the job anyway, no reason not to get a jump on it."

"Perfect. And then I can jump you," he said with a grin.

"What about work?" I asked, glancing at the car he'd been tuning up.

He turned to look. "I'll have this finished up early afternoon. That'd leave us plenty of time to drive down, get checked in, and still be early for clubbing. I only have two appointments for tomorrow, and I can reschedule those."

"Okay, that works. I have a couple other jobs I need to work on, and I have a client meeting in St. Pete at one. I could be ready to go after that."

I finished my coffee, and we agreed to touch base around lunchtime, so we could make plans. Seth pulled me into the office and gave me a goodbye kiss worthy of a porn film. I left weak-kneed, hard as hell, and wondering what he had in mind for the hotel room.

* * * *

At two-thirty, we put Matilda's top up to cut the wind, and headed south. Seth eased his seat back and took a short catnap, and I spent the time going over everything I knew about Serrano's notebook and what I thought it might mean. Not like I really had a clue. It wasn't the first time I'd headed into a job without much to go on, but I knew eventually we'd get that first break, and everything else would start falling into place. It almost always did.

About an hour into the drive, my cellphone rang and I took it out and answered without looking. "Martini."

"I'd love one, thanks," Teresa said in my ear, and I swore silently. This was not the best time to be hearing from her, since the only thing she and I had talked about recently was the Serrano case, and I didn't want her knowing I was working on it.

"Better not let your husband hear you talking like that, or he's gonna get jealous and kick my ass."

"Oh, please," she scoffed.

I preferred not to know which she thought was laughable, her husband kicking my ass, or the idea she might actually be interested in me.

"So," she said, "I understand you did a vehicle repossession on Darryl Serrano just a couple nights before he died. You neglected to mention that little detail."

"I didn't think it was important. I sure as hell didn't drown the guy."

"Well, why don't you let me be the judge of what's important, hmm?" Teresa sounded just a little too shrewd, and I could tell her bullshit senses were tingling. That was part of what made her a good cop, she could spot a line of crap a mile away. She also wasn't any fonder of coincidence than I was.

"I'm sorry, what was that?" I asked, raising my voice. "I must be switching towers or something, you dropped out there for a minute."

"I said, tell me what you got, and I'll let you know if means anything."

"What? You're breakin' up pretty bad, I didn't catch that."

She raised her voice to match mine. "Dino? Where in the hell are you?"

"I'm really sorry, Teresa, I'm barely getting anything here, you're all static. I hope you can hear me, I'll call you later when I'm home." Then I snapped the phone shut and tossed it onto the dashboard.

Seth was awake and looking at me with a sly expression. "That was cheap," he said.

"Yeah, I know. I just didn't want to explain the whole thing to her and make a big deal out of something that might be nothing. She's too hard to lie to, so I opted for the easy way out."

"Telling her the line was full of static *was* a lie, Dino."

"But I only had to pull that one off for a few minutes."

"You're a sneaky son of a bitch."

"It's a job requirement."

Chapter 15

Earlier, while I was waiting for Seth to finish with the Chevy, I'd looked up the address for The Shark Pond. I'd also found a decent looking hotel that was probably within walking distance, and made a reservation for us. Although I was getting more used to the idea of Seth and me together, there were still a few things that threw me for a loop, and getting us a room knowing what would happen there was one of them.

The Shark Pond was wedged into one of the less fashionable corners of South Beach, a fact that made me want to claw my eyes out, but had Seth wired with anticipation. As it turned out, he made relatively frequent runs down to this part of Miami and knew his way around pretty well. He was able to help me pick my way through traffic, and find both the club and the hotel. I locked the car, and we went inside to check in. I don't know if it was in deference to my reaction in the garage that morning, or something else, but Seth hung back until I got on the elevator, and slipped in with me. I didn't say anything, because I still had no idea where we stood on that issue.

The room was nice. Simple and clean, but stylish, and I liked it. I doubted Seth cared either way, as he tossed his duffel bag on the bed and announced he was going to take a shower. "You want to join me?" he asked, peeling off his shirt.

I had to think about that for a minute, and I admit I was damned tempted. Not only did he look good, but the thought of sharing a hotel room had been on my mind all afternoon. So had the job, though, and I figured it would be wise to put that first. "Business before pleasure," I said, "or we might never get there at all."

"And that would be a bad thing?" He slouched against the wall and unbuttoned his jeans slowly, making me start to reconsider.

"Yes," I told him resolutely, "that would be a bad thing. Get in there."

Elle Parker

He gave me an incredibly adorable pout and disappeared into the bathroom.

It didn't take us long to get ready, in spite of Seth's screwing around, which I enjoyed. He's so easy going about nearly everything in life, and he's very comfortable to be around. Soon, he looked trendy and hot, and I looked more stylish, but hot.

It was early yet, so we had dinner in the hotel, then set off in the direction of The Shark Pond. The night was balmy and mild, with a light breeze off the ocean. As jobs go, it was a pretty sweet one for the moment, and I was having a good time. I found myself picking up the energy and excitement of the people around us. Seth spent the entire walk gawking at the scenery and pointing out all the hottest T&A like some kind of tour guide.

"Do you think I'm incapable of noticing these things for myself?" I asked him.

"Yes," he said. "You are the most bizarrely asexual person I've ever met. If I hadn't seen it for myself, I'd be worried you didn't have a dick at all."

"Well, you know there's no problem there."

Seth snickered. "You ever heard the phrase 'use it or lose it?'"

"Why don't you let me worry about that, all right?"

"Oh, man." Seth grabbed my arm and moaned indecently. "Check out the *ass* on that chick. Don't you just wanna sink your teeth into that?"

"You are a pig," I told him.

"Hell, her date's even better," Seth said, as a good-looking guy in his twenties trotted across the street and gave the girl a kiss before walking away with her.

"You wanna sink your teeth into him too?"

Seth smirked. "Something, anyway."

"Am I supposed to be charmed by this?" I asked. "Are you like this on all your dates?"

"I might feel bad," he said, "but you actually looked."

"Of course I looked. I am human, you know."

We walked five blocks and ended up on the sidewalk outside The Shark Pond. It was a smallish place with murals of underwater scenes on either side of glass double doors. Along the bottom edge were planters full of shrubs that had seen better days, and over the doors was a curved, black awning. Most people were walking right past, but occasionally someone would go in or come out.

After ten minutes or so of watching the crowd and scoping out the surrounding area, we went inside. The interior was like the outside, done up in varying shades of blue, green and black, with glitter sparkling from the walls and ceiling. The bar was wave shaped and glowed deep blue off to one side of the room, while the dance floor was washed in green and blue light that oozed from one color to the next in a slow ripple. It wasn't exactly my kind of place, with the pulsing music and black lights, but I was impressed with the effect.

There wasn't a huge crowd yet, but there were a few groups here and there. Seth went up to the bar, and I followed, trying to check out the nooks and crannies of the room without being too obvious about it.

We sat down on stools and I turned to watch the floor, while Seth studied the offerings behind the bar. The bartender passed by us with a "hi" sign that said he'd be with us in a minute, and Seth started studying him instead. He was lean and pale, with old jeans, a white tank top, and some kind of scruff on his chin that passes for a beard with guys of a certain age.

When he finished with the girls at the end, he came down and leaned on the bar in front of us, smiling broadly. "I'm En, what are we drinking tonight?"

"N?" I asked. "What is this, Sesame Street?"

He gave me an arch look and said, "That's fucking hysterical. Think that up all on your own?"

"Yeah, I did, actually. Bring me a beer."

Seth smiled at him and said, "Why don't you surprise me."

En sized him up for a minute and said, "I think you'd really like Sex With an Alligator."

"Dude, you have no idea..."

That earned Seth a sexy grin, and after En shoved a beer at me without bothering to ask what kind I'd actually like, he put a drink shaker on the bar and started to fill it with various types of liquor, all of which glowed in the black lights of the bar. Boy, did this guy read Seth right. He gave it a good shake and set two tall shot glasses up on the bar.

He cast a sidelong glance at me and asked Seth, "You with him?"

"Oh, yes."

En put another shot glass up and filled each one about half full of puce colored liquid. Then he took a bottle of blood red liqueur and poured some down the inside edge of each glass so it settled at the bottom. Finally, he added something to the top, making the whole thing layered. It wasn't exactly the bartending as performance art you hear about, but it was still kind of impressive. Not nearly as impressive as Seth was making it out to be, but noteworthy nonetheless.

After En slid us each a glass, he and Seth toasted and tossed them back in one quick swallow. How Seth can do that, but choke on whiskey, I'll never know.

Since this guy was currently our most likely source of information, I raised my glass to them both, put on my game face, and downed the shot. It wasn't all that bad, but I sincerely hoped I wasn't going to have to do any more to prove to him I wasn't ready for the walker and ear horn just yet.

While En fixed another round, he made the usual light conversation. "So, you guys are a couple of new faces. I haven't seen you around before."

"Yeah," Seth said with a casual air. "We don't get down this way that much, but you know, when you get a chance to take advantage of the action, you don't pass it up."

En smirked and gave Seth another shot.

I tried to cut to the chase. "We're lookin' for a guy named Darryl Serrano, you know him?"

A shadow crossed En's face, and his manner toward me went distinctly cold. "Is he a friend of yours?"

"Fuck, no," I snapped. I could easily read the guy's attitude on this one. "The son of a bitch owes me money. A lot of it. And I aim to collect one way or another."

The threat of violence against Serrano clearly put me back in the good graces of our bartender, because he offered me another round of the alligator shit.

"No thanks," I said. "Beer's just fine for me. So, can you tell me if he's been around lately? Someone told me he hung out here."

En shook his head. "Haven't seen that fucker in months. He used to work for the owner once in a while, but not anymore, I can tell you that." If he knew Serrano was dead, he wasn't letting on.

"That's not a real big surprise now, is it?" Seth scoffed, downing his second shot. "Guy's a class-A moron."

En laughed. "The shit that always got to me, was his stupid cloak-and-dagger crap. Nothing was ever easy or straightforward with him. It was like everything had to be a game, you know?"

"A game?" I asked.

"Yeah," En said dismissively. "Four phone calls when one would do, cryptic notes, sneaking around everywhere. Shit drove me crazy. I used to hate it when Ollie would ask me to send Darryl on errands, because it turned into such a fucking hassle."

"Ollie...that your boss?"

"Yeah. He pawned that shit off on me because he didn't want to deal with it himself."

The crowd was starting to grow and business was picking up. A second bartender had come on duty and was working down at the other end. En brought me another beer, and glanced at the clock on the wall. "I'd better take my smoke break before it gets much crazier in here, or I won't get the chance." He gave Seth an especially rakish grin and took off.

Seth polished off his fourth shot. Or maybe it was his fifth, I'd lost count. He grinned at me and said, "You hang tight for a bit. I think I might have a chance to get a little more dirt on Serrano, here."

"Yeah," I said, leveling my gaze on him. "I think you mean get a little dirt on your knees, don't you?"

Seth gaped at me and I had to laugh, because it's not often I can shock him. "Dude, I can't believe you just said that out loud."

"Don't get me wrong," I said, "I really admire your dedication to the job."

He smiled as he slid off his stool and started walking backward toward the hall where En had disappeared. "No worries, baby, I'm all yours tonight," he said with a saucy wink. "This is strictly business."

Since it appeared I was going to be on my own for a while, I took my beer and opted for wandering the crowd. I wanted see if there was anything that might give me a clue as to what Serrano did for them, or why he liked to hang out there.

There wasn't a hell of a lot to see that I thought would help us. I saw a few small-time drug deals go down, which stood to reason. That was regular trade all over South Beach. I worked my way along the edge of the dance floor slowly, trying to look more like I was scoping out the action, and less like I was casing the joint. Must have worked, because I caught a fairly pretty, young woman checking me out.

I nodded and said, "Hi." She smiled at me and went back to talking to her friends.

I was about to move on and maybe get another beer, when the back door opened and En came in, followed by Seth. They were talking about some band I'd never heard of, and I imagined that was probably just as well.

Seth looked fairly smug, which I took to be a good sign. He stopped next to me and said, "You ready to head out?"

"I am," I said, tossing my empty beer bottle into a garbage can at the end of the bar. We thanked En and started to pick our way through the crowd.

Out on the sidewalk, Seth turned to me with a huge grin and said, "Boy, have I got some great shit for you."

"On Serrano?"

"Yep." We started walking back toward the hotel. "En wasn't kidding when he said Serrano was a total crackpot. All that shit about games he used to play? Turns out the guy had some *serious* James Bond delusions. Like, he spent most of his time practically play-acting spy movies."

"He'd pretend he was James Bond?"

"Not by name exactly, but En said he carried around some kind of stupid spy gear he bought off the internet, like little cameras and stuff. And he wouldn't let En give him orders directly, he'd refuse to listen unless En called him on his cellphone so he could duck out of sight, be all sneaky about it."

I rolled my eyes. Crackpot was a polite word for Serrano. "The guy leads the life of a peon," I mused, "so he tries to spice it up with imaginary games, make it more exciting."

Seth nodded. "Well, it was about to get a whole lot less exciting. The club owner was starting to get sick of all the bullshit, and Serrano was on his way out. En told me he was going to get fired."

"I suppose he saw it coming, decided to split town instead."

Details were starting to click into place, bit by bit. Now we had some kind of a handle on Serrano, and a clue as to how the guy operated. I felt the satisfying rush I always did when I got a toehold on a case.

"You're right," I told Seth. "That is some good stuff. Knowing Serrano's taste for spy games might shed some light on those codes of his."

Seth beamed at me. "Does that mean you're feeling especially grateful to me right now?"

"As a matter of fact, it does. I would say business is concluded for the day. We'll start trying to break the codes tomorrow. With the VIN numbers, and this new information, we've got a good starting point and it's looking promising."

"Excellent." He lit up and rubbed his hands together with glee. "There's a fantastic club I want to take you to, just a couple blocks from here. Let's go."

He turned and crossed the street, rather than heading down the sidewalk like I'd expected. I ran to catch up with him. "Club? I thought we were going back to the hotel."

He gave me a horrified look. "The night is still young, Dino. Come on, man, live a little."

"Yeah, but your kind of club? I don't know."

"Dino," he said, stopping to nail me with a stare. "I ate dinner with candles on the table. Now, you're gonna sit in a club and have a drink and maybe even dance, got it?"

"I got it, I got it," I said, holding up my hands. Dancing, I knew, was nothing even remotely resembling what I'd been taught, but he had a point, and I figured turnabout was fair play.

It was dark out, or as dark as it could be with all the neon around, and the party that was South Beach surrounded us. South Beach is a little like being on Mars, and you never know what in the hell you're going to see.

Seth's club turned out to be farther than a couple blocks, and from the outside it didn't look like much. It was a plain, concrete building with a blue awning that said *Tease* on it. Inside, it was more interesting. There was a bar that looked like an English pub, with men sitting around in fat armchairs having drinks. I thought I could probably have a decent time in spite of the volume of the music, but Seth pulled me straight through that room and into something more like I'd been expecting in the first place.

There were a lot more guys in this one, younger too, and at least half of them were shirtless. The music pulsed so loud it made my insides feel weird. Seth immediately started bouncing to the music. He told me to stay put, and I watched as he made his way up to the bar. I noticed several other guys watch him too, and I wasn't sure if I liked that or not.

When he came back, he was carrying two tall drinks. "What's that?" I hollered above the din.

"Long Island Iced Tea," he said, pressing close so he could talk by my ear. "They're two for one right now. You'll like it, everyone likes them."

I took a sip, and it wasn't bad. Better than Alligator Sex or whatever En had fixed us. Seth raised his eyebrows in question, and I nodded, which made him smile. I felt his hand slide along my back and saw that a couple of the guys who had been watching him, were now looking at me rather enviously. I definitely liked that.

Seth gave me a nudge and steered me deeper into the room, pointing ahead of us. There was a stage featuring a well oiled guy in gold lamé underwear, gyrating in the most unlikely way. I glanced back at Seth and rolled my eyes. He laughed and took up a stance behind me, watching around my shoulder. He had one hand on my waist and was still rocking his hips along with the music, which was just fine with me. I could be a good date and watch strippers for a while. The song changed and they brought out a different guy, who was a little more my type. I'd only ever really looked at naked men on-line before. Having one on stage right in front of me was a completely different experience, but I liked it.

Actually, all around me would be a better description, because it wasn't just the guy on stage. Lots of them were half naked and dirty dancing or making out. I guessed this was part of Seth's plan to loosen me up about us, because he was suddenly way handsier than he'd ever been. I realized he was touching me constantly, rubbing or caressing anywhere and everywhere. He was practically glued to my side too, which was probably a good thing. If he wasn't, I'm sure he'd have been hit on relentlessly.

When we finished our drinks, Seth took my glass and set it on a table, then led me through the crowd again. We came to a set of stairs and joined the steady stream of guys going up and down.

"What now?" I asked, as we paused while traffic sorted itself out.

"There's a bar up here you'll like a lot better," he said, glancing at me over his shoulder. He grinned and leaned back against my chest for a moment, before people started moving again.

His enthusiasm was infectious and I tried to soak it up, although I felt awkward as hell. It wasn't so much that I was out of place. I mean, aside from the eleven million shirtless college boys, there were drag queens and plenty of older guys, some real freaks, and quite a few women. But I was definitely out of my element.

It might have been different if I was working, because I can play a part, and I'm not really myself. This, though? This was all me, in a gay bar, with my best friend.

Seth was right. I did like the upstairs room better. It was a long open veranda, with comfortable chairs and sofas to sit on, and the most relaxing ocean breeze blowing through. The music was still loud, but it wasn't nearly so pulsing, and we could talk if we kept our heads together.

Again, he went to the bar and came back with drinks. Same as before, but stronger, if possible.

"Are you trying to get me drunk so you can take advantage of me?" I asked. We settled onto a sofa in a pleasantly dim corner.

He smirked. "I'm trying to get you drunk so I can drag you out onto the dance floor in the next room."

"Ah," I said, and took a good long swallow of my iced tea.

Seth wedged himself as close as he could get to me without sitting in my lap and proceeded to tell me all about the club and several of his adventures in it. I'm guessing there are a lot of them he left out.

I began to feel the alcohol go to my head, and I was far more relaxed than when we'd walked in. Seth probably thought so, because he left off whatever story he was in the middle of and put down his glass. He shoved me back against the cushions and kissed me hard and dirty.

Instinct took over and I pushed him back, bracing my hands on his shoulders. "Hey, hey!" I said, looking around in a panic.

He gave me a stern look. "Dino. We are in South Beach, Miami. I could do you out in the middle of the street and people wouldn't even notice."

I was willing to bet they would, but I got his point. They weren't holding Bible school out there.

He slipped an arm around my neck and settled against me. "Look around," he said. "Who in the fuck is even going to give us a second glance? Except maybe that guy at the end who's been checking you out."

I ignored that last part, and looked around obediently. There were, of course, lots of other guys doing exactly what we were doing.

Seth continued. "Gay guys come to gay bars to do what everybody else does. Haven't you ever made out with some chick in a bar before?"

"No," I said, looking back at him, "I haven't. That's not really my style. And I don't date 'chicks.'"

"You don't *date*," he said with a wicked smirk.

"Yes, I do." I took a sip of my drink. "You should see the hot mechanic I'm sleeping with."

"Asshole," Seth murmured in my ear, right before he licked it.

This time when he kissed me, I let him, and pulled him into my lap, holding him tight against me. He responded with a lot of moaning and enthusiastic wriggling. It got to the point that I had to smile. "Are you taking this seriously?" I asked.

"I'll take it seriously later. Right now I'm all about having fun." He jumped up and drained his drink, then held out a hand. "Time's up, let's go!"

"You're not talkin' about the hotel, are you?"

"Nope." He snapped his fingers.

"All right." I let him pull me to my feet. "Just...be gentle with me."

* * * *

The dance floor was actually pretty small, but it was packed with the same assortment of half naked guys and drag queens that filled the other rooms. The music was louder, but better, since there was a live DJ working this one. Strobe lights pulsed in time to the beat. So did the crowd.

Seth picked up the rhythm and started dancing as we worked our way through the throng of people. There was a low wall around the edge of the dance floor, and I found a place along it where I could lean and watch. Once he got onto the floor, Seth cut loose and I was surprised to find out he really could dance. He's lean and coordinated, and he moved effortlessly.

He caught me staring and licked his lips, pouring it on thick for my benefit. I gave him an encouraging smile. I wasn't the only one noticing him. A couple of the guys on the dance floor picked up on him, and started to do a seriously dirty bump and grind with him. Seth could put the hired dancers downstairs to shame. Even without the gold underwear.

Eventually, he came over and pulled me away from the wall, so he could use the same moves on me. I know I looked like an ass, completely out of place, but Seth's energy was infectious, and his sex appeal was in full force. I wound up like several other guys in the room, willing to do just about anything to keep his interest fixed on me.

Tease definitely wasn't my scene, but I do have moves, and I managed to modify what I knew into something more or less passable. Apparently, it was good enough for Seth, because he seemed to approve.

I held my own for a while, but I was starting to get a headache. I pulled him close and leaned down to his ear. "Come on, let's get out of here," I said.

He got a smoky look on his face and nodded, rubbing up against my hip one last time before making for the stairs.

* * * *

The walk back to the hotel was as big a circus as the walk from it, only Seth was louder, ruder, and dirtier. That was all right, though, because so was the rest of the crowd. He was absolutely right—we could have had sex right there on the street and no one would have cared a bit.

"This is a side of you I don't think I've seen before," I told Seth, as he flirted outrageously with a group of guys who were hanging out on the sidewalk, teasing everyone who went by. He was silly and sultry, and fit in naturally with the people and the surroundings.

"Dino, you have no idea. I can be *extremely* gay when I want to be."

He sounded extremely gay when he said it, and I was amazed at how that suited him just as well as the tough guy in a bar fight, or the hardworking mechanic, or the pig with the pizza and beer.

Once we hit the elevator, he turned all that silly, sultry attention back on me...and then cranked it up a notch. It was all I could do to keep him dressed until we got to the room.

Inside, he kicked off his shoes and jumped onto the bed, bouncing as he pulled his shirt off over his head. He twirled it around on one finger and danced like he had in the club, all thrusting pelvis and writhing body.

I went over and turned on the radio on the bedside table, scanning the stations until I found one playing the same kind of techno-crap they had in the club.

"Come on," I said, "let's see you take it all off."

He matched the beat of the music and treated me to a striptease far more interesting than the ones I'd seen earlier. When he unbuttoned his jeans and eased them down over the tops of his thighs, I saw he wasn't wearing any underwear. My growing hard-on sprang to full attention, and I said, "I wish you would have told me that before."

"Well, if you weren't so uptight, you would have found out for yourself."

"I am not—"

"Dino, don't even try to argue it," he said with a smile. He finished out the song, dancing with his jeans half off, then dropped down onto his butt so he could kick them the rest of the way off. "Your turn," he said, giving me a wink.

"Oh, no. Not a chance," I said, holding up my hands.

He shook his head and got off the bed, coming to undo my shirt buttons. "I just meant get naked, not the dancing part."

"Ah," I said, watching his hands as he took my shirt off.

I let him undress me while I looked him over. I'd never actually seen him completely naked before. Sure, I'd seen him shirtless plenty of times, and even wearing nothing but a towel. But I'd never seen that long stretch of pale skin, unbroken from his neck, down the angle of his hip bone and along his leg. He was gorgeous, but I felt bizarre, like I was out of line for looking.

I put my hands on his shoulders and ran them down his arms, tracing the muscles with my thumbs. He was hot and a little sweaty, and I could smell it on him, earthy and raw, mixed with aftershave and cigarette smoke and the scent of arousal.

He was working on my belt buckle, but I sat down on the edge of the bed so I could study him closer, trailing my fingers down his smooth torso. He went still and let me explore, resting a hand lightly on the back of my neck. When I pressed my mouth to his stomach, he moaned and leaned into me.

This I could do. I'd spent the better part of the evening feeling awkward, but this I could do. I could stop thinking altogether and lose myself in the physical. I slid my arms around him and pulled him against my body, reveling in the feel of skin against skin, and the solid weight of him. He was hard, and excited, and I could feel his chest swell with each heavy breath. I ran my hand over his ass and down the back of his leg as far as I could reach.

"Oh man," he said, kneading my shoulders with his fingers. "I really like this silent, intense thing you do. You have some serious focus goin' on."

"Yeah," I said, kissing a slow path across his chest.

"Come on, stand up, I want you naked and on the bed, like...now." He was breathless and getting more than a little intense himself.

I got up and dropped my pants, using my feet to pull my socks off. The second I was done, Seth pushed me onto my back and crawled up over me. I never got the chance to notice if I'd feel weird being naked in front of him. By that point, we were both so turned on, I didn't care.

He straddled my hips and lay down on top of me, half kissing, half licking my neck. "Holy hell, Dino, you feel good."

I agreed with him, but for the moment, I couldn't speak. I was completely unprepared for the experience of being skin to skin, all over. "Holy hell" didn't even come close to what I was feeling. All I managed was an inarticulate moan.

"That good, huh?"

"Oh, yeah."

The hard length of Seth's cock pressed into my belly, radiating heat. He pushed up onto his hands and knees and started to deliberately rub it against me, sliding over my skin in long, light strokes. A tease. An even bigger tease when he shifted so he was brushing against my cock, over and over. It was a hell of a sensation and sent shivers down my spine.

The light from the desk gave me a remarkable view of what he was doing, and I watched, mesmerized. When I glanced up at him, I saw he was just as taken with the sight as I was, which excited me even more.

"Jesus, Seth," I moaned.

"No shit," he said, panting. "You are fucking hot, Dino."

So was he. His body was taut with the effort of controlling his motions, and his face and chest were flushed. His cock was making us both slick.

Things were moving fast, and I got nervous. "You gotta' know that I'm not really sure what comes next, here, right?"

"Just follow my lead." He spit into his hand and coated both our cocks with it.

"Classy," I said, running my fingers along his thigh.

"When have you ever known me to be classy?" He lay back down on top of me, pushing one arm under my neck, and grasping my shoulder with his other hand. I liked that a lot, because I was able to touch him almost anywhere I wanted.

His face was mere inches from mine, and he flashed one of his dark looks, before he shoved down hard with his hips. Our cocks ground together, trapped in the damp heat between us. He arched his back and did it again, which made my skin go hot and my spine tingle. My breath caught in my throat, and I could only stare at him with dumb pleasure.

When he did it a third time, I met him with a thrust of my own, and both of us moaned out loud. "Oh, shit, Dino, that's the ticket. Keep it up."

We found a rhythm that worked for us and rubbed against each other eagerly. It felt amazing, and I was desperate for more. I had to have him harder, closer, tighter. Anything to feed the desire he'd created. I wrapped my arms around him and pulled him down, planting a hand on his ass to hold him close as I drove hard against him.

"God, yeah," he moaned, clutching my shoulders tighter. "This is one of my favorite ways to fuck."

He writhed in my arms, reminding me of the way he danced. The hot rush of his breath warmed my neck, and his thighs squeezed me as he pumped his body, our cocks sliding together relentlessly. I braced my feet on the bed, straining upward each time he thrust against me. I still had a buzz from the drinks at the club, and it heightened the experience, making my head spin as waves of pleasure washed through me.

Seth looked as turned on as I was. Soon he was moaning steadily, and the bliss turned into a look of deep concentration, eyes squeezed shut and brows furrowed. His hips jerked erratically, and he clawed at my shoulders with his fingers.

"Come on, Seth," I whispered, butting my head against his lightly. "Come for me. I wanna see you lose it, right here."

"Fuck, Dino, I'm about to," he groaned.

The hard, wet slide of his body reached a fever pitch, and he cried out, holding on tightly as he rode it through. The effort he put into it, and the sudden warmth of his climax, was enough to pull me right along with him. I came hard, grinding my cock against him with fierce need.

When it was all over, we lay in a tangle, panting hard, but grinning stupidly. I hooked an arm around his neck and pulled him close so I could plant a kiss on his forehead. "I can see why you like that so much," I said. "It was incredible."

"Yes, it was." He rolled over onto his back and stretched with a satisfied hum. "You want to shower off with me and get some sleep?"

"Sure, just as soon as I can move."

He got off the bed and grabbed my ankle. "Come on, ya big dinosaur, you can make it."

I did, just barely, and when we fell back in bed, I was out like a light.

Chapter 16

I woke up the next morning, disoriented by the unfamiliar room. Reality returned in the form of Seth snoring from the other side of the bed. I pulled one of the pillows out from under my head and tossed it at him, bouncing it off his face. The snoring stopped, and the pillow came flying back.

"It's too early for that kind of shit," he groaned, rolling over.

I looked at the beside clock. "It's eight-thirty. Time to get moving. We have a lot of work to do today."

"Nrrgmmph."

I crawled out of bed and went to peer through the window. It looked like another bright and pleasant day in Florida, so I went to start a pot of coffee and take a shower.

When I got done, Seth was just coming in the door with a fistful of loose change and a bottle of something bright blue. He was half naked and his hair was a bigger mess than usual. I wasn't sure he was entirely awake yet.

"You went out in the hall in your underwear?" I asked him.

"All the X-rated junk is covered," he said, squinting. "Are you done in the shower?"

"Yeah, it's all yours."

While he got into functional shape, I poured myself a cup of coffee, dried off and got dressed. I grabbed my computer bag from the corner of the closet and unzipped it, setting up my laptop on the table.

Seth finished his shower and came out wrapped in a towel, chugging the last of his blue stuff. He paused by me, bumping my arm with his hip, then rummaged around in his duffel bag and disappeared again with his shaving kit.

My stomach growled at me, unhappy about the assorted kinds of weird alcohol I'd poured into it. I went to the nightstand and dug out the room service menu.

When Seth came back, he looked over my shoulder. "What'cha got there?"

"Breakfast." I stuffed the menu into his hand. "Order me the vegetable omelet."

"Jesus," he said, reading it. "Do they come and spoon feed you? For six bucks these pancakes better suck me off before I eat them."

"McCann's footin' the bill, I don't plan on starving." I sat down at the table and started to leaf through Serrano's notebook while my web browser loaded.

Seth picked up the phone and dialed room service. He ordered my omelet, a pot of coffee, steak and eggs, two pancakes, and a large glass of milk, then gave them our room number. Afterward, he grabbed the remote and turned on the TV. "So what's the game plan for this morning?" he asked.

"I'm gonna run these VIN numbers, see if any of them are legit. If they are, maybe they can tell us something."

"Shit, I hope so," Seth said, perching himself on the end of the bed.

He clicked through the channels erratically, rejecting each one in turn. A random assortment of words spilled from the TV—partly sunny, recommended daily amount, checked into rehab, coming up next. It was enough to drive me crazy.

"Would you pick something, already? Or you could help, you know."

"There's not a lot I can do right now, Dino."

"Get a pad of paper out of my briefcase, you can take notes."

He nodded, but couldn't resist clicking the remote a couple more times. The shrill sound of a woman screaming erupted from the TV, followed by gunfire. I rolled my eyes.

"Hey! Check it," Seth said, standing up and pointing at the screen. "It's James Bond. Speak of the devil."

I looked over, and sure enough, a good-looking man with a handgun was chasing some arch villain through the streets of a dated looking European city. I was about to comment on the coincidence, when there was a knock at the door and the muffled call of "Room Service."

Seth opened the door and led two waiters in, each one carrying a tray holding silver topped plates. I was especially interested in the one who had my pot of coffee, and I went to snatch it while he unloaded the food on the dresser. Seth signed the room charge and tipped them, then quickly flipped up all the tops to find his food.

I took my omelet and went to make room for it on the table, while Seth grabbed his plate and sat down in front of the TV.

"You're actually going to watch that?" I asked.

"I'm doing research."

"Right."

I sliced off a bite of egg with my fork and ate it while I pulled up the AutoSafe website I use to trace VIN numbers. It's one of about a dozen websites designed to help the average used car buyer avoid getting stuck with a lemon. For thirty bucks, you can plug in the VIN of the car you want to buy and find out about nearly every accident and repair job it's been through. You also get a report of each time the car changed hands officially. All this information comes in pretty handy for private eyes too, and I buy the unlimited account.

The first one I ran came up invalid. I reached into my briefcase for a pad of paper and a pen and tossed them at Seth. "I thought you were takin' notes for me," I said.

"Yeah, yeah, yeah," he said, wedging a forkful of pancakes into his mouth.

While he chewed, he set down his plate and picked up the paper. He looked like a chipmunk when he turned to me and raised his eyebrows.

"First page is a bust," I told him. "The VIN's no good."

He jotted that down and went back to watching Bond.

I flipped the page and entered the next VIN number. This time, I got a hit on a 1996 Chevy Caprice. "Hey, here we go," I said to Seth, poking him with my foot.

He put his empty plate on the dresser and came to read over my shoulder. The car had been registered in Georgia, sold twice, been reported in a minor accident, sold again and reregistered in Florida, and finally listed as salvage. Not surprisingly, the final location was Miami.

"Want me to write all that down?" Seth asked, reaching for the pad.

I shook my head. "Not yet. I can save this to a file until I run the rest of them, if even half of these are for real, there's going to be a lot of information. It would be better to sort it out when I'm done."

He looked relieved and put the paper and pen on the table. Then he went back to watching the movie. Calling it research wasn't all that dumb under the circumstances, and I said so, telling him to pay attention for anything about Bond that might actually give us a clue.

"Well," Seth said, "I bet if we asked any of the chicks Serrano knew, they'd tell us he thought he was some kind of player."

"I could say the same thing about you," I said as I typed in the next set of digits.

Seth smirked. "No. If you asked about me, they would tell you that I *am* a player."

I smiled, because from what little I knew, he was right. I was pretty sure I didn't want to know a whole lot more.

The next VIN was a hit too, and I scanned the report, looking for similarities. The only thing I could find was this car ended up salvaged in Miami also. I saved it and ran the next one. It was a dud.

On the TV, some blonde was being fragile and irritating, and giving Bond a hard time about something. He was trying to explain the situation to her, but she, of course, was having none of it.

I stood up and watched as Timothy Dalton chewed up the scenery, trying to act as though he'd been drugged. "Let's hope he didn't get his inspiration from the worst Bond ever."

Seth snorted and turned back to the TV. I finished running the VIN numbers.

At the end of an hour and a half, I had a list of a dozen bogus numbers and four real ones. The movie ended before I was done, and Seth prowled around, alternating between watching me, making faces out the window, and juggling his tennis shoes.

"Okay, that's the last one." I pulled a fresh sheet of paper off the pad and copied down the codes for each of the VIN numbers that led to an actual car. I also copied the one page that didn't fit the pattern of the rest of them. It had no VIN, and I was reasonably sure it had a real purpose. I got up to stretch and use the bathroom.

When I came out, Seth was in my chair, looking through the notebook. I poured myself the last cup of room service coffee and sat on the corner of the bed.

He turned to me. "Well?"

"The only link I see is that all the real VIN numbers are for cars that have been salvaged in Miami."

"There's no way that's a coincidence," Seth said.

"Nope. I don't think so."

"So what the hell does it mean?"

"Well, whatever this is about, McCann wanted it real bad. Maybe enough to kill for. I don't think a lot of junked cars fit the bill. But, when you think of it, wrecked cars aren't a bad place to hide something if you don't plan to leave it too long."

Seth jumped up and rubbed his hands together gleefully. "All right then, let's get cracking. Where are we going first?"

I looked at him warily. He was completely wired and going stir-crazy, and I didn't think he was going to like my answer. "I have no idea."

"What?" He frowned at me. "But you ran them, you said they were all salvaged, so where are they?"

"They're in Miami. That's all I know. They don't list final resting places, just the last thing reported to the DMV."

He flopped back in the chair and stared at me.

I smiled. "You want the computer or the phone book?"

"Say what?"

"To search salvage yards," I explained. "If he hid something in wrecked cars, I would imagine the rest of the code is what we need to find the cars."

He looked about as excited by that as I expected him to be. "I'll take the computer."

"Fine," I said, getting up to pull the phone book from the nightstand. "But stay off the porn sites, I don't want you fucking up my hard drive."

"What the hell do you take me for?" he groused as he twisted around and pulled the laptop in front of him.

"I'm serious. No porn."

He flipped me off over his shoulder.

I brought the yellow pages to the table and sat down in the chair opposite him, turning to the Auto section and scanning the columns until I found salvage yards. There were at least twenty of them.

"What are we looking for?" Seth asked, over the top of the screen.

"Get a list and start looking for anything that might match something in Serrano's notebook."

He made a face. "That's like looking for a needle in a haystack!"

"Welcome to the reality of detective work, my friend."

I read through the listings a couple of times, getting familiar with them and looking for things that might have appealed to Serrano, something that would make him choose a particular place. I even looked for Bond references. I didn't find any.

Across the table, Seth scrolled through computer screens and muttered irritably to himself. I suppressed a smile. Usually, when he helped me out, it was bar fights, tailing people, and repo work. The fun and interesting stuff. He'd never spent a sweltering afternoon at City Records with me, or sat through three hours of computer searches brainstorming keywords.

I thought maybe location was a key, so I jotted down the addresses for a couple of likely looking places, choosing them based off how flashy their ad was, and flipped to the maps in the front of the phone book. I found the street index and ran my finger down the columns to find the first one. It was in section K-four on page fourteen.

My brain started to get the kind of itch that happens when an idea is just out of reach. I paused to see if it would come, but nothing happened. Turning to page fourteen, I followed the side bar down the page to row K. Again the itch. Still no idea. As I scanned the top of the page and found column four, it finally hit me.

"Son of a bitch," I said, smacking the phone book and leaning back in the chair.

Seth looked up. "What's the matter?"

"I got him," I said, giving him a huge grin, which he cautiously mirrored back at me. I could tell he wasn't completely ready to believe anyone could make sense of a wacko's scribblings. "I figured out another piece of the code, and it's a doozy."

"So, spill."

I knew damn well he was chomping at the bit, and if I was right, we weren't too far from going somewhere. I turned the phone book so he could see it. "Look at the first line of each code," I said. "They're map coordinates."

"Like longitude and latitude?" He looked deeply skeptical.

I shook my head. "Like atlas markings. The top and side bars you use to zero in on a certain spot on the map. The first bit is the page number, and the rest shows you where on the page to look." I demonstrated with the one I'd just been looking for.

Seth's eyes got wide and a slow smile crossed his face. "Hot damn."

"We better hope like hell he used the Miami YellowBook, because if these refer to any other map, we're screwed. I can only imagine how many different maps cover this area, we'd never figure it out."

"Only one way to know," Seth said, shoving my notes at me. "Page fifteen, M-eight."

I turned the page and we both leaned in as I followed the M row to the eight column. I grabbed a pencil and outlined the square of map we were interested in. "Looks like we got twenty-fifth through twenty-eighth avenues crossed by ninety-ninth street through a hundred and second. So let's see if there's a salvage yard in there somewhere."

Seth slid the computer into the center of the table and started scrolling through his list slowly.

"There's one on a hundred and first," he said, pointing at the screen. He clicked the link for it and a Google map popped up. The little flag showed us it was nowhere near the part of the city we were concentrating on. He swore.

"I have an idea," I said, pulling the computer closer. I used Google Maps to search for salvage yards in the area, which got me a map covered in little flags. Using the phone book as a reference, I zoomed in on our square. Flags started dropping off the edges of the map as the scale got larger and larger. Eventually, only one flag remained, and it was well within the section we wanted. I clicked on the flag and all the information for M & H Auto Sales & Salvage popped up on the screen. Seth let out a whoop and slapped me on the back.

"You're a fucking genius," he said. He grabbed the page of notes and held it up next to the screen. "And Serrano's not. Look at the second line of the code. It's the freakin' address."

He was right. The second line of code was 993827. M & H was located at 9938 NW 27th Avenue. I shook my head and smiled. I also got that rush again. It's one hell of a feeling, and I will never grow tired of it. Sometimes, it's the only thing that keeps me pushing forward until I finally solve a case.

I took the sheet from Seth and set it down, labeling the parts of the code we'd figured out—map, address, VIN. I did that for each set, so the information started to look organized and meaningful.

Seth got up to get himself a glass of water and came back, looking significantly more interested in the whole process now that it was producing something.

We used the same method to track down each of the other salvage yards. Having the address line made it quick and fairly simple, and within twenty minutes we had all four yards, with names, complete addresses, and phone numbers. I put all the information on the sheet with the codes. I also marked each one on the phone book map and tore the pages out. Normally, I hate jerks who do stuff like that, but desperate times call for desperate measures.

Seth took the paper from me and looked it over. He pointed at the last one, on the bottom of the page. "What's that? We don't have anything down for it."

"Got me," I said, stretching. "It's the only set that looks like that, so I figured it was important."

I wanted more coffee and had to make do with the crappy boil-your-own that came with the room. Still, it was better than nothing.

At the table, Seth bent over the computer, chewing his lip and typing. I sat down on the bed and watched. "What'cha doing?" I asked.

"I was looking at this last code, and the first line looks just like the address lines of the salvage lots. I'm trying to see if I can pull something up."

I looked at our notes. The top line for that code was 8592124. It made sense to me, we still had nothing to go with the car key or the card. Seth was searching the map for either 24th or 124th, but wasn't getting very far. His idea was sound, but what we'd done before wasn't going to work without knowing what part of the city to look at.

"Try whitepages dot com," I said.

He pulled up the site and shook his head. "That won't work, Dino, it's asking for the name of the place, and all I have is the address. Maybe."

"Click on this tab that says 'reverse lookup,'" I said, pointing it out to him.

"You sneaky bastard," he said as he started to enter in various combinations of the address numbers we had.

On the third try, he got a listing for EZ Mini Storage. Bingo.

"Nice work," I said. "You wanna bet there's a BMW in there that fits this key? Do a map search on it now."

I added the new information to our sheet and marked the storage unit on the phone book map. Seth looked exceedingly pleased with himself.

"Now can we get the hell out of here for a while?" he asked, turning sideways in the chair.

"Yup, put your shoes on." I tossed them over.

"You know, this stuff with the maps and the squished up addresses and everything, it's completely redundant. First of all, if you hide something that important, aren't you going to remember where? And if you have the addresses right there, you don't really need the map numbers too, do you?"

"Remember," I pointed out, "he was role playing. It's a game. He may not really need to look them up on the map, but he does it because it feeds the fantasy that he's some kind of secret agent."

"What a nut job."

I tossed the notebook and papers into my briefcase, and put away my computer. We packed our bags as well, and I stopped by the dresser to pick up my wallet and car keys. Seth shoved a ball cap on his head, shouldered his duffel, and we went down to check out.

Chapter 17

At around eleven in the morning on a weekday, the traffic in Miami is already pretty heavy and starting to pick up for the lunch hour. That meant slow going for much of the drive. Three out of the four salvage yards we were looking for were at the edges of town, situated where there was more room to spread out. We decided to hit the farthest one and work our way back. Serrano had us going in all directions anyway.

Seth drove because I couldn't stand another minute of him fidgeting, drumming his fingers, or otherwise going crazy on me. Miami was easier to bear if I didn't have to actively deal with it, and he was smart enough not to abuse Matilda when I sat within arm's reach of his throat.

That left me free for navigating, and I had both a Florida road map and the phone book pages on my lap.

"Where to first?" Seth asked. He had one hand on the wheel and the other draped over the side of the car, aviator sunglasses on, and cap turned backward.

"Lester's Auto Salvage."

"Hrm. Wonder if he's anything like Ed."

"No idea," I said, reading the map. "Take the next exit up here. You're gonna turn left at the top."

He hit the turn signal and floated over onto the ramp, pulling to a stop at the light. It took us another ten minutes to get to 27th, then five more cruising along until we spotted the salvage yard.

We parked at the far end of a dirt patch out front and walked along the fence. Seth peered in at the cars, getting a feel for what was in there. He pulled his hat off and put it on the right way, mashing it around until it sat right.

A bell jingled as we went in, and a large man in a dirty union suit came through a door connecting the front office to the shop. Country music drifted in behind him, sounding tinny in the concrete acoustics.

"What can I do ya for?" he asked.

Seth smiled and readjusted his cap. "I'm looking for the right front fender of a ninety-five or ninety-six Chevy Caprice. White if you've got it."

"Well, now, I know I have a few of those out there. Probably got something that'll fix it."

"I sure hope so," Seth said. He jerked his thumb at me. "His wife is a picky bitch, and she's not going to settle for just anything."

The guy gave me a knowing nod and said, "Ain't that always the way. They'll have our nuts in a wringer one way or t'other."

"Tell me about it," I said.

We followed him through the side door, and he pointed out the section of the yard we needed. "Most of the Chevys are over in that corner there, running down the hill. There's a few good Caprices in there. Take a look at the ninety-seven too, I think there's at least a couple. Fender from one of them oughta' work, I think."

"Thanks, man," Seth said, and we started off down the center driveway. Behind me, I could hear the guy singing along with Willie Nelson while he hammered on some old car part.

When we were well out of earshot, Seth asked, "What's Serrano's code for the Caprice?"

I pulled the sheet of notes out of my back pocket and unfolded it. "The parts we haven't figured out are R-nine, seventeen and one-three-two-two-zero-nine."

"Whatever the fuck that means," Seth said.

He paused at the top of a small rise, and we looked out over the long rows of battered and broken cars, snaking through the grass to the left of the driveway. They made neat lines like some kind of automotive farm crop. With any luck, somewhere out there was the reason we'd been through a whole lot of trouble.

"R-nine, seventeen," Seth mused, folding his arms over his chest. "We know Serrano was a moron, and we know the rest of his code was simplistic and redundant, so what the fuck does R-nine, seventeen mean?"

"Are the spaces for the cars marked? Like some parking lots?"

"Shit, no," Seth scoffed. "Not usually. Most of these places are loosely organized by type of car, but that's about it. Old codgers who've been around forever have it all in their heads. Some of the newer or bigger places keep computerized inventories, but that wouldn't help us. Unless Serrano had access to that information, and I highly doubt it."

"All right," I said, putting on my sunglasses to cut the glare of a few hundred windshields. "What's R, then? Road?"

Seth smacked his forehead. "*Row!*" He looked like he was considering smacking me too.

"Row nine," I said, nodding. A thrill was creeping up my back, and I grinned. "Car seventeen in row nine, maybe?"

Seth looked smug. "Sounds pretty freakin' obvious to me."

I turned and looked back toward the front gate. The cars there were more jumbled, and it was harder to make out what actually constituted a row. Seth had a finger in the air and was counting to himself, turning as he passed where we stood, and looking out ahead of us.

When he hit nine, I said, "Lead the way. Let's see if you're right."

"That red Monte Carlo," he said, pointing. "I think that's the row."

We set off down the drive, walking fast, but resisting the urge to break into a dead run in case the old guy was watching. No one gets that excited about fenders. Taking a left at the Monte, we both started counting. When we hit seventeen, we stopped and stared. It wasn't a Caprice. I counted again to be sure, but the car seventeen spaces from the end was a rusted out Impala. Damn.

"Shit," Seth said.

I turned and looked behind us. That one was a truck. When I turned back, Seth was already trudging through the tall grass between the cars to the next row over. Sure enough, there on the other side was a green Chevy Caprice that had seen better days. Plus one very bad day. The front end was crumpled and the windshield smashed into a tight spider web of cracks. One of the back doors was missing. I had a feeling someone didn't walk away from this one.

Seth snatched the notes from my hand and went around to the driver's side, cupping his hand over the glass to compare the VIN to what we had.

"You really think that's necessary?" I asked, figuring that if we'd gotten this far, it had to be the right car.

"You want to waste an hour searching this pig and find out we were barking up the wrong tree?"

"No, not really," I said. "Are we?"

Seth straightened up. "Nope. It's a match. Can you believe this? It's like we're in a fucking Indiana Jones movie."

"I think that was the idea." I took a look at my watch. It was just after noon, and the sun was beating down hot and clear. There wasn't even a hint of breeze, and I could feel the sweat forming on the back of my neck.

I wasn't looking forward to crawling around in a stale, overheated car full of native wildlife.

"Where do you want to start?" Seth asked.

"Let's try the trunk, seems logical."

Seth had brought a small pry bar from the tool kit in my car. He needn't have bothered, though. One look at the back end showed it was too banged up for the trunk to close properly. He lifted the lid, and we both peered in.

The spare tire was missing, as well as the jack, and there was little else of interest inside. The carpet was bunched up and the cover of the tire well was askew. Seth started pulling off fuse hatches and interior panels, reaching into places I didn't even know existed. I stood back and let him work, deferring to his expertise.

After ten minutes he stood up and dusted off his hands. He looked hot and irritated. "There's nothing here, Dino."

"Son of a bitch." I wiped the sweat off my brow with the back of my hand. "All right, let's get to work on the rest of it."

Seth took the driver's side and I took the passenger, both of us reaching under seats and prying up the corners of door panels. I even checked the glove compartment, but that seemed a little obvious, even for Serrano.

"What if we're wrong?" Seth asked from down by the brake pedal where he was feeling around behind the dashboard.

"Too much of it fits so far," I said. "There's no such thing as this much coincidence."

"What if it's something really tiny like a jump drive full of secret files or whatever?"

"I doubt it. Too risky to leave something like that to the heat and the elements. Besides, I don't figure him for that kind of thing anyway. Not enough smarts for computer crime."

I stretched out on my stomach in the grass so I could look underneath the car. I hoped like hell he hadn't buried his prize, or something equally obnoxious. I also hoped nothing was crawling into my clothes while I searched.

"Well, fuck me sideways," Seth said from inside the car.

I sat up. "Is that a request, or did you find something?"

"Can't it be both?" he smirked.

"I don't know, sounds painful. What have you got?"

Seth pulled up the front edge of the driver's seat upholstery to reveal a long, jagged gash in the foam padding underneath. He grinned and raised an eyebrow. Reaching in with his fingers, he felt around carefully, face set in heavy concentration. After a moment, he eased out a slim, gray cashbox about eight inches wide. It had a combination lock on the front, formed by a row of six small tumblers.

He put it on the seat and said, "I'm willing to bet this isn't a first-aid kit. Can I assume the last part of the code is the combination?"

I took a look at our notes. "Try this," I said. "One-three-two-two-zero-nine."

Seth turned the box to face him, dialed in the numbers with his thumbs, and clicked the latch. The lid popped open with an audible snap, and he grinned. So did I. He opened the box slowly and let out a low whistle.

"I'll be damned," he said. "Would you look at that."

I was looking. There in living color were three fat wads of cash and a veritable toy box of various drugs. There were rolled up baggies full of pills, tiny amber vials of things both liquid and powder, and sheets of paper that appeared to be stickers but were far more potent.

"Oh, I fucking hate Miami," I said.

Seth poked through the drugs and said, "Looks like mostly Ecstasy, K, and acid."

"You know what you're talkin' about."

He shrugged. "I hang out in clubs a lot, I see what goes on."

"You ever do any of this?" I asked.

"I'd never have anything to do with acid, but I've tried the others. Fun, but not worth all the bullshit. I'd rather get drunk and have a good time the old fashioned way."

I nodded. I was glad to hear it. Although I'd never had any particular worries, if I had to pick a personality type that would be attracted to drugs, Seth's was certainly high on the list.

I got up out of the grass and brushed myself off. "Close that up and stuff it back where you got it. We're done with this."

Seth snapped the box closed, wiping it clean with the tail of his T-shirt. "Don't have to tell me twice. There's enough here to get us both put away for dealing."

"Exactly. I have no intention of running around Miami with a stash of drugs. Especially not for some schmuck who probably knew exactly what he was sending us after. I'm betting Serrano was a runner for McCann *and* The Shark Pond, and he double crossed somebody."

"Yeah, and he got killed for it." Seth pushed the box back into the seat and pulled his cap off, raking his fingers through his hair. "How exactly are we going to avoid the same fate?"

"By playing stupid. We go back and tell McCann that we're sorry to have to break it to him, but it looks like dear old Darryl was messing around in the drug trade. We tell him where we found the stuff and suggest that he make an anonymous tip to the cops. Then once we're out of his hair, he can go pick up his shit and everyone's a winner."

Seth held out a hand so I could help him to his feet, and grabbed a quick grope in the process. "Are *we* planning to call the cops?"

"No, we are planning to put as much distance between this and us as possible. It's not my job to make up for the failings of the Miami police department."

"I'm cool with that," he said.

We walked back to the office and thanked the old guy. I made a point of calling to him through the open door of the auto shop, rather than going in. I didn't want him getting another good look at our faces on the off chance we got connected with McCann's deal.

Chapter 18

Back in the car, I took out my cellphone and McCann's business card, and dialed his number. When he answered, I said, "Yeah, this is Dino Martini. Listen, I'm in Miami right now, and I have a report for you. Is there someplace we can meet?"

"So soon? I'm impressed, Mr. Martini," he said.

"I know you and your family were very anxious to get things taken care of, so I gave it my complete attention. I understand what a difficult time this must be for you."

Seth rolled his eyes.

"I appreciate that," McCann said. "I have a short meeting in a few minutes, but I'll be free after that. There's a nice bistro nearby that I like, we can meet there. Say, four o'clock?"

"Sounds all right to me." I jotted down the address he gave me and told him we'd be there.

After I hung up, we found the spot on the map and figured out how to get there. The restaurant was up in North Miami, on the waterfront, and was actually named Harbor Bistro.

Rush hour starts early on Fridays, so the drive took us every spare minute we had. Even so, we arrived first. We took a table where we had a view of the door. The place was pretty swanky, and the waiter seemed like he wasn't sure we belonged there, but he was polite anyway. We ordered drinks, and Seth ordered an appetizer of cheese, smoked fish and crackers.

Fifteen minutes later, McCann strode in, looking pleased and relaxed, and not at all like a man in the midst of great personal loss. He managed to plaster that on by the time he got to us.

"So," he said, after he sat down and ordered a drink for himself. "You've made some progress already."

"A lot of progress, actually," I told him. "I don't think you're gonna like what I discovered."

He sighed and gave a painful nod. "I was afraid of that."

"I'm sorry to have to tell you that it looks like your brother-in-law was dealing drugs," I explained, keeping my voice low. "The codes in the notebook led us to his stash."

McCann kept a somber face, but his eyes positively gleamed. "Oh, dear, that's...that's really very unfortunate. What did you do with it?"

"We left it there," I said. His eyes stopped gleaming. "As soon as we realized what we were into, we put everything back the way we found it, and called you right away."

"I see..." He concentrated on straightening his silverware.

I had already put the package back together the way it started, and I pulled it from my briefcase and laid it on the table in front of him.

"This is as far as we're willing to go." I set a slip of paper on top of the package. "That's the address where we found it and a description of where it is. This is a matter for the police now."

"The police?" he said, picking up the paper and reading it with interest.

"Yeah. My suggestion is that you call the police and explain what you know. They have anonymous tip lines you can use if you're concerned about getting the family name involved."

He glanced up at me. "You didn't notify them yourself?"

I shook my head. "I didn't feel it was my place, what with it being a delicate matter and all. I'll let you decide what to do about that."

"That's very kind of you," he said, gleaming again. "You've done a fine job."

"Thank you," I said. I gave him the hotel bill and gas receipts and he gave me five hundred dollars to cover those, plus the day's work. He didn't even bat an eye.

As far as I was concerned, it seemed like a good idea to get out of there before McCann started asking any more questions. I didn't bother to give him my notes on the other salvage yards. If I wasn't doing the cops any favors, I sure as hell wasn't going to turn around and do it for the bad guys.

We stood up and said our goodbyes as McCann pocketed the package, and left him to pay the bill.

Outside, Seth asked, "Do you think he bought it?"

"Yup. I think he's a smug bastard who's too impressed with his own acting skills to even consider that we might have thought he was lying. He's got no reason to doubt us."

I pulled McCann's money out of my pocket and handed two hundred to Seth. "Here, you earned that."

"Did I earn this today, or last night?" he asked with a dirty grin.

I gave him an exasperated look, but humored him. "If that was for last night, I would have given you all of it."

"Yeah, and don't forget it either." He stuffed the money in his pocket and climbed into the car.

* * * *

The trip home was quiet and uneventful, which is exactly what you want after a job like that. We took turns driving, with me doing the first half and Seth taking the second. I know I fell asleep at some point, because I was woken up by Seth's catastrophic music blasting from the radio. He was singing along with it and beating time on the steering wheel. I smacked his hand.

When we got back to Madeira Beach, he went straight to the garage and pulled into the lot. I climbed out and stretched, and Seth came around the back of the car. Without warning, he grabbed me by the front of my shirt and pulled me into a brutal kiss that just about knocked me on my ass. He shoved me against the car and started grinding on my hip. Fortunately, it was already dark out.

When he broke for air and started to suck on my neck, I said, "Driving my car gets you wired?"

"No, fucking you in Miami gets me wired. I've been thinking about it for an hour, and I'm hard as a rock," he panted. He yanked on my shirt and started dragging me after him. "Come on, you're gonna fix it."

"Whoa, wait a minute. Where are we going?"

"Upstairs," he said, pulling me across the parking lot.

"Oh...no way," I protested, putting on the brakes. "You know I've become extremely fond of getting naked with you, but there is no way in hell I'm going to do anything of the kind in your disaster of a bed."

He snorted and tried pushing me instead. "It's okay, Dino, I cleaned it all up again. It's been good since you helped."

"You're lying." I braced myself at the foot of stairs. "You're just saying that so I'll go up there, then you're gonna shove me down and pounce on me and not let me up until you're done."

"All of that is true except for the lying part. My bedroom really is clean. We'll have to kick a path to get there, but I promise the sheets won't scare you. Now, get the fuck up the stairs."

The mess wasn't the only thing I had reservations about. It was Seth's domain, and I had the definite impression things got pretty wild when he brought people up there. The thought sent a chill down my spine, but also turned me on.

Seth growled with frustration and said, "In about eight seconds, I'm gonna do you right here on the stairs."

That thought was kind of hot too, but I turned and trotted up to the apartment, Seth right on my tail. He pushed past me so he could unlock the door. Inside, he didn't even bother with lights, he just dragged me through the mess to the bedroom, shoved me into it, and slammed the door behind us. He grinned at me and kicked off his shoes, and I suddenly felt like a rat in a trap.

He peeled off his shirt as he crossed the room, tossing it and flipping on the stereo, which came alive at top volume. It was like being assaulted. The song had a driving beat, with lyrics screamed out of the speakers, rattling the windows. I've heard explosions that were more musical.

I hollered something about turning it down, but Seth shook his head. "No way, man. It's my rules now."

"It was your rules last night," I hollered back.

"Still is, Dino." He looked wicked and feral, and my mouth went dry. I had no idea what the hell I was in for, but I wanted to find out. I locked eyes with him and pulled my sweatshirt off over my head. He smirked... and attacked me.

Without warning, he shoved me onto the bed and jumped me, pinning my shoulders down and kissing me recklessly. He dug his feet into the mattress and rubbed his hips in crude circles against my groin. The sensation was electric, and I grabbed him by the waist, pulling him down harder. He moaned loud enough to hear over the music.

He got up on his knees, tearing at my pants. I tried helping, but it was clumsy work, wrestling each other between wet, sloppy kisses. We slid off the bed in the process. By the time the song changed to something equally ear splitting, we were both naked on the floor.

Seth made a grab for my cock, stroking it as he panted in my ear, "Get back on the bed."

Then he was gone, digging through the drawer in the bedside table, while I did as I was told. He climbed on top of me with a condom and plastic bottle clutched in one hand, rubbing our erections together with just enough friction to drive me crazy. I threaded my fingers in his hair and rolled over him so I could claim his mouth. He moaned and humped my leg like a dog.

Before long, he struggled to get free and pushed me onto my back, straddling my hips. He stuck the condom in his mouth and tore it open with his teeth, spitting the wrapper on the floor. It occurred to me I had no idea which one of us he intended it for, and I hoped he remembered I was new to all this.

Whether he remembered or not, it was me he rolled the condom on to, and I was hugely relieved. Among other things, I didn't want to blow the mood by having to remind him of my inexperience. I could deal with being on the giving end.

The driving pace of the music made everything seem frantic, and I was concerned we were going a little too fast, but Seth was absolutely focused on what he was doing. If I didn't know for a fact he was stone-cold sober, I would have guessed he was on something. He'd gotten me ready and was fingering himself, eyes squeezed shut. He took deep, ragged breaths. I sat up and kissed his neck, biting and licking his skin the way he did to me.

"Oh, fuck, Dino," he moaned, shoving me down so we could get on with it.

He slicked up my cock with more lube and moved so he could slide down on it. I held still and watched him, aroused beyond belief, letting him do whatever he wanted. He moved so slowly, muttering, "Oh fuck, oh fuck, oh fuck, oh fuck..."

I put my hands on his thighs and stroked encouragement. It was all I could do to control myself.

As he got used to me, he started rocking his hips, barely moving at first. It felt so good I was shaking. He got bolder, and I realized I could join in, which was a good thing because I was on the verge of going insane. I held onto his waist and started to thrust at his pace, following his lead. It was amazing, and I hate to admit it, but the music was the perfect backdrop.

We were getting into it, moaning and writhing on the bed, when all of the sudden he stopped. I got confused and wondered if maybe I missed something, because he actually eased off me and made like he was going to get off the bed.

I grabbed his arm and gave him a questioning look, which he answered by leaning down and saying, "You want more, you're gonna have to take it."

"Excuse me?"

He grinned darkly and patted my cheek. "You heard me."

"You mean like grab you and hold you down and literally take it?"

"Yep, that's what I mean," he said, twisting out of my grasp and pulling just out of reach.

He crouched there, daring me to attack him, but I said, "I'm not gonna do that. It's crazy, you're not even healed up from your real fight."

"Do not start with that shit, right now, Dino. I swear, I'm fine."

"When I can't see bruises, then you're fine." I know people play those kinds of games all the time, and it wasn't so much that I was opposed to it, but I didn't think I wanted to start out with one. It felt like we were skipping huge steps in the process of switching from friends to...whatever we were becoming.

"Are you gonna fuck me or not?" His voice carried an edge of frustration, but he still gazed at me with hunger in his eyes.

That was a challenge I could meet. I took hold of his arm and pulled him to me. "Yeah, I am," I said, kissing the side of his neck, "but you're gonna lie down here and let me do it right. My way."

"Does that include knee pads and safety goggles?"

"Fuck you," I snapped, but inwardly I was relieved.

He sounded less irritated, and rubbed his cock against my thigh, impatient. "Yes, please, I'm dyin' here."

I started to push him down, but he stopped me and said, "No, wait. I wanna be on my knees, so you can actually fuck me."

"Yeah, sure, I can do that." I was damn near breathless at the thought of doing that.

He arranged himself while I found the lube and got ready again. When he was in position I pushed into him as slow as I could manage. My efforts were wasted, however, because he shoved back onto my cock with a ragged moan, and tried to start running the show again.

"Harder, Dino, I won't break. Come on, dude."

"Give a guy a chance, will ya?" I grabbed hold of his hips and held him still, so I could catch up. He may have been all about fast action, but I needed a little more time. I wanted to enjoy the buildup, and savor the thrill of being inside him.

He clutched at the blankets and gave me about fifteen seconds to appreciate anything before he took up his previous pace, forcing me along with him. I quit trying to fight it and fucked him, matching pace with the music and letting it set the tone. He wanted it rough, and I did my best to give it to him. It worked better than I expected, and we fell into a steady rhythm. He felt great beneath me, all hot slick skin and lean muscle. It wasn't long before I lost it, driving into him while I held his hips so firmly, I probably added to his collection of bruises. He met me thrust for thrust, and his steady stream of commentary assured me he liked it. I came hard, panting uncontrollably and moaning Seth's name. The aftershocks shuddered through my whole body.

While I tried to catch my breath, Seth reached back and grabbed my hand, pulling it around so I could stroke his cock. As soon as I started, he groaned and swore, shoving back against me until I fucked him even harder. That put him over the edge, writhing between my hand and my body for what seemed like ages, until he finally slowed to a stop and dropped on the bed, gasping for air.

I hovered over him, making sure he was okay, and marveled at just how sexy he really was. As first times go, I'm not sure I would have chosen to get rough like that, but as he said, we were playing by his rules. I brushed the damp hair off his forehead and he smiled at me without opening his eyes.

"Son of a bitch," he muttered. "That was fucking fantastic. I didn't think you had it in you."

"I am capable," I said. "It's just not my usual order of things."

"I know," he told me, rolling onto his back. "You have this whole code of conduct deal or whatever. Is there a handbook I should read?"

"You know what? Shut up."

"I'm sorry." He wound his arms around my neck and pulled me down on top of him. "You're an old-fashioned guy, I get that. I actually like that, Dino. It's hot."

"Yeah, all right."

It's impossible to get mad when you're still buzzing from an intense orgasm. Seth's body was warm and comfortable under me, and I preferred to use what energy I had left kissing him. He allowed me to be as slow and old-fashioned as I wanted, and that was apology enough.

It was late and we were tired, so I left to get something to clean up with, and by the time I got back, he was sound asleep. I took care of us both and went to turn down the music. It took some work, but I managed to get him roused enough to get under the covers, then he was out again. I climbed in next to him and curled up along his back, feeling exhausted, satisfied, and completely out of my league.

Chapter 19

I woke up early the next morning, disoriented and tense. Beside me, Seth snored softly, one arm shoved up under the pillow and the other draped loosely over his stomach. When he shifted and rolled to his side, I saw he had crease marks on his cheek from the pillow. God, he looked so young.

He looked like the shirtless college boys in the club in South Beach. Hell, he *was* like the guys in the club. That was his world, wild all-night parties, heavy drinking, crazy sex, then do it all over again the next night. What the fuck did I think I was doing?

It was the first time in my life I can remember actually feeling old. We all joke about it from time to time, but this was real, this was me feeling old and like an ass for trying to be something I wasn't.

Suddenly, I felt ridiculous being in his bed, so I got up. I went and used the bathroom, then hunted around until I found my clothes and got dressed. I was putting on my shoes when Seth rolled over into the middle of the bed. He made the usual waking-up faces and pried one eye halfway open. He spotted me and frowned. "What'cha doin'?"

"I have a lot of stuff to get done today," I said. "I'm going to head home."

"What time'z it?"

"Early. Go back to sleep."

"Mmm," he murmured, eyes already drifting shut again. "I'll see you later, 'kay?"

"I'll give you a call," I told him. He was already sound asleep.

* * * *

I drove to the bakery with the good coffee and bought some breakfast, then went back to my place, letting myself in quietly so I wouldn't wake any of the ladies. I shouldn't have worried. Ruth's bicycle was gone, and the downstairs hall smelled of eggs and toast. My stomach growled.

I ate half my breakfast, but it wasn't sitting right. I was still tired, and mentally drained, so I crawled in bed and slept for a couple more hours.

It was a little after ten when I woke up. I reheated my coffee and sat down at the desk to take stock of my day. There were several cases in my current workload that only required computer time on my part. I separated those into one stack, figuring the state I was in, that would be the best use of my time.

Even at that, I found I couldn't focus very well. I decided to see if the ladies were around, so I put on a clean shirt and went to find them.

Downstairs, the whole gang was sitting out on the patio, drinking iced tea and having a lively conversation about something they didn't exactly see eye to eye on. When I went around the corner, I discovered the debate involved planters for a garden they were planning.

"Ruth, you just *can't* have a bunch of cornstalks and beanpoles all over the place like some Farmer Brown. They'd be horribly ugly."

Ruth laughed and said, "I'm not planning to grow corn, Della. There are plenty of ornamental vegetables that flower magnificently. They would look perfectly beautiful *and* make practical use of the some of the space. I want to grow herbs too."

"Adele," Della pleaded, "can't you talk some sense into her. Those garden society ladies will think we're a bunch of hicks."

"Why don't you put a lid on the Southern drama," said Adele. "This isn't *Gone With the Wind*. I like Ruth's idea."

Della flapped her hands and made a little pouting noise. I decided that was a good moment to make my presence known.

"Good morning, ladies," I said cheerfully, slipping my hands into my pockets and strolling over to where they sat.

"Dino, darling!" Della jumped up and gave me a warm hug and a pat on the cheek. "We haven't seen you in *days*. How are you? Come sit down, you should have some tea."

I sat in an empty chair, while Ruth poured me a glass. Adele said hello, and Fern stared. I smiled at them all and said, "Things have been fine. I just got back from a couple days in Miami, working on a job. Didn't turn out to be much, but it paid all right."

"It still sounds exciting," Ruth said.

Della sat in her chair and leaned toward me. "We were just planning our garden. Don't you think that masses and masses of beautiful flowers are just the thing?"

Ruth intervened and explained, "We got to talking with one of the women in the Gulf Beaches Garden Club the other day, and she agreed to bring a few of her friends to help us design a garden out here. We're going to have them visit on Tuesday."

"And Ruth wants to embarrass us all by telling those society ladies that we want to plant *vegetables*."

Adele piped up. "Where do you keep getting this society shit? It's a garden club."

I took a sip of my tea and measured my words. Finally, as gently as possible, I said, "Della...you don't really think you can plant a society garden in the back yard of an old hardware store, do you?"

"Oh, don't be *silly*, I just want to start getting invited to all those lovely garden parties. But that's not going to happen if they think we're planting crops out here."

I laughed and shook my head. "My ma used to grow herbs and stuff in our backyard, and it always looked pretty to me. Aren't urban vegetable gardens supposed to be the big thing now? Politically correct or whatever?"

Ruth laughed this time. "That's true, and there's nothing as tasty as homegrown veggies." She gave me a conspiratorial smile that suggested she was grateful for my support.

I stayed for a while to finish my tea and listen to them talk about what they wanted to plant. They also spent a lot of time discussing how they were going to entertain their "society" garden club guests on Tuesday afternoon. It was a pleasant break from the constant whirlwind going on inside my head.

* * * *

Upstairs, in my apartment, I saw Seth had called my cellphone while I was gone. There was a voice message, but I didn't listen to it right away. It would be his usual "Give me a call or stop by" with some newly added innuendo mixed in. I'd deal with it later.

I worked steadily for about an hour and a half, then went downstairs to smoke in the storefront. That wasn't the best idea in the world, since it left me too much idle time to think about Seth. I spent ten minutes mentally reliving the night in the hotel room and felt old all over again.

When I couldn't take it anymore, I went back upstairs to work. After a while, Ruth tapped on my door, and I invited her in.

"I was just heading up to cook a little lunch, and I thought I'd stop and see what you've done with the apartment," she said, looking around with interest. She gravitated to the desk where my paperwork was spread out and ran a hand over the wood. "This is stunning. Where did you get it?"

"It was my granddad's. Ma gave it to me when he died. It's pretty great."

She stayed a few more minutes, checking out the place, then gave me the kind of shrewd once over only mothers can do. "Della and I are going to get some pizza and wine and watch a couple of movies tonight. Why don't you come join us?"

I gathered she sensed my mood and thought I needed a little cheering up, which wasn't entirely wrong. It might be good to get my mind off current events for a while and relax, and the truth was, the set up around there was beginning to remind of me home.

"Yeah, I'll probably come over," I said, "if I get enough work done."

She smiled. "That's fine. You can join us whenever you want."

I thanked her and saw her out, then sat down and buried myself in my work. If there was one good thing that came out of the day, it was that I made a lot of money. At the end, I had six full reports, complete with invoices, ready to mail out.

When I went over to Ruth's, I left my cellphone behind and made a mental apology to Seth. I just wasn't ready to deal with that yet.

Chapter 20

Pizza and wine with pleasant ladies was a pretty good escape from my troubles for a while, but Sunday morning brought the full weight of them back down on me. I tried to stay asleep as long as I could, but by nine, I had to admit I was awake. My brain was going to start working whether I liked it or not.

I went through the motions of coffee and shower and breakfast, intentionally dragging my feet just to use up time. I felt restless, like I had an itch I couldn't scratch, but my motivation to do anything at all was completely gone. I had no focus.

That's how I ended up wasting the entire afternoon at the Backroom Bar watching guys shoot pool out back, nursing beers, and ignoring my cellphone. I didn't want to think about Seth, but he was on my mind anyway, and I knew I had to figure out what I was doing. I couldn't keep avoiding him forever, and I didn't want to. But I needed to get back to a place where things felt normal again. I was exploring the possibility of going back to being just friends, when Seth himself plopped down in the chair opposite me.

"So this is where you've been hiding out," he said. He looked mildly irritated, but not exactly pissed off. "Do you know how many bars I've been to in the past two days?"

I shook my head. "I was working all day yesterday."

"Is your cellphone broken?"

"I was just real busy, Seth, I'm sorry. I had a lot of catching up to do."

He shot me a look that said he knew I was full of shit, and went to stick his head through the bar window to ask for a beer. She handed one out to him and he came and sat down, taking a sip.

"I'm a little surprised," he said. "I thought a freak out of this size would have been reserved for when I nail you, not the other way around."

He had a wicked glint in his eye, and with one sentence, he brought back the memory of Friday night so strong I could practically feel his skin against mine. I felt old and out of touch all over again, and I needed that to stop. I didn't want to know what it felt like when *he* finally realized I wasn't in his league.

"Look, Seth...I don't know about this." The words tumbled out of my mouth before I even thought about it.

Seth smirked and dismissed me with a wave of his hand. "What are you talkin' about? Things are cool."

"No, they're not. Sooner or later, the novelty's going to wear off and you're gonna decide I'm just not your speed."

He paused with his bottle halfway to his lips. "Dino, don't."

"You know I'm righ—"

"I'm serious. Don't do this." His eyes were boring into mine. "What? Are you still hung up about the age thing?"

"It's not just age, it's everything that goes with it."

"What the hell does that mean? I thought things were great. We've been having a blast."

"Yeah, it's been one big party," I said. "I'm sorry. I thought I could do this, but I can't."

"Dino, that's crap. You know you were into it. You can't possibly try to tell me that you realized you don't dig men after all."

"It's not that. I'm just pretty sure you and I won't work in the long run, and we should cool it before we both regret it."

He quit arguing with me and stared for a moment. His eyes were like ice, and his mouth pressed into a firm line.

"That's great," he finally said, barely audible. "That's just great." He got up and walked back through the bar, leaving his beer half full on the table.

I don't know what I was expecting to happen, but I didn't like leaving it that way, so I jumped up and went after him. If he knew I was behind him, he didn't show it, and he let the front door swing shut in my face. I caught it and followed him out into the parking lot, in the fading light.

"Seth, come on," I said. "I told you in the beginning it wasn't such a great idea. Let's just go back to the way things were before. I wanna stay friends."

In the blink of an eye, he whipped around and decked me so hard, I landed in a heap on the ground, gravel digging into my shoulder. Pain exploded in my head, and I groaned, blinking to clear my vision. I tasted blood. As I rolled to my back, I swiped a thumb over my mouth and found I had a split lip.

I was still dazed when Seth dropped on my stomach and grabbed a handful of shirt, raising his fist to take another shot. I reached out to block the blow, catching his arm and holding it at bay. We struggled in the dirt, ending up locked in a stalemate.

"You son of a bitch," he seethed. "You're so damned convinced I'm gonna kick you to the curb, that you had to do it to me first. What happened to all your bullshit about not doing flings and taking this stuff seriously?"

He ignored my attempt to answer. Instead, he gave me one final shove and stood up, muttering, "Asshole," before he trudged off in the direction of home.

I didn't think it was a good idea to go after him again. It wasn't just anger I saw on his face, there was hurt too.

I sat up and gathered my wits before trying to stand. That was the hardest punch I'd taken in a long time, and I was going to be feeling it for a while. Aside from my head and jaw, there was the throbbing pain in my shoulder where I'd hit the ground. I felt like shit inside and out.

* * * *

When I got home, I stopped in the kitchen and drank a shot of whiskey. Then I went into the bathroom and took a look at my face in the mirror. My lower lip was starting to swell, and there was blood smeared on my chin. My left cheek was red where he'd hit me. By morning I'd probably have a pretty good bruise.

I got out the bottle of ibuprofen and swallowed a couple with water from the tap, then grabbed a washcloth and soaked it. As I started to wash my face, I thought about the last time I'd had to clean up after a fight. Ironic that it ended the same way it began. That time, I'd wound up with Seth in my arms, and even though I was caught off guard, I knew damn well I liked it.

I liked it, and deep down I still wanted it. Problem was, I'd just made sure it would never happen again.

"How fucking stupid are you?" I asked my reflection.

It was fear that drove me to do it, plain and simple. Seth was absolutely right about that one. I was afraid he'd get tired of me and leave. I'd also been afraid of him getting close in the first place, because I just don't usually let people get that close.

On top of everything, if I was being completely honest with myself, I was surprised by the idea of being gay, and maybe that scared me a little too. I'd never seriously thought of myself that way, and that's a pretty big leap of self-perception right there. It's a far cry from being attracted to guys once in a while.

I thought about the look on Seth's face when he'd left the parking lot and considered for the first time that I might have been wrong. He wasn't just ticked off because he'd lost a fuck buddy, he was genuinely hurt. I'd treated him the way I was afraid he'd treat me, and not only did I throw away what could have been a hell of a good thing in my life, but I'd probably lost a friend as well.

The thought made me sick to my stomach, and I had to splash cold water on my face.

The whiskey, on top of an afternoon of beer, made my head feel heavy and slow. Which had been the idea, of course. Fix it so I'd fall asleep as quickly as possible. I went into my bedroom and got undressed. Unfortunately, I lay in the dark feeling miserable for hours, torturing myself with both the good memories and bad.

Chapter 21

Mondays are shitty enough without having lost your best friend, and I was in a foul mood all day. I made it through two meetings barely clinging to this side of civility, but I put the fear of God into some kid I caught leaning on my car. I nearly beat the crap out of a guy I was supposed to be pumping for information.

By three o'clock in the afternoon, I'd had it and called it a day. I picked up some Chinese food for dinner later on and went home to sulk in front of the TV. I checked my messages several times during the day, but Seth never called. I didn't really expect him to.

At nine, I finally got sick of the dull ache lodged in my chest and decided to get thoroughly drunk. I took down the bottle of whiskey, but it was almost empty. There was no way I had enough to do the job. The refrigerator had two beers in it, and the only other liquor I had in the apartment was half a bottle of amaretto. You *can* get hammered on amaretto, but I don't recommend it.

I grabbed my keys and phone, and went downstairs to make a liquor run. There's a decent liquor store up the road in Redington Beach, so I went there and bought more whiskey.

On the way home, I found myself driving past my turn and toward the causeway instead. I was headed for Seth's garage, even though I knew I couldn't face him, and I was pretty damn sure he didn't want to see me anyway. I pulled up out front and parked on the opposite side of the street, out of range of the street lamp. I shut the car off and sat for a minute, trying to figure out what the hell I was doing.

Both garage doors were up and the shop lights were on. I could hear music drifting out and the occasional sound of the air wrench. Seth came out from behind a gray sedan and went to dig through one of the tool chests. He wore jeans and a dirty T-shirt, no coveralls. I wanted to touch him.

The ache in my chest twisted hard, and I reached for the bottle. I cracked open the seal and took a healthy swig of whiskey. My jaw was sore when I opened my mouth, and my lip was still tender. I drank it anyway.

I couldn't bring myself to go in and talk to him, but I couldn't leave either. So, I leaned back against the door and put my feet up on the seat, getting comfortable. I took another drink and watched him work. He changed out some filters and a belt, then got down under the car to change the oil. I sat there for a long time, just watching and drinking. Wishing I wasn't so damn stupid. Wishing I knew what was wrong with me.

I wanted him. That was never really in question. Whether or not I could deal with it was the problem, but *not* having him turned out to be far worse. I didn't care anymore what kind of fear might come with seeing him. I'd live with it or deal with it, if I could just have him back. I didn't know what that might take, though.

He moved slow, subdued, and I wondered what he was thinking. Did he hate me now, or did he want me back too? I watched him wipe his hands off on a rag and disappear into the office. I sincerely hoped he wasn't getting ready to close up for the night, because I didn't want to go home. I drank more whiskey and waited for him to come back.

My cellphone rang and startled the shit out of me. My heart hammered in my chest as I reached for it. "Yeah?" I answered.

"If you think I don't know you're across the street getting drunk in your car, you're wrong."

I didn't know what to say. His voice sounded flat and dry, but I didn't hear any anger. "Ah...well..."

"Dino, get your ass in here, would you?" He hung up and I was left staring into the garage, torn between hope and fear. He probably didn't hate me, at any rate.

It took a few minutes for me to work up the nerve to get out of the car, during which time, Seth came back into view and glanced out at me before leaning over the engine of the sedan.

I walked across the street to the garage, which would have been considerably easier if the ground wasn't slanted so sharply. My head spun, and I was grateful when I could grab hold of the door frame and work my way in. Mission accomplished, apparently. I made it to the stool and sat down.

Seth turned around and leaned against the car, folding his arms over his chest. He looked at me, wary, and I met his eye. Neither one of us spoke.

"What's goin' on?" he asked finally.

"I don't know." I tried to find words for what was happening inside my head. "I don't know what I'm doing, Seth. I didn't know what I was doing yesterday, either. Maybe you're right about me freaking out."

He nodded and chewed his lip. "Turns out you might not be the only one."

"Oh?"

"I thought about the stuff you said yesterday, and realized that maybe I gave you pretty good reason to think you're not my speed or whatever. I did a damn good job of it, actually."

He looked nervous, and I wondered what he was getting at. I kept my mouth shut, for fear of saying something stupid, and waited for him to go on.

"There's another side of me that you haven't seen before," he said, coming over to me. "And you should have."

He cupped my face in his hands and kissed me long and slow. There was nothing lewd or playful about it, just clear, strong affection. I slid my arms around him and held him close, something I didn't think I was going to get to do again.

He kissed my cheek and whispered, "I love you, asshole."

As soon as the words were out of his mouth, he squeezed his eyes shut, shaking his head with a pained expression. He opened his eyes and looked straight into mine. "I love you, and I think I have for a while now."

I stared at him, stupidly speechless, afraid I might not be hearing him right.

"That's my freak out," he explained. "I told you that you weren't just some fling to me, and I meant that, I know how you are. But the serious part, that's new for me. I didn't show it like I should have." He bit his lip. "Hell, I couldn't even say it without getting cocky."

"You said it fine."

"Well, if I'd said it sooner, we could have avoided what happened yesterday."

I smiled ruefully. "I'm not so sure about that. This is hard for me no matter how you slice it. It's gonna take me some time."

"So, we freak out together."

"That might work." I ran my hand along his forearm. "How long?"

"Hmm?"

"You said you think you've loved me for a while. How long are we talkin' about?"

He flushed and looked a little guilty. "Probably longer than you'd like to know about. It was getting dishonest."

"Why didn't you say something, then?"

He shrugged. "I wasn't sure. Plus, the same thing you were dealing with. You just don't fuck your best friend."

"And what changed?"

"I finally figured you weren't fucking anyone else, so I might as well go for it." He flashed me that wicked smile, but there was a warmth in his eyes that was new.

"Prick," I muttered.

"I know." He was idly running his fingers through my hair and looking kind of curious, as if he didn't know he would like it. His gaze drifted down to my bruised jaw, and he winced, touching it gingerly. "I'm sorry about that. I was totally out of line."

"Yeah, well... It's good to know I've been relying on some serious backup."

I had gotten to the point I wasn't holding him so much as clinging to him. Whiskey is one of those insidious things that creeps up on you long after you've stopped drinking it, and I was approaching significantly drunk.

My head spun, and I rested my face on his chest, inhaling the scent of motor oil and grease. Beneath those, Seth himself. I tried to sort my feelings for him out of the whorl of my thoughts, but I couldn't pin them down. I'd never let myself think about it very hard.

"I need you," I said against his shirt. I'd figured out that much. "I still don't know what I'm doing, but I know I need you."

"I'll take that." He wrapped his arms around me and rubbed my back.

"I'm probably just gonna keep fucking it up."

"Yeah, me too."

"And you still want to do this?"

"Yep." He pried me loose and held me at arm's length, looking me in the eye. "I'm not expecting perfection here. Everyone's relationship gets messy."

"When the hell did you become an expert?"

He raised an eyebrow. "Now who's the prick?"

I grinned and tried to focus on him, but I was losing the ability. I also had a little trouble sitting up straight.

He shook his head in amusement. "I think we need to get you home, buddy. You are drunk as hell."

"Yes, I know. I did that."

"Can you sit on your own for a couple minutes? I've gotta' close the place up."

"Okay." I grabbed hold of the vice bolted to the workbench.

Seth gave me a loopy, affectionate kind of grin and went to shut the doors and turn the lights off. He came back slipping on a sweat jacket.

"Come on, I'll drive you," he said, pulling me to my feet. I could stand reasonably well, but I couldn't steer for shit, so he draped my arm over his shoulders and led me outside.

We wove an inelegant path to my car, and he opened the passenger door and pushed me into the seat. He buckled the seat belt across my lap, gave me a quick kiss and went around and got in behind the wheel.

"Keys," he said, holding out his hand.

While I fished around in my pockets looking for them, he picked up the whiskey bottle and held it up to the light. It was just a little over half full. "How much of this have you had?"

"I jus' bought it."

"That's great," he said, rolling his eyes. I was having trouble getting the keys free of my pants, so he put the bottle in the backseat and helped me get them loose.

"I thought you weren't ever gonna speak to me again," I said, trying to explain.

"Not possible. I would never abandon Matilda."

It only takes about three minutes to drive from his place to mine, but the fresh air on my face felt good and staved off a vague sense of nausea I'd been feeling.

When we got there, Seth hauled me out of the car and started herding me to the front door.

"You have to be quiet," I said. "We don't want to wake up the ladies. I don't think I want 'em to see me all drunk like this."

"It's not really me we have to worry about, Dino."

"Shit, am I too loud?"

"Yes. Shut up."

We managed to get upstairs and into my apartment without incident, and without waking anyone that we knew of.

Seth led me straight to the bedroom and pushed me onto the bed, where I flopped on my back. It was an incredible relief not to have to hold myself up anymore, and I melted into the blankets, while Seth messed around in the living room. The hall went dark.

He came back pulling his shirt off, which he dropped on the floor, and reached for his jeans. I watched him strip down to nothing and climb on the bed. He started unbuttoning my shirt, and I figured since he had that covered, I could do what I liked. I ran my hands over his body, enthralled with his skin.

"Dino...could you work with me, here?" he said, stopping to look at me.

"What?"

"Pay attention. I need you to pull your arms out of your sleeves."

"I'm busy."

"Oh, Jesus," he muttered as he wrestled me out of my shirt. He got up to pull off my shoes and socks, then went for my belt. "The sooner we get you undressed, the sooner we can get to the fucking part of the program."

I smiled at the thought, but said, "I hate to break this to you, but I'm probably too drunk to fuck."

"You think so?" he asked, dragging my pants off me.

"Well, when you get to my age, things stop working after a certain poi—"

"'Cause you've got a hard-on."

"I do?" I looked down, and sure enough, there it was. I was amazed. "Cool."

He stretched out on my chest, warm and heavy, and kissed me. It was a slow caress of his lips against mine, both of us trying to make up for our own stupidity. It made me dizzy all over again.

"I do love you, you know," he said. He'd learned a new trick and wanted to keep trying it out.

"I know." I reached up to stroke his hair. "I think I could love you too."

"That's good, I want you to."

"Yeah, me too." It was true, and I had a feeling it wouldn't take very long. I just hoped I could make it that far.

The last thing I saw was Seth straddling my hips so he could fit our cocks together. He pressed down on top of me and started moving, but the rest is a blur of hot breath and slick skin. I'm ashamed to say I don't remember much beyond that point.

Chapter 22

The first thing to reach my consciousness was white hot pain originating from my left eye. It hurt so bad it glowed, and it took me a few minutes to realize the sun was shining in my face. When I moved my head, things got better. There was still pain, but it was at a much more tolerable level.

After taking a physical inventory, I sifted though the memories I had of the night before. I remembered the drinking, the garage, and Seth. Pieces of our conversation started to fall in place, and I remembered he said he loved me. Then I remembered him naked in my bed.

I turned to reach for him and ask what else had happened, but there was no one there. Just me in my empty bed. In my drunken state, my mind had cooked up what I wanted to see. I'd dreamt it all.

But then I smelled coffee. Bad coffee. My stomach turned, but I knew I hadn't made it, so the prospect that Seth forgave me was still a sound one.

I sat up slowly and swung my legs over the edge of the bed with the intention of going to find him. Instead, I saw a note propped up against my lamp along with a big glass of water and a bottle of ibuprofen. The clock read eleven o'clock. No wonder the God damned sun was in my eye.

I picked up the note and unfolded it.

> *Hi,*
> *I hope your hangover isn't half as bad as it should be. I had a 7 AM appointment this morning, and didn't have the heart to wake you. I'm not sure if I could have anyway, so you probably needed the sleep. I tried making coffee for you. I have no idea how it turned out. It's not supposed to be a science experiment, dude. Come on over to the shop when you wake up.*

Love, Seth

I smiled. Not a dream then, which was good, but no Seth to find in my kitchen, either. That was probably for the best, since I stunk like old booze and sex I couldn't remember.

I got showered, shaved and dressed with a minimum of fuss, and went to the kitchen to find out if Seth had destroyed my coffee grinder. What I found was a pot of weak looking coffee sitting in the maker, still heating. It smelled old and burnt, which stood to reason since it had been made about four hours before. It was clear Seth had tried to clean up after himself, but there was still a fine mist of ground coffee on everything in sight. I was glad I'd slept through it.

I poured out the bad coffee and gave the counter a quick wipe down with a rag. I decided coffee out would be a good idea, and I'd pick up some breakfast too. My headache was almost gone, and with something solid to settle my stomach, I'd feel better than I had a right to.

I drove back to my old neighborhood and a little mom-and-pop grocery store I like, called Donadio's. Rosa and Dominic are the mom and pop that run the place. They'd have the paper, good coffee, and some fresh doughnuts at the small bakery counter that was Rosa's main contribution to the business. It reminded me of New York.

"Hey, it's Dino!" Dominic bellowed as I came through the door, jingling the little bell that hung on the inside of the doorknob. He was sitting on an overturned milk crate, pricing cans of soup and lining them up on the shelf in front of him.

"Morning, Dom," I said, reaching to shake his hand.

Rosa poked her head through the bakery counter window and waved at me with a dish towel. "Hi, you," she said. "Had your breakfast yet? I've got some nice cinnamon buns today."

"That sounds great, Rosa. I'll take three of them. And some coffee, please."

"Hungry boy today," she said, shaking open a white paper bag.

"Two of those are for Seth. You could probably put your rag in there and he wouldn't know the difference."

She laughed. "You could stand to put a little meat on your bones. Can I put four in here?"

"Yeah, sure, why not." I could always save it for later, and Rosa's rolls were not to be missed.

I pulled a newspaper off the rack and put it on the front counter as Dominic came around to ring me up. "How's business?" I asked him.

"Oh, I can't complain. Things keep pretty steady. It's good." He punched at the buttons on the old cash register. "And you? Where did you end up after they tore down the apartment building?"

"I'm over in the north end of town, on First. It's a nice place with a bunch of old ladies for neighbors."

Rosa carried over the bag of rolls and a cardboard cup of coffee. "I gave you some cookies too," she said. "Those are on the house."

"Thanks, Rosa, you're too good to me. You're gonna have me lookin' like Dom before you know it."

She grinned and poked her husband with her elbow. "You could do worse."

I paid Dominic and stuffed my wallet back in my pocket. I tucked the paper under my arm and picked up the bag and coffee. We said our goodbyes, and I went out to the car.

I was anxious to see Seth and try to get back to something approaching normal. A new normal, and far from perfect, to be sure, but we could deal with that.

I pulled into the lot at Ed's and parked next to the tow truck. With the paper and rolls in one hand, and my coffee in the other, I headed for the side door. I was surprised to find it locked. I checked my watch. It was a quarter to twelve, a little early for lunch, and Seth was supposedly expecting me.

A guy in his mid-thirties poked his head around the corner of the building, saw me, and came over looking put out. "Are you the guy that runs this place?" he asked.

"Nope, sorry. But I know him. He must have stepped out for a minute. He lives upstairs, I'll get him for you."

The guy shook his head. "I don't have time for that. My wife is waiting, and we have to be somewhere. Could you give him my card and the keys? I'll leave it parked out front. It's the blue Buick. Have him call me when he gets back."

"Sure, no problem," I said taking the keys and card from him. Nice to know I look trustworthy.

He got into his wife's car, and she roared away with more force than necessary.

I turned and trotted up the steps to beat on the door. "Hey, lazy ass!" I hollered, pounding with my fist. "Get back to work, you're pissin' off people right and left here!"

I paused and listened for the sound of Seth crashing through the rubble. Nothing.

I knocked harder, confused. "Seth! Come on, this would be a really bad day to be fucking around with me."

I contemplated kicking in the door, but my cellphone rang. I pulled it out and breathed a sigh of relief as I looked at the screen. Seth.

"Where in the hell are you?" I asked when I flipped it open. "I'm standing here beatin' on your door."

"You remember how we thought it would be a good idea to get our noses out of McCann's business?" he asked. His voice was gravely, and he sounded tired.

"What's going on, Seth? Where are you?"

"That's a really good question. I don't know exactly, but I met some pals of McCann's. A couple of 'em might be Snake and Tango, but they don't look smart enough."

I heard the distinct sound of the back of a hand hitting someone's face, and Seth groaned in the background as someone else came on the line.

"Mr. Martini," said a smooth voice I instantly recognized. "You've been holding out on me. Either you're not as good a detective as I thought, or you still have information that belongs to me. I decided to balance the scales."

Fear shot through me, and I pictured Seth bleeding on the floor of the bar. "Where the fuck did you take him, asshole?"

"You're a smart man, you know how this works."

"Yeah, I give you what you want, and then you whack my friend anyway. And probably me too, for good measure."

"You've been watching too many action films. I'm proposing a simple and civilized exchange. No one needs to get hurt if you cooperate."

"Tell that to Darryl Serrano."

"That was very unfortunate, but it wasn't my doing. Mr. Serrano was never good at choosing his friends carefully."

"Yeah, I can see that," I said.

"Are we going to deal or not? I don't have all day."

"All right, fine," I said, going down to the car and tossing the rolls and newspaper in the backseat. I turned around and leaned on the fender. "What've you got in mind?"

"It's a lovely day, Mr. Martini. I'm thinking you should take a drive." He sounded relaxed and friendly, like we were making plans to play golf. "You can come down to Miami and visit me, and we'll take care of business."

"God, I fucking hate Miami," I said, rubbing my forehead with my fingers to keep calm. It shouldn't have mattered, but knowing Seth was that far away made the whole situation worse. "Where?"

"I'll get in touch with you in a few hours. No sense in clouding your thinking with too many details. You just come to Miami."

"Let me talk to Seth."

I wasn't surprised when he chuckled and said, "We'll see you later, Mr. Martini."

The line went dead, and I was left staring at the gravel in the parking lot. I was scared, and I felt like shit. Seth was in trouble because I couldn't keep my nose out of stuff, and I deeply regretted the day I ever laid eyes on that package.

* * * *

The drive down to Miami was uneventful on the outside. No cops to speak of, and nothing else to slow me down or cause trouble, so I made good time. On the inside, my mind was a tangle of thoughts, berating myself for getting us into this mess, concerned for Seth, and steeling myself for what I might face when I got down there. Not even the radio could calm me down, and I finally shut it off and drove in silence, letting the wind whipping around my head numb me for a while.

I took the turnpike straight into Miami and kept on until I had to pull over to fill my tank. I also put on my holster and gun. When I was done, I stood outside, leaning on the car, wondering what in the hell I was supposed to do next. It was sunny and hot, but a breeze tugged at my shirt and threw the scent of gasoline and exhaust in the air. It had been four hours since they'd contacted me, and I was getting antsy. I took out my cellphone and stared at it, wondering if I'd be violating McCann's rules if I called him instead. It's not like I didn't have the number.

Fuck it. I flipped open the phone and dialed Seth's number, assuming they would have his phone right there. I was right, because it was answered in two rings.

"Are you getting impatient, Mr. Martini? I did say we would contact you."

"Yeah, well, I'm here, so let's get on with this, all right? Where do I need to go?"

"We're holding your friend at an abandoned warehouse down by the waterfront. I'll give you directions."

"Abandoned warehouse? What do you take me for? I show up there and Seth and I are fish food. How about we try for someplace a little more public?"

"This isn't the old west, Dino. May I call you Dino?" I could hear the smirk in his voice. "We're not going to gun you down in cold blood. That would merely create unnecessary complications, and I'm too busy a man for that."

"Fine then. I'm standin' right across the street from a big steakhouse called Axel's Grill. Why don't you come meet me there? You can do business and take care of lunch all at the same time. Very efficient. You know, for a busy man like you."

"Knowing how you think, perhaps I should be worried about walking into a trap," he said.

"I don't give a shit about you and your little penny-ante drug operation. If I did, I'd have already called the cops. I just want to get my friend and get the fuck out of town, got it?"

"And what about him? He doesn't seem to share your reasonable nature."

"Put him on the phone, I'll make sure he behaves himself," I said. "Seriously, though, bringing him to a steakhouse is the best way to keep him in line."

There was a pause and faint footsteps, then Seth's voice. He still sounded tired. "Hey dude," he said. "What's going on?"

"I'm trying to convince them to meet me somewhere a little more in our favor. Our friend there doesn't think you'll cooperate. Haven't you been playing nice?"

"Fuck no. Someone snatches me at the fucking crack of dawn and doesn't give me breakfast? I tend to get a little cranky."

"Well, knock it off, because it would be nice if we could get out of this smoothly. Are you all right?"

"Yeah, mostly."

"You in any shape to fight if it comes to that?"

"Sure, if I'm not tied to a chair."

That was apparently as much as the thugs were willing to let him share, because McCann came back on the phone. "Do we have an agreement? We'll come to you if you can assure us of cooperation on both your parts?"

"Yeah, all right. I can't help you if you piss him off, though."

"We'll see if we can avoid that," he said. "I pick the venue, however. A restaurant is a little *too* public for us to be able to speak freely. I have a compromise I think is sufficient."

"What's that?" I asked.

"We'll bring Mr. Donnelly to a hotel, and you can meet us there. I'll call you with a room number as soon as we've checked in. That way, we can do our business privately, but you can be assured of some measure of protection. Although, I say again, if you cooperate, you won't need it."

I considered for a moment. "That doesn't sound like much protection to me."

"That's the best you're going to get," McCann said, getting impatient. "Give us half an hour to work on your friend, and I'm sure he'll be able to convince you."

"No," I said, cringing at the thought. "I get it, I'll be there. Just give me the details."

McCann told me to wait for his call and hung up, leaving me standing in the parking lot, helpless. I thought about Seth, and memories of him in my bed alternated with ones of him bruised and bloody. I felt sick. Didn't seem like we could catch a break lately.

Chapter 23

Half an hour later, I was headed for the Days Inn Airport, room 115. There was to be a man waiting for me at the side entrance. I still would have preferred to meet somewhere with a lot of handy witnesses, but McCann was calling the shots, and the fact that I got him to compromise at all was something.

The Days Inn was about as posh as you'd expect from a hotel located three miles from the airport. Which is to say, it wasn't at all. I was surprised it had a pool. I pulled into the parking lot and shut off the car, taking a couple minutes to gather my wits and put on my game face.

When I was ready, I stuffed Rosa's rolls into my briefcase, got out, and strode toward the side door with as much ass-kicking attitude as I could muster. I waved to a couple getting into their car and said hello. As I approached the door, a garden-variety thug, complete with tight black T-shirt and sunglasses, got up from his spot on the stairs inside and let me in. He had an ugly fresh cut down his cheek and a fat lip, and I thought I recognized Seth's handiwork.

I gave him a knowing smirk and said, "You wanna show me the room, maybe let your boss know I'm here?"

"He knows," the guy said. "Second to the last door on the right."

I walked down the hall with him hot on my tail, which didn't look remotely suspicious, and rapped hard on the door. My plan was to call as much attention as possible to our presence, so if something did go down, someone might notice. It was weak, but it was the best I had at the moment.

The door swung open and there stood McCann looking every bit as poised and refined as he had when I'd first met him. He slipped his hands into his pockets and rocked back on his heels. "It's good to see you again, Mr. Martini. I trust you had a nice drive?"

He stepped back and held the door for me, but I stalled long enough to nod at two pretty girls getting off the elevator. The thug gave me a shove, and I shoved him right back, curling my hand into a fist in case I needed it.

McCann sighed heavily and regarded us both with a deadpan expression. "Is it possible for any one of you to do so much as scratch an itch without resorting to physical violence?"

"Isn't that what you breed 'em for?" I asked, pushing past him into the room.

My gaze went immediately to Seth, who was bound like a calf and lying on the bed. There were new bruises on his face and blood on his shirt. He had a cloth gag tied in his mouth, and managed to look exhausted and pissed off at the same time. When he saw me come in, the look changed to relief, and he tried to smile.

The thug caught up with me and grabbed my arm. "You want me to frisk him?" he asked McCann.

"That won't be necessary. I have no doubt that Mr. Martini is armed, and given the job he's about to do, that's probably just as well for his sake. We're not going to have any trouble, I don't think."

I broke free and went around the side of the bed to pull the gag from Seth's mouth, brushing the hair off his forehead in lieu of being able to kiss him. "How are you doin'?" I asked.

He grinned and said, "I've been better. I think one of these guys might be Rick's big brother."

That suggested more injuries I couldn't see at the moment, and I winced. "You gonna be all right?"

"Nothing a little TLC won't fix," he said with a wink. I marveled that he could be making come-ons at a time like this, but it meant he wasn't hurt too badly, and for that I was extremely grateful.

"Untie him," I said, straightening up and looking around the room. McCann had needed three thugs to get Seth there, even bound, and not one of them looked like they'd appreciate having him loose again.

"Fat chance," said the one with the cut on his face. "He stays just the way he is."

"Chicken shit asshole," Seth snapped. "Somebody better fucking untie me, because my hands are numb, and I have to take a piss. Don't think I won't just flood the bed if I have to."

I cocked my head at McCann and said, "Whatever happened to being civilized?"

"You did assure me that he would behave," McCann said, nodding at one of the thugs. "It's on your head if he doesn't."

I gave a Seth a stern look while the guy cut through the ropes and he nodded at me, wisely refraining from any snarky comeback.

Once free, he sat up on the edge of the bed with a miserable groan. He rubbed his wrists and tried to stretch, flexing his ankles. It made me ache just to watch him, and I felt terrible. I helped him to his feet and kept him steady while he crossed the room.

The head thug took up a post by the bathroom. "Door stays open."

"He likes to watch," Seth said to me with a smirk.

McCann went to the dresser where there was an ice bucket, glasses, and a bottle of scotch. "Can I offer you a drink?"

"Fine," I said, following him and looking around, "then let's get this show on the road."

The room was standard discount fare. It had beige everything centered around a big beige bed.

He handed a glass to me, and one to Seth, who had come out of the bathroom, moving easier as his blood got flowing. Seth looked at it skeptically, but drank some when I nodded that he should. It would dull the aches and pains until we could get something better.

I took a seat on the end of the bed and sipped what turned out to be some fairly top shelf scotch. Seth came and stood next to me. I asked, "What the hell is this all about?"

"Don't play coy, Mr. Martini. You and I both know you found significantly more from that notebook than you reported to me."

"What makes you think that?" I asked. "Serrano was pretty small time, and that stash was nothing to sneeze at."

"Because I know how much there was supposed to be," he said, gazing at me flatly.

I shrugged and reached for my briefcase, pulling out the pages of notes we'd made on the locations of the other wrecked cars. There wasn't any point in playing cat-and-mouse with him. McCann looked over the sheets, and for the first time, I saw his refinement slip. He seemed irritated and made a pained grimace as he read.

Finally, he shook his head and handed the pages back to me. "You certainly have your work cut out for you," he said, taking a sip of his drink.

That was a new twist. "Excuse me?" I narrowed my eyes at him, afraid I knew exactly what he was getting at.

McCann gave me a smug, oily smile. "Retrieving all that is going to be a highly dangerous job, and I have no intention of sending my men after it. Unfortunately, they were spotted going after the first stash, and now we are surely being watched carefully. You, on the other hand, are unknown to our rivals and should be able to slip in undetected."

"Not a chance," I said, shaking my head. "That wasn't part of the deal. There's no way in hell I'm carting a load of drugs around Miami for you."

I glanced up at Seth who didn't look the least bit surprised. In fact, he looked distinctly apologetic, and I realized he knew what McCann had in mind. I started to do some fast thinking.

"Listen," I said, "there's no way I can pull off a job like that on my own. I'm gonna need Seth with me. It's strictly a two man deal." If he wasn't willing to put his own guys at risk, then he'd have to give me Seth, and that gave us a whole lot of opportunity.

"I completely agree with you. However, before you attempt to do anything rash," McCann said, "I think you should have a very clear picture of what's at stake."

He had an ominous look I didn't like one bit, and something told me he was holding all the cards. He tapped a couple buttons on the cellphone he held, and we heard the ring of a call over the speaker.

"Yeah, boss?" came the answer with a crackle of static.

"I'm having drinks with Mr. Martini and his friend, and we'd like to hear a report on your assignment." McCann held my eye the whole time he spoke.

The guy on the other end sounded bored as hell. "Them old ladies spent all morning fucking around out in the yard with tables and chairs and shit, and now they got some other ladies there and they're having some kind of a tea party or some shit."

The picture suddenly became *very* clear to me and I jumped up, slamming my glass on the table and grabbing McCann by the tie. "If you hurt one gray hair on a single one of those nice ladies, I'm going to tear you limb from limb, you sleazy little cocksucker."

All three thugs made a grab for me, but Seth got there first and pulled me back. He said to McCann, "Dino's very big on chivalry and shit like that. Threatening ladies is about as low as it gets in his book."

McCann smoothed out his tie and took another drink. "That was precisely the idea. I find that with the right leverage, you can get anything done."

Seth pushed me back down on the bed, and I shot him a glance. "You knew this was coming."

"Yeah, I heard them planning it, and there wasn't a fucking thing I could do about it. It's a shitty gig, I know that, but we can pull this off. Let's just get it done, all right?"

I was so pissed off I had to fight hard to think clearly, but I could see Seth had a point. It didn't matter to me if we furthered the Miami drug trade or not, and if McCann got what he wanted out of us, I didn't see why he'd feel the need to hurt any of my neighbors.

I turned to glare at him. "Do I have your word that you'll leave them alone if we do this?"

"They'll never even know they were involved," McCann said. "I'll shake on that."

I shook his hand, because some guys get very serious about that kind of thing, and I had the sense he was one of them. I could keep the ladies safe if I was willing to play ball, and I wasn't going to let them down.

"Fine," I said. "Spell it out for me. I wanna know the whole story, so I know what we're heading into."

McCann poured me another splash of whiskey and gave my glass back. He settled into his chair and got comfortable, crossing his legs. "I own a popular nightclub here in Miami, and I make an excellent living at it. Part of the reason for that is I make sure my club offers all the amusements people look for when they go out for a night of fun, as well as an attractive hassle-free setting to do them in."

"You mean drugs."

"I mean upscale designer drugs, companions, private rooms, secluded spaces for a little romance. All the natural outcroppings of a place where people come to drink and dance."

"So, drugs, hookers and probably a few other things frowned upon by the Miami PD."

"It's a competitive market, and I have to offer what the people want." His expression was completely unapologetic.

"How do Serrano and his notebook fit into all this?" I asked.

McCann's face darkened. "Darryl Serrano was employed by one of the seedier clubs I often do business with, The Shark Pond. You've been there. He generally acts as a courier when we purchase supplies from them."

"He's your drug dealer." I loved how he was putting a respectable spin on everything like we both didn't know just what the hell he was talking about.

"He was a runner. He didn't have the brains or the attention span to deal drugs," McCann said. "He did, however, have barely enough street smarts and reckless stupidity to do an end run around my man during the last drop. He made off with a substantial amount of my money and the equivalent in his employer's designer drugs. He's made a lot of people very angry."

"How much are we talking about?" I asked.

"One million dollars."

Seth whistled. "Of each?"

McCann nodded.

"Is that why you killed him?" I asked, tipping back the last of my drink. "Did you kill the guy that let him make off with your money too?"

"My man was taught a hard lesson and let go," he said. "As for Serrano, he was alive when my boys left him. He was extremely unhappy and not incredibly coherent, from what I understand, but we got the information about the notebook out of him. We thought that would be all we needed."

"Who killed him then?"

McCann raised an eyebrow. "I really couldn't say. But if I were to hazard a guess, I'd think it was the other party he screwed over. They're an unsavory bunch, and their methods are crude and extreme."

"I see. And you want to wind up with the drugs *and* the cash in the end?"

"Exactly," said McCann. "And if we can do so without alerting the denizens of The Shark Pond, then so much the better."

"So, now you're gonna do the double crossing."

"Not at all. It was their employee who broke the rules in the first place. With him gone, and the merchandise still at large... Well, as far as I'm concerned it's fair game. I'm quite sure they view it that way too, and I would be out my money if they found it first."

I mulled that over. "You have any idea if they're looking?"

"They would be stupid not to be," McCann said. "I suggest you watch your back."

"All right, here's the way it's gonna work," I said. "We'll scope out the other sites to get a feel for them, but we are *not* goin' after this stuff until it's dark. I want as much of an advantage as possible."

"That's understandable. You can return here when you're finished, and I'll collect my property then." He stood up and brushed the wrinkles from his suit. "Well, I've taken up enough of your time. I'm sure you'll want to get to work right away. The room is yours to use, of course, and I'll have a few of my men keeping tabs on your progress, to make sure you stay on track."

Seth made a face, and I had a feeling he was about to say something rude, so I cut him off. "Just make sure they stay the hell out of our way."

"You'll hardly even know they're there," McCann said smugly.

He and his men walked into the hallway, and I went to the peephole. I looked out to see the four of them in a hushed conference before McCann and two others strode down the hallway as if they had somewhere to be. The other guy had the slower gait of someone who'd just been assigned stakeout duty.

Back in the room, Seth was pacing like a caged dog. "This stinks, Dino," he snapped. "How in the fuck are we supposed to get anything done with those pricks all over our backs?"

"Relax," I told him, catching his arm to take the barely touched drink out of his hand before he sloshed it all over the bedspread. "They want us to get the job done, so I don't think they'll give us a hard time as long as they know we're workin' on it."

I finally had him alone, and I wanted to tell him how sorry I was, how scared I'd been all morning, but it didn't seem like the best time.

"You hurt bad?" I asked, running a hand over him slowly. I was checking for injuries, but I didn't mind when he took it as a caress and pressed up against me, resting his forehead on my shoulder.

"Not really." He looked up me and grinned. "And I got even."

"Yeah, I saw that." I touched his bruised lip with my thumb. "Did it ever occur to you that you could save yourself a lot of pain?"

He shrugged. "What's the fun in that? You got anything to eat? I'm starving. Those assholes didn't feed me."

I didn't need to answer him, because he was already rooting through my briefcase. He found the bag from Donadio's and pulled out a roll, stuffing it in his mouth as he turned back to me. He ripped off one bite and swallowed it whole, then tore off another.

"Hey," I said, "don't scarf those down like a mangy dog, those are Rosa's."

"And they're great," he mumbled through a mouthful. In fifteen seconds he'd eaten one entire roll and took a second one from the bag.

"I'm serious. It's alarming to watch you eat that way. You're gonna choke yourself."

He paused for a moment, looked vaguely ill, and then belched obnoxiously.

I shook my head. "You are disgusting."

"I haven't eaten anything since last night, Dino, I'm about to pass out here."

"Not likely," I said. "So tell me what happened."

"Hey, there's cookies in here."

"Give me one of those."

He handed me a cookie and said, "Those fuckers are sneaky. One minute I was Joe Mechanic about to open up for the day, and the next, I got some thug cramming something in my mouth. I woke up a while later in heap on the floor of a van driving who knows where."

"They drugged you?"

"Yeah, but I got even for that too. I puked on their carpet."

"Shit, I'm sorry..."

Seth shrugged and ate another cookie. "I felt fine after that. They took me to some old warehouse and kept me in the van until Slick in the Suit showed up and started asking me about Serrano's notebook. I gave him the party line, which was that we only knew about the one stash of drugs and he should feel free to go fuck himself. Then me and the boys played a fun game of 'beat the shit out of Seth' while Slick messed around with my cellphone."

"That's when I got the call?"

"Yep."

"Did you spend the next three hours antagonizing them?"

"Of course I did, what do you think? Had to entertain myself somehow."

I shook my head. Seth wadded up the empty bag and tossed it in the garbage can. "Got any cash on you?" he asked. "I saw some vending machines when they dragged me in here, and I want a sandwich."

"Sure," I said. McCann had left the room keys on the dresser, so I took one. "I'll walk down with you."

Once we were out in the hall, I said, "I think we'd be wise to assume the hotel room is probably bugged, and by now they would have had time to bug Matilda too, if they're going to."

"I wish I could tell you," Seth said. "The way they had me on that bed, I couldn't see much of what was going on. What do we do about it?"

"Nothing. Just keep it in mind and don't say anything you don't want them to hear. Either write it down, or save it until we're somewhere clear. Trying to find or destroy the bugs would just piss them off, plus they'd probably do it again anyway. Better to let them think we don't know."

Seth nodded and said, "Can I spend all my time talking about how ugly and dickless they all are?"

"Sure, knock yourself out."

One of the vending machines sold toiletries, so I got some Tylenol for both of us, and a sandwich since I hadn't eaten either. Seth got an egg salad made on fluorescent orange bread that was supposed to taste like cheese. He also bought a bag of chips, a package of Oreos and two of those horrible energy drinks he likes.

"It's no damn wonder you barfed in their van," I said, when he dumped it all on the table in our room.

"Dude, I *wish* I could've had orange bread and Oreos. That would have been awesome. If they try anything tonight, I'm going to try to take a gut shot."

"Well, stay the hell away from me then," I said, unwrapping my food.

Seth wolfed down his lunch, then stalked around the room with a scowl on his face. He grabbed a handful of ice out of the bucket on the dresser and started flinging cubes at the wall. "This is gonna be one long ass afternoon, Dino. I don't know if I can hack it, I just want to get out there and take care of this."

"You need to settle down and pull yourself together," I said, looking up from my notes and folding my arms over my chest. This was not the time I wanted to be dealing with one of Seth's minor meltdowns.

He turned and started pelting *me* with ice cubes.

I swatted at them and said, "Stop that, asshole."

He had the good grace to look mildly chagrined and dumped the rest of the ice back in the bucket. "Look, we know where everything is, why don't we just go get it and be done?"

"Because we only *think* we know where everything is, and I don't want to have half a million bucks worth of drugs in my possession when we hit a snag we weren't ready for."

I got up and stopped his pacing, rubbing his neck to calm him. "We're gonna head out right now and check on the other cars, make sure we know where stuff is and what it's going to take to get it. All right?"

He nodded reluctantly. "Yeah, all right. I just need to let the food kick in. I'll be fine once we get moving."

"Okay, then, let's go."

Chapter 24

The first stop on the agenda was Auto Parts Unlimited, where we were in search of an older Buick Riviera. We pulled into the lot and parked near the back. I studied the top of the surrounding wall and the corners of the building that housed the main office. There were no cameras or other obvious security devices, just a few halogen spotlights that probably stayed on all night. A sign by the main entrance announced *Lyle Taggart, General Manager*.

As we went inside, I checked the office door for any kind of alarm system and was surprised to find nothing. Apparently, Lyle and company relied on the power of good old-fashioned locks and the decency of humanity.

We ran the picky wife routine again, and followed Serrano's clues to the car in question. It was a blue Riv with only one remaining door and no front seats.

"Where do you want to start?" Seth asked.

"Why don't you look inside while I try to get the trunk open."

I went around to search the back end of the car. The paint was scratched and dirty, and there was rust dotting the edges and seams. I tried simply lifting the trunk in case it wasn't latched, but nothing happened, so I felt along the lip. Just to the right of center was a chewed up spot that was dented and flared.

"Hey, Seth," I called. "I think I got something."

He backed himself out and stood up, brushing dirt and bits of safety glass off his jeans. "Good, because I really doubt there's anything inside, it's destroyed in there."

"Look," I said, pointing to the damage on the trunk lid. "This has been pried open."

He bent down to look at it closely, flicking away some of the chipped paint with his fingernail. "Yup, not very much rust, either. It wasn't all that long ago."

He reached into his jeans and took out his pry bar. With one good yank, he popped the trunk open and raised the lid. It took some work, but we found the box hidden underneath the flooring. The contents were the same as the first one we'd found. Seth gave a low whistle and shook his head.

"Okay," I said, "close that up and stuff it back where you got it. We have two more to find, and then we have to come up with a game plan."

Seth snapped the box closed. "Why don't we just take this with us now so we don't have to come all the way back out here?"

"No way. I don't see how we could get it past the front gate without someone noticing, and I don't want it with us now anyway. We come back tonight and do this under the cover of darkness. We're fucked if we get caught, and I want every advantage we can get."

* * * *

A-1 Auto Salvage & Towing was a little harder to find than the first lot, because it was down a small side street, and we missed it the first time. Although this yard was smaller than Unlimited, it had twice as many cars, at least. More than half of them were stacked two high, and I hoped like hell we weren't going to have to start scaling wrecked automobiles.

On the plus side, our luck seemed to be holding well in the security department. I cased the area as we walked toward the office and didn't see anything more sophisticated than the motion lights and gate lock. There was a fairly tough looking dog on a chain, sleeping in the sun by the entrance. I couldn't place the breed, but he was on the smaller side of huge and looked like he had a lot of teeth. It didn't take much hard thinking to realize he was probably let loose in the yard at night. We'd have to consider that in our plans.

The other thing that gave me cause for concern was the house located right next door. The worn, sandy path between it and the office building made it pretty clear the business was owner operated and they lived on the premise. Another slight complication.

This time, the box was hidden in the engine compartment of a late model Thunderbird, and was a bitch to get at. We stuffed it under the seat, instead, to make things easier when we came back.

When we tracked down the final box, we found it in the wheel well of a rusted Geo Hatchback. In each case, I paid close attention to the security measures the salvage yards used, and any potential obstacles to getting in and out quickly.

"I got a hunch about why he picked the yards he did," I told Seth as we stood under the island canopy of a gas station, filling up the tank.

He leaned on the side of the car, hands stuffed in his pockets. "Yeah? What's that?"

"Easy to break into."

Seth smirked. "No shit? That would be fucking convenient, wouldn't it?"

"It looks that way to me. I mean, think about it, he's just a dumb schmuck who wants to play at being a secret agent. He doesn't want to get caught at it, so he scopes out a bunch of places and goes for the ones he figures are easy marks."

"Sweet. I finally have a reason to appreciate his delusional tendencies."

"They're all older, small-time operations. None of them have cameras or decent security systems. It's about time we caught a break."

I left Seth to keep an eye on the pump while I popped Matilda's hood and checked the oil, washed the windshield and made sure the tires had enough air. We used the restrooms, bought a couple of candy bars and got moving again.

"Next stop on Moron Serrano's Magical Mystery Tour, EZ Mini Storage," Seth said. He pulled out and turned right, following the directions I'd given him.

I slid the page of notes out of the stack and laid it on top. The code for the storage unit was shorter and simpler than the others.

8592124
27272727
361429

We knew the first line was the address and were able to find it without any trouble. The one he'd picked was right off the Regan Turnpike, and I wondered if he'd planned it for a quick getaway.

Seth turned into the parking lot and pulled off to the side. A sheet metal fence ran all the way around the outside of the storage lot, ending on either side of the office building. To the left of the building was an automatic gate with a drive-up card box on the side.

Seth pointed to it. "Key card?"

"That would be my guess." I reached into my briefcase and took the key card out of Serrano's envelope, dropping it in the palm of Seth's outstretched hand.

He put the car in gear and eased up to the box, sliding the card into it. The box beeped, and there was an audible click from the gate, then a motorized whir as it rolled open. We drove in, and it closed behind us.

"Now where?" Seth asked, pausing to look both ways.

I showed him the paper with the code. "You wanna bet we're looking for unit number twenty-seven?"

He snorted and said, "You're shitting me."

"What else do you get out of that? They're all two digit numbers from what I can see."

"Wow," he said, following the directional signs to the twenty-one through thirty section. "He must have really been scraping the bottom of the barrel when he came up with that one."

"Probably burned out his last two brain cells," I said.

Seth rolled to a stop in front of twenty-seven, and we both turned to stare at the unit door. I grabbed Serrano's key ring and the notes, and got out of the car. Seth came around the front end to stand beside me.

The steel hasp on the side was fastened by not one, but two locks. One was a standard issue black and silver combination lock, and the other was a gold padlock.

"Well," Seth said, "what do you think is behind the door? A lady or a tiger?"

I shot him a glance. "That is a surprisingly *literary* reference for you."

"I resent that."

"You know I'm right," I said, trying the small gold key. I was hoping it fit the padlock, which would make sense given Serrano's style.

Luck was holding with us, and I grinned when the lock snapped open. I had bolt cutters that would have gotten us in, but I generally prefer the easy route if I can get it.

Seth looked over my shoulder. "One down, one to go."

"Yeah. Here," I said, handing him the paper, "read me the combination."

"Thirty-six, fourteen, twenty-nine."

That worked too, and we raised the garage door. Seth let out the kind of low moan he usually reserved for sightseeing in bars. The door was barely halfway up when he ducked inside to explore.

"A motherfucking Z-four," he groaned, running his hands along the sides of a gleaming black convertible two-seater sports car, top down. "Three point oh liter, two hundred twenty-five horsepower, dual overhead cam. Twenty-four valve, inline six cylinder engine with double-VANOS variable valve timing. Shit, Dino, have you ever seen anything so gorgeous in your entire life?"

"Yes, I have, and she's right behind us so watch your mouth."

He went back to fondling the car, muttering things about struts and transmissions. When he made his way around to the driver's side, he reached in and popped the hood. As soon as he lifted it and disappeared from view, the moaning started again.

I rolled my eyes and folded my arms. "You two want to be left alone for a while?"

"Yeah. About ten minutes will do just fine. Wait, better make it fifteen, I want it to last."

"Shut up and see if this key goes to that car," I said.

He dropped the hood and practically danced back to the driver's door as I tossed him the keys. The way he jumped in and slid down into the driver's seat, I felt like I should be averting my eyes. Three seconds later, when the car roared to life, I'd forgotten any such concerns.

"This is excellent," I said, going over to the side of the car. "I'm willing to bet we're looking a decent chunk of McCann's stash right here. He's probably gonna have a shit fit."

"I wouldn't say that McCann having a shit fit was excellent, Dino," Seth said, looking up me.

"Well, I don't give a rat's ass. I didn't spend his money. This is good for us."

"Why?"

"Because now we don't have to run around Miami with a pile of drugs in a car that's registered in my name, that's why." I stopped and waited for the implication to hit Seth.

He froze in the middle of stroking the steering wheel and turned to gaze up at me over the top of his sunglasses. The gleam in his eye was complete, unadulterated lust. He opened his mouth to say something, but was speechless for the first time since I'd known him.

I grinned. "Yep. You get to ride in this car tonight."

"*Ride?*" The gleam turned instantly cold. "What the fuck do you mean 'ride,' Dino?"

"Okay, okay," I said holding up my hands. "You can drive. You didn't really think I would try to get between you and a hot car, did you?"

He eyed me sharply for a long moment. "I would hope not."

I had to laugh. "You are so fucking easy..."

"Look who's talkin', baby."

For a few minutes, we were able to forget about the trouble we were in and toss shit back and forth like we were in Ed's garage changing Matilda's oil. It was refreshing, and I needed it. In spite of the spectacular progress we'd made, there were still quite a few details I hadn't worked out yet, not the least of which was how this adventure ended. That had been nagging at me all day. I was struggling with my impression of McCann as a practical man, versus the risk of letting us go knowing what we did.

"All right, listen," I said, checking my watch, "it's getting late, and we have a couple of things to take care of before tonight. I think we should get moving."

"No problem, I could really use some dinner soon."

"Yeah, we don't want you starving to death. You really should eat more. Growing boy like you."

"Har, har," Seth said, climbing out of the car. He slipped the keys into his pocket and readjusted his sunglasses.

We pulled the unit door shut, and I secured it with the padlock only. We had the key, and I didn't want to have to screw around with a combination in the dark. Then Seth took us back to the hotel.

Chapter 25

Halfway between the car and the door of the hotel, Seth brushed up against me and said in a low voice, "I could use a little bit of that TLC right about now..."

I glanced at him and he was looking up at me through his eyelashes with the barest hint of a grin on his face. It was one of the damnedest looks I'd ever seen.

"Absolutely not," I told him. I sincerely hoped I'd see it again sometime in the near future when I'd be able to enjoy it.

"Why the hell not?" Seth frowned at me. "We've got to kill a few hours before we can even think of getting started on the job."

"Because I'm pretty sure that room is bugged, and there is no way we're screwing around in there."

"Oh dear God," he said, snorting with exasperation and looking up at the sky. "Do we really give a fuck if McCann hears us gettin' all hot and sweaty?"

"Yes, we do, and it's not because I'm a prude." I cut him off with a look and went on, "He used our friendship as leverage against me. How dangerous do you think it would be for you if he knew how things really stand?"

"This sucks," he said, kicking a plastic bottle cap on the ground. I wasn't sure if he actually agreed with me, but it seemed he wasn't planning to argue, and for that I was grateful. I'd already fucked up and landed him in a lot of trouble, I wasn't going to do it again if I could help it.

"We both could use some rest anyway," I said. I held the side door open for him. "We've got a long night ahead of us, and we're gonna need to be sharp."

In the hotel room, I arranged what we'd need for the job, and packed up my computer and briefcase to stash in the car when we left. I didn't want anything left behind we'd have to come back for. The minute we handed over McCann's stuff, I planned to hit the road and get out of Miami as quickly as possible.

Seth lay on the bed, propped up on one elbow and watching me quietly. When I was finished, I draped my jacket over a chair, kicked off my shoes, and went to join him. He smiled and shifted to make room for me.

When I settled my head on the pillow, he leaned over me with a grin and put a finger to his lips in a silent "shh," before he kissed me long and slow. He edged closer and slid a leg up over mine. Every move he made was deliberate, intent on not making a sound.

The experience was surreal, and he was obviously pushing it after the conversation we'd just had, but after everything that happened in the past few days, I wasn't about to let go of him. I'd spent too much time fearing I'd lost him, one way or the other, and it was good to have him right there with me.

He went too far, though, when he slipped open the button of his jeans and eased the zipper down, quiet as a mouse. I narrowed my eyes in warning, but he took my hand and pulled it to his straining hard-on. I shook my head and started to pull away, but the look on his face stopped me. There was no trace of cocky game playing, or any kind of challenge, just plain and simple need. He looked tired and beat up and tense, and I realized he was only looking for some release and a chance to wind down.

That I could do for him, and I kissed him softly as I slid my hand into his underwear and caressed his cock. He was hot and hard, damp in the confines of his jeans. When I started stroking him, he blew out a ragged breath and bit his lip. His mouth fascinated me, and the lines of concentration on his brow. I watched his face until he curled in closer, muffling his thick panting against my shoulder as he struggled to keep quiet. He wrapped an arm around my waist and thrust erratically when I worked him faster, trying to up the tension as much as possible.

In spite of the circumstances, or maybe because of them, it was one of the most erotic moments I could remember. I was hard, and I wanted him so much, every instinct I had was urging me to push him down and take him. My heart and my mind may have struggled with the concept of dating Seth, but my body had been on board from the first moment he touched me.

When he seemed close to coming, I tightened my hand and pumped him hard and fast. He pressed closer still, rubbing his body against mine, and trapping my hand between us. Moving was somewhat awkward, but it blocked the noise, which was good. When Seth came, his body jerked, and his mouth fell open in silent moans that ghosted hot breath against my neck.

I stroked him lightly until he calmed down and finally slumped against me. He let his head roll back so he could smile lazily at me, still breathing hard. I was pleased to see no traces of tension left on his face. I met his gaze and held it, trying to show him I'd meant it when I said I could easily love him.

He rubbed a hand down across my erection and back to my belt buckle, but I stopped him and shook my head. He frowned and looked at me quizzically, raising an eyebrow. I leaned to whisper in his ear. "You can owe me."

I kissed him to show him I meant it, and he seemed to accept that, because he got up and went into the bathroom. I was too concerned with the events ahead of us to have enjoyed it, and I still thought it was taking a hell of a risk, so I was just as willing to wait until we were home.

When Seth came back, his jeans were buttoned and he was carrying a wet washcloth, which he used to wipe traces of come off the front of my shirt. When he was done, it barely showed at all. I took the washcloth and tossed it into the corner.

"You really should try to get some sleep," I said quietly, pulling him down next to me.

He settled in with one arm wrapped around his stomach and the other hanging loosely over me, his head resting on my shoulder. Within five minutes he was asleep.

* * * *

Around eight o'clock that night, I lay on the bed staring up at the hotel ceiling, watching the blinking red light on the smoke detector. I never did get any sleep. My mind was too busy replaying the day's events and running potential scenarios for the outcome. I forced myself to lie there anyway, figuring some rest was better than nothing at all. Seth appeared to be out cold, but it was hard to tell because he was so quiet.

At eight fifteen, I couldn't take it anymore and got up. We'd set the alarm clock for nine, which would leave us plenty of time to go out for dinner and get ready.

On impulse, I grabbed my cellphone and my cigarettes and let myself into the hallway as quietly as I could. I took the long way around and went out through the lobby, away from the prying eyes of McCann's thug. They were only making a token showing of it anyway.

In front of the hotel was a matching pair of huge potted palms, and on either side of those were cement benches. I chose one and sat down, lighting a cigarette and taking a long drag. I smoked about half of it and tried to clear my head, which was easier with a nicotine buzz going. Accomplishing that for a full two minutes probably did more for me than the couple hours I laid on the bed.

I flipped open my phone and dialed Ruth's number, taking another drag while it rang. An airplane roared overhead and curved toward the runways.

On the fourth ring, she picked up. "Hello?"

"Hey, Ruth, it's Dino," I said, blowing out smoke.

"Dino! How nice to hear from you." I heard a squeal of delight in the background and Ruth said, "Della's here. She says to tell you hello."

I smiled. "Say hi for me."

Ruth chuckled and said, "I think you'll get to yourself. She'd like to talk to you when we're finished."

"Sure," I said. "That'd be great. Listen, I just wanted to make sure everything was okay there."

"Well, of course it is. Is something worrying you?"

"No, not really," I lied. "I was just wondering how the garden party went and if I can look forward to fresh veggies or bouquets of flowers."

"You'll have both," she told me. "We're going to have plenty of space, so we reached a compromise."

"That's great. Everything else like normal around there?"

"Yes. Dino, is there something going on we should know about?"

"No, no, I'm sure everything's fine." I reached over and crushed out the butt of my cigarette in the sand of a small garbage can. "I'm down in Miami and just wanted to check up on things. It's what I do, don't sound so suspicious. Della would eat this up with a spoon."

"Mmm," Ruth agreed, sounding mildly amused. I could hear chatter as she passed the information along. Then she said, "The police were here looking for you today."

Damn it. She'd been waiting to spring that on me, I could tell.

"Female?" I asked. "A detective?"

"Yes." She sounded surprised that I'd guessed.

"That's Teresa, she's a friend of mine. It's okay, we've just been trying to touch base and haven't had much luck lately. I'll call her when I get back."

"I think you should. She didn't seem very happy about missing you," Ruth said. "She also seemed to be acting in an official capacity. She asked me quite a lot of questions about you and where you've been the last couple of days. Are you in some kind of trouble?"

"Nah," I said, trying to sound as casual as possible. "We're working on a case together, and she's ticked because I haven't had time to meet with her about it."

"I see," she said, which in my experience is female for 'I don't believe a word of that crap.' Ruth was a shrewd one, all right.

"Everything's fine, Ruth. Just take care of yourself, okay?"

Her tone was quite a bit warmer when she said, "I'll say the same to you, Dino."

"Yes, ma'am, I will."

She said goodbye and handed the phone over to Della who immediately gushed, "Dino, darling, how *are* you? Are you enjoying Miami? I just *adore* Miami. All those barely dressed boys on the beach, I could just sit there for days and days."

"You can have them, Della. I hate Miami. I can't wait to come home."

She laughed and asked, "When will that be, sugar?"

"Tomorrow, I hope. That's the plan anyway."

"Well then, I'll make sure to have something hot and steamy waiting for you," she said, and then added saucily, "And maybe I'll bake too."

"Della, you slay me."

When I finished talking with them, I hung up and lit another cigarette. It made me feel better to know things were going all right there. It was also good to get a reminder of why I was doing this. A little something to strengthen my resolve.

After a few minutes, I took a deep breath and dialed Seth's cellphone number. McCann answered immediately. "Dino. I was beginning to wonder when I'd hear from you."

"Oh, cut the crap. You know where we've been and what we've been up to."

"Yes, I do," he said smoothly. "And I understand things are going well. I really am quite impressed. You're saving me a great deal of trouble."

"I'm just that kind of guy," I said, although I really didn't have it in me to banter with the asshole. "We'll get started in a few hours. I figure we'll probably be done around two or so, depending on how things go. I got one condition, though."

"Really. And what is that?"

"No tail for this. I don't want your guy fuckin' things up and blowing this for me."

"My men are very professional—"

"Bullshit. At least one of your men screwed up enough to put all of us in this position to begin with. Seth and I are on our own, or we're not doing it at all, and we'll find some other way to keep you off my neighbors."

I heard McCann take a deep breath, and I knew it galled him to give in. "All right. We'll do this your way. It would be safer to distance myself from it anyway."

"Good," I said. "Make sure you're ready when we are. I'm not dragging this out any longer than necessary."

"Just return to the hotel when you're finished. I'll be waiting for you there."

"Fine," I said, and I hung up on him.

I finished my cigarette, and on my way back through the lobby, I stopped at the hospitality table and got a cup of coffee. It was old, but it was the restaurant coffee, and it wasn't too bad. Plus, it was hot, which can't always be said for coffee that's been sitting around a while. I sipped it carefully as I went back to the room.

Inside, Seth was up and moving and had evidently been to the vending machines, because he was chugging down a green energy drink and eating a candy bar.

"Where were you?" he asked.

"Out front having a smoke. I called and gave a report to McCann, and I told him to call off the tail."

While I spoke, I grabbed the pad of paper off the table and jotted down: *Called Ruth, everyone's fine.* Not that I figured McCann would care, but I didn't like the idea of him listening to anything involving my neighbors. I showed it to Seth.

"Excellent," he said with a nod. "I was thinking about dinner. There's this great little Cuban restaurant I've been to a few times. Teofilo's. It's down in South Beach, and the food is incredible."

"My favorite part of town."

Seth grinned. "You can't deny the scenery's nice, and it beats the hell out of fast food, right? You'll like it, trust me. My treat even."

I raised my eyebrows. "Twice in one month? You must be getting soft."

He narrowed his eyes. "You in or not?"

"Yes," I said. "Yes, I'm in. I'm starving. That sandwich was crap."

Chapter 26

Teofilo's was a small, rundown place with green stained-glass windows. The floor and furniture were all bare wood, giving the room a rustic look. Two large ceiling fans hung down on poles, turning slowly to keep the spiced air moving. It smelled like heaven. There was still a decent sized crowd, but we were able to get a table right away, and soon we had a couple of beers.

Lively music played in the background, along with the usual restaurant noise of a dozen conversations, the clattering of silverware, and the occasional hiss and sizzle from the kitchen. It was almost possible to forget the situation we were in, save for the apprehension sitting in my gut and the guy in the corner. McCann's thug had slunk in right behind us to grab some dinner while the getting was good. I sincerely hoped McCann planned on keeping his word and pulling the guy when things got started. For the time being, I was willing to ignore him.

I took a sip of beer and said, "We need to stop at a drugstore and pick up some sleeping pills, and then run by a drive-thru for a hamburger."

Seth's gaze darted toward the corner. "You're gonna drug the guy? What do we care?"

"We don't care," I said, frowning at him. "This is for the dog at A-1 Auto. Even if he's not the type to take a chunk out of my ass, I don't want his barking to wake up the neighbors."

"Yeah, good luck with that," Seth said. "Every dog I've ever met would hork down the burger like it's starving and then spit the pill on the ground. I have no idea how they do it."

"Well, shit. Got a better idea?"

"Booze. Knocks them right out if you can get them to drink enough. They seem to really like the fruity stuff like strawberry flavored rum or lime vodka."

I tilted my head and eyed him. "And you know this how?"

"Ed's dogs," he said with a smirk. "They come sniffing around when I have parties out back sometimes and get into people's drinks. It's never Cuervo or Jack Daniel's they go for, it's always the sweet stuff."

"And you let them."

"Well, no, of course not. I wouldn't waste good booze on the mutts. They wait until no one's looking."

"Okay," I said. "We skip the drugstore and hit a liquor store, instead."

We paused as the waiter brought our meals and set them down in front of us, the plates steaming enticingly. I leaned forward and inhaled deeply, humming with anticipation. Seth looked pleased with my reaction.

"Actually," he said, "we're not that far from The Shark Pond. We can get a burger from the diner across the street, and then stop in there and get a couple shots to pour on it. It'll save time."

"Uh-huh."

"What? It's not like we have all night."

"Well, yes, we do have all night. I think you just want to see that bartender again."

"He's just eye candy," he said with a grin. "Eat your damn dinner."

We agreed not to ruin an excellent meal with talk about McCann and his shitty job. Instead, we spent the time talking about cars, us, football and beer. We didn't rush either, enjoying our meal to the fullest and even going so far as to order a dessert of papaya topped with cream cheese. We also had Cuban coffee, which was about all I needed to die happy. It occurred to me that might be a distinct possibility, but I pushed the thought out of my head and had a second cup. If it weren't for the nasty situation we were in, it would have been a decent dinner date.

Seth must have read my face, because he grinned and said, "I want to do this again when we don't have thugs and drug dealers snapping at our heels."

"Yeah, me too."

Eventually, there were only a few tables left with people at them, and the staff was reaching that state of tired politeness that screamed "Get Out," so Seth paid the bill and we left.

We crossed the street to the all-night diner. The crowd there was livelier, being mostly twenty-somethings starting a night of club hopping. Raucous laughter came from several different tables. There were two free stools at the counter, so we sat down.

A blond waitress came over, my age or a little younger, cute in a bookish sort of way. She had glasses and a short haircut, and looked more like she belonged in Minnesota than Miami. When she greeted us, she sounded like maybe she *was* from Minnesota.

"Hi, there," she said. "Are you having a nice evening? Can I get you a couple of menus?"

"No, thanks," I told her. "We just need a hamburger to go."

"Just one?" she asked, looking between the two of us.

"It's a treat for my dog."

"Lucky dog!" she said. "You know what the dog said when its tail got run over by a lawn mower, don't you?"

"Ah, no?"

"Won't be long now!"

Seth groaned, but I gave her a smile. "Do you have one of those big Styrofoam boxes you could put it in?"

"Yeah, sure," she said, and hustled off to put in the order.

A couple of obviously drunk young men came in and sat down next to Seth, giggling and clutching at each other. The waitress came over and watched them with amusement.

"Nice night for barhopping," she said. "Did you hear about the two peanuts that walked into a bar?"

They gaped at her curiously, and Seth buried his face in his hands.

"One of them was a salted!"

The two drunk guys busted up laughing and seemed to think that was the funniest thing they'd ever heard.

While she was handing out menus and working her way down the counter with a coffee pot, Seth leaned close and said, "Is she for real? What the fuck?"

"Come on," I said. "I think it's kind of cute."

"Yeah, but you don't date, you wouldn't know."

"I think you're cute sometimes."

Down at the end of the counter, she rang up someone's bill and said, "Do you know how you stop an elephant from charging? Take away his credit card!"

"For fuck's sake," Seth muttered. "Just shoot me now."

"Be nice." I jabbed him with my elbow. "She's packing up our burger."

She carried over the box and set it on the counter in front of me. "I have a friend who's a vegetarian, but I say if we're not supposed to eat animals, why are they made out of meat?"

Seth winced and rolled his eyes. "Oh my God," he muttered.

She turned and fixed him with a rather piercing gaze, and I thought I could detect a wicked gleam in her eye.

"Hey," she said, nodding at him, "how does a farmer find a sheep in the tall grass?"

Seth merely raised an eyebrow at her.

She smirked. "Very satisfying."

The stunned look on Seth's face was priceless. He stared open mouthed for a minute and then said, "Come again?"

"Only if the sheep is very docile," she shot back.

I laughed out loud and put a ten dollar bill on the counter. "Keep the change, and thank you *very* much."

"You betcha," she said with a wink.

Seth was still staring at her in shock, so I grabbed the box and dragged him out of the diner.

Out on the sidewalk, he finally found his tongue. "Dude. Did your cute little waitress just jump straight from kindergarten stuff to sheep fucking jokes?"

"Yes, she did," I said. "You should have seen your face. She got your number, all right."

"Wow. That is...that is actually kind of hot."

"See? I would know."

* * * *

We figured we were about six blocks away from The Shark Pond, and it would be easier to just walk than to try to move the car. It was a nice night, which I was extremely thankful for, and the fresh air would do us both some good. The general atmosphere was wilder than it had been the last time.

This time, we didn't bother hanging around outside the club, but went right in. The club was much busier and louder, and it took some work to make our way to the bar. We had to hang out for a few minutes before a spot opened up and we could squeeze in.

En was working again, pouring drinks with both hands, and Seth gave him a wave. He smiled brightly and flipped a bottle in the air before putting it away. When he finished the round he was serving, he wiped his hands on his jeans and came down to where we stood.

"Well, well, look who's back," he said, leaning on the bar. "Just couldn't get enough, I guess?"

"Something like that," Seth said, grinning slyly.

"Too bad I already had my break. What can I get you guys tonight?" He was a bit less gregarious this time, and I imagined that had a lot to do with the crowd and how busy he was. No time for screwing around.

"I'll take an amaretto on the rocks," I said.

"Red Bull."

En looked at Seth. "Red Bull and..."

"Just the Red Bull. I'm driving tonight."

"Good looking *and* responsible...nice."

Seth shrugged and gave a humble little nod I knew was pure bullshit. He's never had a humble moment in his life. He leaned in and said, "We do need about five shots of lime vodka for the hamburger, though."

That gave En some pause and he narrowed his eyes at both of us. I lifted the lid of the Styrofoam box slightly so he could see inside.

"I get it," he said. "You skipped the drinking and went straight for the drugs."

Seth smirked. "No, seriously. I have this buddy who's always pulling shit on me—pranks and stuff—and I need to get even. He's been watching his girlfriend's dog, and she's due back tomorrow morning, so I want to get the dog drunk as shit and leave him holding the bag."

"That is so fucked up," En said with a big grin. "You are an evil little bastard."

He put a can of Red Bull up on the bar for Seth and went to fix my drink. When he came back, he had a glass for me and a bottle of Smirnoff lime vodka.

"Here, give me that," he said reaching for the box. He looked at me. "I gotta' say, you don't really look the type for shit like this."

I shook my head. "No, no, this is not my show. I just came out for some dinner. I'm going home and heading to bed like normal people do."

They both laughed at me. En opened the box and grabbed a long bar straw, which he used to poke about fifteen holes straight through the hamburger. He tossed that and picked up the bottle, pouring vodka slowly over the top to let it soak in. I was impressed with the effort he was putting into it. When he was done, the whole thing was a glistening, soggy mess sitting in a quarter-inch deep clear puddle. Carrying that back to the car was going to be a treat.

I took a drink of my amaretto and said, "You're a real professional, that's a hell of a job."

En nodded. "Damn straight. I don't do anything half-assed."

He took the bottle down to the other end of the bar and put it back up on the lighted platform with the rest of them. I closed the hamburger box and took another sip of my drink, when something caught my eye.

The club manager had cornered En and was talking to him. That in itself wouldn't be unusual, but what made me notice was he was pointing at us, and it was clear we were the topic of conversation.

"Oh, I do not like this," I said, poking Seth with my foot.

He raised his eyebrows in question, and I cut a glance to where En was.

He looked at me and mused, "I don't know. The guy probably saw the stunt with the burger and wanted to know what the hell was up. They're probably talking about what to charge us for it."

"I hope you're right. We could have raised a few suspicions asking about Serrano the other day. En may not have known he was dead yet, but I'm willing to bet the manager did."

"Shit. I wish I'd thought to tell him to keep that to himself."

I shrugged. "No real way to do that without making him suspicious too. Don't worry about it. Let's get the hell out of here as quick as we can, though."

"Anytime, man. I can take this with me."

I waited until En worked his way back to us and said, "What do we owe you?"

"Twenty bucks ought to cover it," he said. I gave him twenty-five.

He gave Seth a steamy look and said, "Next time you come around here, be early."

Seth smirked. "Will do. You can count on that."

"Good luck with your dog intoxication. Hope that works out for you."

"Thanks, I could use it."

Chapter 27

Back at the car, I let Seth have the keys, mainly because I didn't trust him to transport the swimming hamburger without spilling vodka all over my seats. Thankfully, it wasn't that far a drive to the mini-storage unit, and we were there in less than fifteen minutes.

We let ourselves in with the key card and drove quietly around to number twenty-seven, where Serrano had his car stashed. I jumped out and unlocked the garage door, pushing it halfway up. Seth parked so Matilda's trunk was right by the door. That way we could load what we'd need into the Z4 without calling a lot of attention to ourselves.

Seth shut the car off and came around back. "I'll go open up the Z-four," he said.

"Why don't you put the top up too, I don't want to be that visible tonight."

"I'm on it," he said, and ducked under the garage door.

In the trunk of my car, I put together what I thought we would need with us. I had a duffel bag to carry the boxes, the set of lock picks from my surveillance kit, flashlights, and the stun gun. I also added the pry bar and an extra clip of ammo for my gun. The gun itself, I checked over and slipped into its holster, nestled at the small of my back.

"You almost ready?" Seth asked, sticking his head out the door.

"Yeah." I handed him the empty duffle and the tool kit.

He disappeared with those while I opened my briefcase and got the maps to the salvage yards and our notes with the box combinations. Serrano's package was in there, with the notebook, and I grabbed it, figuring I'd give it back to McCann. None of us wanted any loose ends floating around.

I tapped on the door and Seth peered out at me. "Here," I said, giving him the envelope with the notebook in it, "stick that in the empty bag."

"Right. Is that everything?"

"I think so. You ready in there?"

"Dude, you have no idea." His eyes gleamed wildly.

I pointed at him. "No fucking around tonight, this is damn serious. We can *not* get pulled over for any reason, you got it?"

"You don't need to tell me that," he said with a hint of exasperation.

"Yeah, I think do, Seth. You look about this close to goin' right over the edge on me."

"I'm fine, I swear it."

"All right."

"Nag, nag, nag." He stood up and pushed the door open the rest of the way so we could switch cars.

"Yeah, bite me."

I held out my hands, and Seth tossed me my car keys. He flashed me a big grin as I threw him the keys for the Z4. I shut the trunk and went around to get in the driver's seat, starting her up.

I watched in the rearview mirror, and after the Z4 backed slowly into sight, I jockeyed Matilda around until I could back her into the space. That way, when we were done, we could pull straight out and get the hell out of there.

I shut off the engine and gave her a pat on the fender. "Wish me luck, baby. I'll be back soon," I muttered.

Outside, I pulled the door down and snapped the padlock in place. Seth eased forward in the Z4 and I got in, setting the hamburger box on the floor between my feet. He had the radio tuned to something obnoxious, and after a couple seconds, I realized my seat was heated. Like a little kid, he'd already been messing with the levers and buttons.

"Is this thing sweet or what?" he said, practically purring with lust. "I can't wait to get on the road with it."

"Well, now's the time," I said. "Just keep it cool until we're away from here."

"I said I'd be good, and I meant it. I'll even wait until we're on the freeway to really open her up."

"Within reason."

"Yeah, yeah, yeah."

He drove slowly up to the gate, which rolled open automatically from the inside when a car set off its motion sensor. True to his word, Seth kept it barely over the speed limit through the frontage roads and side streets. When we reached the entrance ramp to the freeway, however, he hit the gas and the Z4 surged forward like a cat. Seth merged effortlessly into traffic and wove in and out, playing with the easy maneuverability of the car. It was the ideal place to let him have fun with it, because at that hour, there were plenty of flashy hot rods zipping around like it was a playground.

"Oh baby," Seth moaned, eyes on the road, one hand on the wheel, and the other on the stick shift. I was willing to bet he'd totally forgotten I was there.

I took a penlight out of my pocket and checked the map. "You've got a nice long stretch on here before you have to worry about any changes. Knock yourself out."

By way of an answer, he cut across two lanes of traffic and sailed past a Maserati before darting back into the center lane.

I settled down into my seat and said, "On the other hand, please keep in mind that this is quite possibly a stolen car."

"I'm keeping an eye out," Seth said.

He was clearly not the least bit worried, and I didn't have the heart to spoil his fun when there was such a good chance it was the last he was going to have for a while. Besides, it appeared he had a pretty good knack for being only the second fastest car on the road at any given time, so if a cop did show up, he'd have bigger fish to fry.

Chapter 28

We headed for A-1 Salvage first. It was the farthest north and easy to get to by freeway. Plus, it had the dog, and I really wanted to get rid of the booze-soaked hamburger. The combination of alcohol and tepid beef is a disgusting smell, and the inside of a Z4 is damn small. I kept tabs on the road signs and let Seth know when we were getting close to our exit.

When I did, he veered across traffic and up the ramp with a squeal of tires. "Hey," I said, "you wanna take it easy?"

"I deserved one last hurrah. From here on out it's got to be granny driving all the way." He coasted up to the intersection and stopped neatly.

"It's got to be inconspicuous driving," I said. "You go too slow and you'll draw just as much attention as if you were speeding."

He gave me an irritated look. "I know, Dino. I wasn't born yesterday. Will you give me a little credit here?"

"Sorry. This is not my idea of a good job. There's no way I can lie my way out of this or pull one over on someone. We get caught, and that's it."

"We won't get caught," he said.

To prove his worth, he drove perfectly the rest of the way. When we reached the lot, he drove down to the end of the street, turned around, and shut the lights off. Moving at a slow creep, he inched quietly back along the far side of the road until we were just past the salvage yard, pointed in the right direction for a fast getaway. A couple of large palms drooped heavily, swaying in the light breeze. Seth pulled over beneath them and shut the car off.

"Let's hope Fido's a booze hound," he said.

I leaned down and picked up the box. "You're the expert here, you wanna do this?"

"No." Seth eyed me and settled down in his seat.

"Fine."

I got out of the car, leaving the door ajar and walked across the road, staying well to the far side of the gate. The only motion lights were right above the office door, and I didn't want to risk setting them off this early. With any luck, they were set to light up if anything came into the parking lot. If they'd been trained on the yard, the dog would set them off every time he moved.

The old chain link gate hung crooked, sagging on worn-out hinges. There was a large gap at the bottom, between the gate and the fence. I crept up to it, hoping not to alarm the dog, and opened the hamburger box. Back in the shadows, I heard a faint jingling and the snuffle of something live. Hello, Fido.

I set the box on the ground and poked it through the gap in the gate, sliding it as far as my arm would reach. I was met with a low, menacing growl, and I yanked my hand out of there before he ate the wrong thing.

"Come here, boy," I called, barely above a whisper. "Come and see what we brought you. You're gonna love this."

The growl became more intense at the sound of my voice, and the dog moved closer. He paced the length of the gate, eyeing me warily. I froze and held my breath. I needed him to notice the burger before he decided to raise the alarm.

"Easy," I murmured to him as he came closer.

He lifted his snout to the air, sniffing rapidly, and started to cast around, swinging his head from side to side. His attention was still firmly fixed on me, but I hoped the smell of food would start to sink in. I crept a little further to the side, trying to draw him toward it. The movement caused him to snarl at me, and I stopped obediently.

This time when he snuffled around, he found the burger and gobbled it up with large savage bites, three of them at the most. When there was none left, he licked the inside of the box, following it through the dirt as his tongue pushed it along. I took that opportunity to back away and cross the street.

Seth was standing by the car watching. "I thought you were gonna have to hand feed the dumb bastard," he said.

"So did I. He was not real impressed with me." I reached into the car to get my notes and tucked them in my shirt pocket with the penlight. "How long until he passes out?"

He held up his hands. "Don't know. He's bigger than Ed's dogs. They usually pass out after about twenty minutes."

"That sucks. I'd like to get this over with."

"This is the hard one," Seth said. "The rest will be a piece of cake."

"Yeah, okay," I said. "Pop the trunk, will ya?"

He pulled the key from his pocket, unlocked the trunk, and lifted the lid. I leaned in and unzipped the tool bag, taking out my lock picks, which I slipped into my back pocket, and the stun gun. I grabbed the empty duffle bag and closed the trunk.

"Here, take this," I said, handing Seth the stun gun. "In case there's any trouble with the dog, you zap him."

Seth nodded and clipped it to the front of his jeans.

For the next twenty minutes, we leaned on the car and watched the shadows across the road, trying to see the dog. I'd hoped he'd just stagger around in front of us and fall over, assuring us a bite-free job, but no such luck. When we went back to the gate, the Styrofoam box was in pieces, and there was no sign of the dog.

"You see him?" Seth asked.

"Nope, so keep an eye out," I said. "Come and hold a light for me."

I slipped sideways along the gate to the padlocked chain in the middle, trying to avoid setting off the motion lights. They cooperated better than the dog. Seth trained the beam of his penlight on the lock and I set to work on it with the slim picks. The lock was old and worn, so it took me longer than usual, but eventually I got it right and it clicked open. I left the lock and chain hanging on the fence, and we eased open the gate and slipped inside, listening for any sign of Fido. There was nothing.

"All right," I said. "This one's the Thunderbird. You remember where it is?"

"Yeah, I think so."

We stuck close to the side of the main road and walked the same path we had earlier that day. I watched for familiar cars. Seth was just ahead of me and looked like he had it under control. He paused to turn and count rows, so I stopped next to him, and in that moment, I heard a chilling sound.

Seth heard it too, because he froze and looked at me. "Is that was I think it is?"

The sound came again, only closer this time. It was the light jingling of dog tags. Seth reached for the taser. When it came again, closer still, the jingling was accompanied by heavy panting and the sound of claws in the dirt.

"Oh, fuck me," Seth said through clenched teeth.

Fido was right next to us. I could make out his form in the dim moonlight, but couldn't see his face. He huffed and whined pitifully, pitching up at the end in a kind of doggie question. I clicked the light on and shined it at him.

He sat down and looked up at us with a dopey expression, tongue hanging out of the side of his mouth. He wagged his tail and reached up at me with one paw, batting the side of my leg. When he did, he tipped to one side and had to scramble to right himself.

Seth snorted with laughter. "He's totally hammered. He wants you to give him another hamburger."

"Sorry, pal," I told him. "That's all I got."

Realizing we were in no immediate danger, we picked up counting where we'd left off and crept through the dark. Fido tagged along, occasionally crashing into my legs. Ten minutes later, the three of us were still wandering around blindly.

"Where in the hell is it?" I snapped.

"I don't know," Seth said. "Everything looks different in the dark. I could swear it was right down here."

"I think we've been down here twice already."

Fido gave a whiney grumble. He was going to be deeply sad when he found out we weren't looking for hamburgers.

Seth shined his light along the row of cars, studying them. "All right, I remember that Pinto at the end. We went around that, and the next row was a bust, but we found it right after that."

He took off with a sense of purpose and I followed, playing back our earlier visit in my mind. We were on the right track, and when we walked down the path two rows over, the terrain looked familiar to me, even in the dark.

"Here!" he said, trotting down the line to the Thunderbird.

"It's about time. Let's do this and get the hell out of here."

Seth eased open the door and reached under the seat where we'd left the box. I unzipped the duffel and stood next to him, so he could slip it inside. So far, so good.

I turned to start heading back to the front gate, but my foot caught on something large and solid. I pitched forward and landed in the grass with a muffled curse, taking most of my weight on my bruised shoulder.

Seth turned on his light, and there in the middle of the path was Fido, sprawled out and snoring softly. At least we wouldn't have to explain why we were leaving without giving him any more treats.

Seth snickered and flicked the light at me. "I told you so," he said.

"You were right." I got up and brushed myself off, and we made for the center drive.

We slipped out, locked the gate, and drove away quietly without any further incident.

"One down, two to go," said Seth as he turned onto the main street, and we joined the ranks of regular night owls again.

"Let's hope the others go a little smoother. We gotta' be faster about it."

"Should be. No dogs to deal with, and the other lots are more organized."

Chapter 29

The next one on the list was Unlimited where our target was in the trunk of the Buick. The game was serious now that we had a quarter million bucks worth of drugs in our car. Getting caught was completely out of the question. I tossed my cellphone into the ashtray so I didn't have to worry about it going off at an inopportune moment.

Breaking in was trickier, since the lock proved to be a bitch. I've rarely met one I can't get the better of, and soon we were in. Unfortunately, not soon enough to avoid setting off the motion lights, but there were enough shadows to hide in, and they had a short range.

Seth was carrying the pry bar this time, in case the trunk had latched again. All we had to do was lift it, and he dove in headfirst to dig under the flooring. We stuffed the box in the duffle bag and left, relocking the gate on the way out.

Back at the car, Seth opened the trunk, and I stashed the bag inside. It now held two of the three boxes and Serrano's notebook. The hairs at the back of my neck prickled. For all our care and precautions, this was still just a crap shoot, and the sooner it was done, the better.

Part of my unease was due to the fact that we were headed deeper into the heart of Miami. The remaining salvage yard was in a much more urban setting. That meant more light, more people, and a strong possibility of more cops. Seth seemed to be feeling it too, because his attention to his driving was faultless and the usual smart-ass comments were at a minimum.

I was watching the side view mirror and noticed a black Mercedes fall into line behind us. At first, I simply kept an eye on it while I gave Seth directions to the last yard, but after a while I got pissed.

"That damned smug son of a bitch," I muttered as I stared at the reflection.

"What's up?" Seth shot me a concerned look and peered into the rearview.

"We're being followed. That prick promised me he'd leave us on our own for this. Asshole."

I grabbed my cellphone and hit the redial, glaring at the car in the mirror while it rang. When McCann answered, I didn't let him finish his greeting. "What the fuck do you think you're doing? I thought we had an agreement."

There was a slight pause. "What, exactly, are you referring to? I've stuck to my end of the bargain so far."

"Yeah? Then why do I have one of your guys crawling up my ass as we speak?"

"What do you mean?"

"What the fuck do you think I mean?" I snapped. "I thought you agreed to pull the tail off us."

"I did," he said. There was muffled conversation in the background. "If you're being followed, it's not any of my men. They're all accounted for."

"And I'm supposed to believe that."

"I think you'd better," he said, sounding cool now. "You've got trouble there, and it doesn't have anything to do with me. I warned you I wasn't the only one who had a stake in finding out where Serrano hid the drugs."

"Shit." I squeezed my eyes shut and rubbed my forehead, because I knew he was telling the truth. "We might be later than we thought." I shut the phone and put it back in the ashtray.

"Well?" Seth glanced over at me.

"McCann's not having us followed. He figures it's the other guys."

"From The Shark Pond?" Seth asked. "How in the hell would they know where we are?"

I thought back to En and the unsettling conversation with his boss. "Because they followed us tonight. They've probably been with us the whole time."

"Shit. Now what?"

"Think you can lose them?"

Seth grinned slyly. "I can sure have fun trying."

He downshifted and stepped on the gas, surging ahead smoothly. Just like on the freeway, he slipped in and out of traffic as if it were a stroll in the park. The only problem was the Mercedes swelled up behind us and stuck to him like glue. Each move Seth made, they followed. If Seth managed to put another car between us, the Mercedes would come charging around the other side.

Seth swerved down side streets and shot through alleys, and every time, the Mercedes would be one step behind. I read the map and shouted directions.

"Son of a bitch," he snapped, taking another hard left. "This guy is like a fucking magnet, and if we keep this up much longer, we're gonna start attracting attention."

The guys in the Mercedes either agreed, or didn't care, because they started to get more aggressive. They roared right up on our bumper, floating from side to side, looking for a chance to come around and run us off the road. Or shoot us.

"Oh, no, you don't, asshole," Seth said, glaring in the mirror. "You're nuts if you think I'm giving you an opening."

His hands were tight on the wheel as he cut them off time and time again. It was clear by the way they charged us, they were getting frustrated. We sped along a street in some industrial area, surrounded by warehouses and truck yards. There wasn't much traffic, which was good for driving, but not so great in terms of being able to blend in.

While Seth concentrated on driving and staying out in front, I tried to keep track of where we were and look for an escape option. I was also watching the guys behind us, hoping to gauge what they had in mind.

"Oh shit." I watched one of the side windows go down and had just enough time to shout "Gun!" before there was a sharp pop and the tinny sound of a bullet hitting metal. I saw a quick flash of sparks.

Seth swore and said, "They are *not* shooting holes in this beautiful car!" He sped forward and dodged around a parked minivan.

They shot a couple more times and missed. Seth was muttering a constant string of foul oaths. He turned right, down a road flanked with brick buildings on one side and a chain link fence on the other. Beyond the fence were rows of semi-trailers and trucks. Out of the corner of my eye, I caught movement at the far side of the lot, nearly a block away. I turned to look and realized we were about to have a very big problem.

"Train," I snapped, just as the red lights started flashing at the crossing ahead of us.

"Perfect," Seth said, leaning forward.

"What do you mean 'perfect'? Take the next left or we're gonna be trapped." The fence ran right up to the crossing, and the tracks slipped through a neat gap in the warehouses. Not an inch of space was wasted.

"I mean this is our way out. Hang on."

"Hang on?" I watched the red and white striped arms fold down across the road. The train was only half a block away and appeared to be closer to the crossing than we were. It moved pretty damn fast for inside the city. I shook my head. "You can't be serious. Do not try to run that train, do you hear me?"

Seth ignored me and mashed the accelerator to the floor.

"Turn left, Seth, now!"

He shook his head slowly. "No can do, Dino. This is the only way."

In one single, terrifying blur of red and white, he swerved hard left, then hard right and zipped around the crossing arms, screeching tires the whole way. I grabbed for the dashboard and my seatbelt strap. The lights flashed red, and the headlight of the engine blinded me through my window. Then came the deafening blast of the train's horn. I shouted a string of Italian curses, while Seth let out a wild cheer like the Dukes of Hazzard.

A fraction of a second later, everything was cool white light and the quiet swish of air along the doors as we sailed down the empty street. My heart was pounding so hard in my chest, it hurt. I whipped around to look and saw only a long chain of boxcars sealing off the street. Through the gaps, the headlights of the Mercedes blinked helplessly, fading in the distance.

I sagged into my seat and let out a sigh of relief. Then I glared at Seth. "You are fucking crazy! Are you *trying* to get us killed?"

"I had it all under control," he said, grinning ear to ear. "You've just gotta' trust me, babe. I know what I'm doing. It worked too, you can't deny that."

"Yeah, well, I'm still not sure I'm not gonna have a heart attack." I clutched at my shirt and took a few deep breaths.

"You're a control freak, that's your problem."

"Excuse me?"

"You do dangerous stuff all the time. You're just getting bent out of shape because this time you didn't have any say in it."

"You're damn right," I said. "I fail to see how that makes me a control freak. It's perfectly rational to not want to get flattened by a train."

"Hey, a little appreciation would not be amiss here." He flashed me his hurt face.

"Amiss? Oh, for Christ's sake." I rolled my eyes. "All right, yes, you lost the bad guys. Very nice work. Thank you for not killing me in the process."

"You're welcome," he said with a smirk. "Besides, I just finally got you into bed, I'm not about to kill you now."

Chapter 30

Once we were free of the Mercedes, Seth resumed his more sedate driving practices, and we took stock of our situation. I'd been able to keep us more or less on course during the chase, and we were only a couple blocks off from where we needed to be. We got to M & H Auto within ten minutes. Seth parked the car around the corner from the entrance, hidden in the shadows at the edge of an alley.

While I got the tool bag, Seth was absorbed with checking out the damage from the gunfire, rubbing his fingers over an ugly bullet hole with a stricken expression.

"It's not like we're gonna have to put her down," I said. "Come on."

He followed me across the street and along the battered wooden fence of the salvage yard. "I seem to recall you being pretty torn up when Matilda got shot."

"That is not your car," I reminded him.

"It's still a crime."

We reached the gate, and I handed Seth the bag. He held his light while I picked the lock, and like each of the other yards, we slipped inside. One last box and we were done. We could head back to the hotel, give McCann his stuff and get the hell out of town.

This yard was arranged a little differently than the others. It had large steel racks that held cars stacked three high, and a couple forklifts for getting them up there. They stood in short rows, lined up one after the other in a huge grid, like a maze. The car we wanted was on the ground level several rows back, almost in the rear corner. Because the yard was laid out so neatly, we had no trouble finding our target. This was the Geo Metro with the smashed hatchback window. I was able to reach right up in the wheel well and fish out the cashbox, feeling like it was about time things started to go our way.

We were turning to head back, when I caught the sound of voices. I paused and listened, trying to get a fix on where they were coming from. Seth stopped next to me. I could see his face in the faint light, and he looked concerned.

Then the beam of a flashlight flickered along the row of cars at the opposite end from us. It was pale and diffuse. They were still near the entrance. Seth and I glanced at each other.

"Shit," he whispered. "Now what?"

"Stick to the shadows and keep still. When they get close, we slip around the end here and make for the gate while they're searching the back of the lot. Fool them into thinking whoever was here is long gone."

Seth nodded, and we both pressed up hard against the side of a wrecked sedan.

The voices grew louder, and I thought I could make out three or four. One of them said, "What makes you so sure this is the right place?"

"Because, you moron, the gate's hanging open."

"Oh, right..." There was a pause where you could almost *hear* the guy's brain cells firing. "Well, what if they're gone already? I didn't see no car."

A different voice said, "They've been locking up after themselves. They're still here. Now shut the fuck up."

I crouched down and peered through the racks of cars. There were a couple of guys within two rows of us, including the one with the flashlight. A third guy hung back a little ways, trying to squint down the rows, and a fourth guy stood squarely in the front gate. Damn.

Seth look plain old pissed now. "How in the fuck did they find us? This is *unreal*."

"I don't know, but we need to get the hell out of here."

He leaned over my shoulder. "We're gonna have a bitch of a time getting past the one up front."

"I know."

"I might have an idea."

"Yeah?"

"The street we parked on runs down the other side of the yard." He pointed to the wall opposite us. "We might be able to bust through the fence. It's a piece of shit. I could probably do it with about three good kicks."

"We'd have to be quick about it, because they'll know right where we are. And we still have to get there."

The guy with the flashlight was just one row away now, and we inched down to the end of the rack, slipping through one of the gaps as he passed us. I gave Seth a nudge, and we kept going through to the next row. Then we started to make our way across, hoping to sneak behind them and reach the fence on the other side.

We almost made it, but the thug at the tail end of the group happened to turn around just as we were disappearing between two racks. Out of the corner of my eye, I saw his hand come up and heard the blast of a gun. The window of a truck shattered right behind me. I pulled my own gun and ducked into the shadows. More gunfire. Ahead of me, Seth did the same, minus a gun.

There was shouting and a lot of commotion as the thugs figured out what was going on and got themselves organized. By that time, Seth and I had put several rows of cars between us and them and were crouching quietly in the dark trying to get our bearings.

Seth leaned over to whisper. "This is what they mean when they say don't count your chickens before they're hatched, isn't it?"

"This is what they mean when they say we're fucked."

The beam of a flashlight played around the ground at the edge of our row, and we started to move toward the other end. Seth stopped short and I bumped into him. I was about to say something rude when I realized there were voices coming from that direction and we were trapped.

I raised my gun to take a pot shot at them, hoping to drive them away long enough to move. Before I could squeeze the trigger, Seth grabbed my arm and pulled me through a gap in the cars. It was a tight fit and we had to crawl over the framework of the center shelving, but in a minute we were standing in the next row over and had a clear path in either direction.

We walked silently toward the end of the row, still trying to go in the general direction of the far wall. The shouts of the thugs were mostly behind and to the left of us again, and I heard a couple more gunshots that weren't even close. That was good. They were confused and didn't have any idea where we were. If we could keep it that way, we'd have a clean path out of there.

Somewhere in the center of the lot, I heard another sound that sent a chill down my spine. I grabbed Seth and whispered in his ear, "You hear that?"

"Sirens. Son of a bitch. When we're fucked, we really do it up right."

"Figures we'd find the only neighborhood in Miami where they don't ignore random gunfire."

Seth said, "No shit. Now we really have to haul ass if we want to get out of here. They're fucking close."

"There's more than one squad car from the sound of it. We're gonna get penned in even if we make it to the fence. We need to keep these thugs occupied long enough so we can slip away. If they stop us, we're screwed."

"What have you got in mind?" Seth asked.

I knelt down and used the pry bar to bust open the lock box we'd picked up and stuffed as much of the cash and drugs into my pockets as I could carry. I handed everything else over to Seth. "Something that'll take them out of the running altogether and let us get out of Miami without them on our tail. Think you can make it to the fence on your own?"

"Sure," Seth said, pulling out the stun gun. "Where are you gonna be?"

"I'll be behind you. Just be ready to take off when I get there. We're gonna want to be quiet about it. No door slamming or squealing tires. They can't know we were here."

"Okay. Just make sure you come back to me. If I'm not allowed to kill you, neither are you." He punched my arm and took off.

The thugs were still chasing around in the dark, hollering to each other and shooting for the fun of it. I wasn't sure they'd heard the sirens yet, which was good news for me. I ducked back through the hole we'd escaped from and eased down toward the center aisle. Glancing around the end, I could see one guy trotting to the back of the lot and another disappearing into one of the rows on the other side.

The car I was standing next to had no windows left, and I saw the rearview mirror lying loose on the front seat, shining in the dark. I reached in and grabbed it. After looking around to make sure no one was going to notice the movement or the reflection, I flung it into the back corner of the lot where it made a fantastic racket, bouncing off the hood of a car and hitting the fence.

Even better was the racket made by the thugs as they fell for it. They all went tearing for the source of the noise, bellowing threats and shooting anything in their path. With all of them distracted, I was able to move from row to row without attracting attention. I hoped the same was true for Seth, and I wished I'd brought a second gun for him. That stun gun wouldn't do him a hell of a lot of good.

It took me a minute to reach the front gate, and I stopped there in the shadows to check the scene. The Mercedes was parked at a careless angle just outside. All the windows were down, which was ideal for my plan. The thug leaning on the front fender wasn't so great, but he was easily dealt with the same way his buddies were, using a rock. While he went to investigate, I crept up to the car and dumped the drugs and cash into the back seat, spreading them out to make it nice and obvious. I made damn sure I got every last little baggie out of my pockets.

Just as I was giving myself a final pat down, a squad car, its lights flashing, came screaming around the corner at the end of the street. The volume of the siren seemed to double. That got the attention of the thugs, both those inside the yard and the one I'd sent down the sidewalk. I had about five seconds to dive for the shadows and get lost before they all converged on the car. If they were hoping to make a fast get away, they were too late. The squad car pulled in, blocking their exit, and two cops jumped out, guns drawn, hollering for everyone to get down.

I ignored that request. If they couldn't see me, they didn't know they were talking to me. I crouched low and raced along the inside perimeter of the yard, until I found the hole Seth had kicked in the fence. I climbed through and found him waiting there for me with the BMW running, passenger door ajar. I got in and held it closed. Seth eased down the street, leaving the headlights off until we got to the corner. My hope was the cops were too tied up with the thugs to notice anything else. At least long enough for us to get out of there.

"Everything okay?" Seth asked.

"I think so. A drug bust will keep them nice and busy for a while, and there's no chance of these guys talking their way out of it."

"The fact that they were shooting up a salvage yard isn't enough?"

"Probably would be, but this'll put a real wrench in the works for The Shark Pond and could gain us a few points with McCann. He might be more inclined to stick to his word if we've just done him a favor."

Seth's hands were tense on the steering wheel, and it looked as if he was having a hell of a time driving like we had no place better to be. "You don't think he might get a little testy that you used his money to do it?"

I'd considered that, but I shrugged and said, "You gotta' spend money to make money. He's a business man, he knows that. And if some of his competition gets knocked out and no one can pin it on him, he's ahead of the game."

Seth turned another corner, and I got a peek down the street at the salvage yard. Another squad car had joined them, and the cops had someone down on the ground in handcuffs already. It looked like they had things under control.

"Okay," I said, "just take it nice and easy back to the storage locker, and we'll pick up Matilda."

He nodded and settled back in the seat.

It took twenty minutes to get there, and they were a damned long twenty minutes. It was work to keep my calm, but I managed, and when Seth stopped outside Serrano's unit, I handed him the keys for the lock and my car.

"What gives?" he asked.

"I want you to drive Matilda, and I'll drive this one. We're not completely out of the woods, and I'd rather be the one in the hot seat if something happens."

"I'm fine," he said with a shrug.

"And you'll be finer in my car, so go. I'm not gonna argue about this."

He sighed and took the keys, and we both got out. I waited until he had the garage door open and said, "Go back to the hotel, we'll meet up with him there. Got a map?"

"Yep. But I'll stay behind you. That way if something does happen, I'll know right away."

"That works," I said.

Instead of going inside, Seth came around the front of the car and grabbed my shirt, pulling me close. He gave me a hard kiss, and I could feel both stress and relief mixed up in it. I wrapped my arms around him and held him tight. For all the witty banter, we both knew we'd just had a pretty close call.

"Waiting for you to come out of that lot was the worst thing I think I've ever had to do," he said.

"Now you know how I felt this morning. We're even."

He snorted and shook his head. "Let's get the fuck out of here."

Chapter 31

The drive back to the hotel was uneventful, and if I wasn't sitting on a fortune in drugs and life in prison, I might have enjoyed it. Seth was right, it was a *nice* car.

I pulled into the parking lot and noticed an upswing in the number of black SUVs around. McCann had arrived and was probably in our room waiting. I made it easy for him and parked next to one of his vehicles. By the time I shut off the car and got out, Seth was pulling in. He parked near the edge of the lot, well away from the thug fleet. I was half tempted to climb in the car with him and call McCann from the freeway, but that wasn't the way it worked.

Besides, I wanted to get a read on McCann's character when this was all said and done, and make damn sure he had a read on mine. If I was right about him, he was a man of honor, however twisted his version might be. Even so, I wouldn't mind leaving him with reasons other than honor to avoid pissing me off.

I got my tools out of the trunk of the Z4 and carried them over to Matilda, where Seth was waiting. I left everything else right where it was. I had no intention of touching it again.

We headed inside, ignoring the thug waiting for us by the stairs, and went straight to the hotel room. We didn't even have to knock. Another thug was ready at the door and let us in. McCann sat in his original spot at the table, sipping a scotch and looking mildly bored with the whole situation.

"I'm sorry I didn't wait for your call," he said. "But it was getting to be about the right time, and I assumed you'd be along shortly. And here you are." He smiled at me in his oily way, and I wanted to deck him.

"Yep. Here we are, and your drugs are out in the parking lot, and we're going home." I tossed the key to the BMW in his lap. "You'll find them in the trunk of Serrano's little toy. I imagine your money probably bought that."

McCann held the key out to the guy standing just behind his right shoulder. "You won't mind if we have a look before you go, will you?"

"Of course not. You're going to find it a little short, though."

"And why is that?"

I had to play it right so I came out doing McCann a favor instead of pissing him off. "We had a little trouble at the end. You were right about who was following us."

He raised an eyebrow and nodded at me, looking expectant.

"The guys from The Shark Pond caught up with us, and we had to find a way to dodge them. Someone had already called the cops, but I wanted to make sure they stayed plenty busy while we took off, and I figured I could maybe give you a leg up at the same time."

"Really? How did you manage that?"

"Well, I had to spend some of your stash to do it." I paused to let that sink in, watching the calculation in McCann's eyes. He showed no sign of his feelings on the matter. "I set them up by dumping some of the drugs and money into their car. Most, if not all of them, have already been hauled off to jail on drug dealing charges."

McCann nodded slowly, musing. "Well, I can see how that would disable The Shark Pond for a short time, but men of that caliber are easy to replace..."

"I thought of that," I said. "I also threw in a book of matches with the club's logo, so the cops would know right where to follow up."

The tiniest hint of a smile touched the corners of McCann's mouth, and I knew that got him. With evidence like that in the car, the cops would be stupid not to investigate, which would seriously throw a wrench in the works for his competitors.

I slipped my hands into my pockets. "I try to always keep a book of matches on me. You never know when they're going to come in handy."

"*Dude*," said Seth, who hadn't heard this detail before. "Is this where you're like Archie What's His Face?"

"Goodwin," I said, rolling my eyes. "Remind me to get you some books for your birthday, would ya?"

McCann's thug slipped in while we were talking and gave a terse little shake of his head.

"I gather you found it a bit short," McCann said to him.

"There's about a quarter of it missing, maybe more."

McCann nodded. "That would seem to corroborate your story, Mr. Martini. Especially if we take Serrano's taste in cars into account. I believe you're free to go."

I took a couple steps closer so I could tower over him. "Before I do, I want your word that you're gonna forget those little old ladies even exist, and you're gonna leave me and my friend alone from now on."

"I told you in the beginning that was the deal. You've kept up your end, now I'll keep mine."

"That's good," I said. "Because if you don't—if any one of them, including Seth, gets hurt in any way—I'm going to hunt you down like the dog you are and make sure you regret it for the rest of your short, short life. And you can have my word on that, got it?"

"Don't give me a reason to hurt any of them."

"I don't plan on it."

McCann smiled placidly, but his eyes were dead serious, and I was pretty sure we understood each other perfectly. "Then you have nothing to worry about. I'm a reasonable man, Mr. Martini, but I suggest you go before I change my mind."

"Fine." I turned to Seth and said, "Let's get the hell out of here."

"You don't have to tell me twice."

Chapter 32

We wasted no time getting out of there, and only paused to put Matilda's top up. Even that was so I could speed on the freeway without the wind choking us both. I was anxious to get back and make sure everything was okay. I considered calling Ruth or Adele, but it was two o'clock in the morning and I didn't think they'd appreciate that very much. Not without explaining the situation, at any rate, and I figured they'd like that even less.

During the first part of the drive, Seth read the map and gave me directions, but once we cleared the city and it was a straight shot home, he stuffed everything in the glove box and shifted so he could study me. He had a seductive expression, and I knew what was coming.

"So," he said, slipping into his extremely gay South Beach tone, "I still owe you from earlier. We could pull over somewhere, and I'll make good on my debt..."

"No, we could not." It came out sharper than I'd intended, and Seth looked taken aback. I sighed and explained, "I want to get home and make sure the ladies are all right. I still don't feel like we're out of the woods."

"Yeah, hey, I can see that," he said, putting a hand on my shoulder. All traces of teasing were gone, and for the moment he was my best friend again. "Why don't you let me drive when we make a pit stop? You didn't get any sleep earlier."

"We'll see. I'm fine right now."

We rode in silence for a while, then he asked, "You think McCann's going to be a problem?"

I thought about it for a minute and tried to honestly pin down my feeling. "My gut says he'll keep his word as long as we do," I said finally. "But the threat is still out there, you know? There's always a possibility, and I don't like it."

"You're just gonna have to let it go, Dino. It bothers you because you know about it, but there's a dozen other threats out there that aren't a problem, because we have no idea they exist."

"What are you, a philosopher now?"

"I am capable of deep thoughts, you know."

"Yeah, well...it's my job to know they exist."

"You're not fuckin' Superman. You can't handle everything, Dino. All you can do is deal with what's in front of you."

"I haven't been managing that too well lately," I said. "Look at the mess I got you into."

"Quit assuming everything is your fault. I could have told you not to mess with that package in the first place, but I didn't. It didn't seem like a big deal to me, either." I glanced over at him in the dim glow of the dashboard lights, and he grinned at me. "And you and I both know it's my own damn fault I got beat up."

I shrugged and nodded. "Yeah, I'll give you that."

"All right, then," he said, leaning back in the seat. "Knock it off with the angst fest. You already had your mid-life crisis this weekend."

"Oh, is that what that was?" I asked, biting back a smile.

"You're fucking forty-one, you dinosaur, you were clearly due."

That forced a chuckle out of me, and I was grateful for the break in the tension.

In spite of that, I was too wired to switch places when we stopped, and I drove the whole way home, speeding as much as I could and keeping a sharp eye out for cops. We were making good time, though, and it would have been worth the price of a ticket. We hit St. Petersburg by five-thirty and were pulling up to my building at six.

The prettiest sight I ever saw was Ruth and Della sitting out on the patio having their morning coffee. I shut the car off and sat there for a minute, letting the relief sink in. Seth was right, and if McCann or his thugs came sniffing around later, I'd deal with that when it happened. We got out of the car and said good morning to the ladies.

"Dino," Ruth said with a smile. "How was Miami?"

"Kind of like an asphalt hell. How goes the garden planning?"

Della set down her cup and clasped her hands. "Darling, it's going to be simply marvelous. We hired a charming young man who's going to come on Thursday and start building the boxes for us."

They offered us breakfast, but we explained we'd been driving all night and just wanted to sleep until noon. Della made a lot of sympathetic cooing noises, which I appreciated, and we made our escape.

Inside, Seth hesitated at the stairs and gave me a cautious look, as if he didn't want to assume anything and start another mid-life crisis.

"Get up there," I said. "You owe me."

He grinned broadly and bounded up the steps two at a time.

I let him into my apartment and went to close the drapes against the early morning sun. When I turned back, he stood in the middle of the room, eyeing me with that dark gaze of his. Desire hit me hard. I wanted him, and I wasn't just thinking with my dick, either.

He came forward to kiss me, and I let him, for a moment. But I was impatient and wanted more. "Come on," I said, herding him toward the bedroom.

I shut the door and pulled the drapes shut there as well, blocking out not only the sunlight, but the whole damn world. This time when he came up to me, I pulled him into my arms and kissed him hard. Since the phone call at the garage, I'd felt like I had a rubber band wound up tight inside me, and now it was finally loosening.

Actually, I'd been tied up in knots all week. I sat on the edge of the bed and pulled Seth's shirt off over his head, so I could get at his skin, pressing my lips to his chest and running my hands up his back. He was warm and smooth and solid, and I needed to feel him more than I thought possible. It hit home to me just how close I came to losing him. He had several new bruises, and I traced them with my fingers until he started getting impatient.

"Dino, come on, man," Seth said, tangling his fingers in my hair and tugging gently. "You're going all mother hen on me again."

"Sue me," I mumbled against the soft line of his stomach.

He huffed and squirmed, but didn't try to get away, which was fine, because I wouldn't have let him anyway. I'd nearly lost him twice, and I was struck with a need to fully appreciate *having* him. I'd been given a second chance, and dumb as I had been lately, I wasn't stupid enough to waste it.

I let go of him and started undoing the buttons of my shirt. "I want you in my bed," I said, pulling it off and dropping it to the floor.

"Yup," was his most coherent reply. "I'm on it."

We stripped ourselves, because we were dead tired and not up to a full-blown seduction. All I wanted was Seth naked and next to me, I didn't care how we got there.

He climbed onto the bed and waited, and I liked the way he watched me as he rested on his knees, eyes shining, but calm. I kicked off my shorts and damn near got tangled in my socks, trying to hurry up and get to him.

When I did, I pushed him to his back and held him there so I could study him for a minute. I knew I wouldn't get completely comfortable with being gay overnight, but it was happening faster than I expected. I trailed my fingers over his chest and stomach, and along the inside of this thigh, absorbing the details.

"Oh man, Dino," he breathed, staring up at me.

"I don't want to have to be afraid for you like that again," I said, settling onto him and nudging his head to the side so I could kiss down over his jaw and along his neck.

"Not that I want you to suffer, but I gotta' say...I kind of like it."

I moved to kiss his throat. "I think I can manage this without putting you in mortal danger."

"Even better," he mumbled, distracted by the path of my hand sliding over his hip.

As I've said, I can learn, and I had been paying attention. I rose up and straddled him, angling my hips to drag my cock lightly over his belly and down along the groove of his thigh. He moaned softly and arched his back, straining for the contact he really wanted. I stayed just out of reach, teasing slowly, and enjoyed the view of him lying naked on my sheets.

I could only manage that for so long. I wanted it as much as he did, and I rubbed my cock tight alongside his. He was hot and hard, and the sensation was electric, making us breathless with anticipation. Seth gripped my arms and pushed up with his hips. He slid his hands down my body and caressed my thighs. He clearly wanted more, but he didn't try to run the show this time. I think it took some effort in his part, but he let me set the pace and the mood.

I wanted it slow, and I wanted to express with my body what I hadn't been able to say yet. My physical self had this all figured out, and it was so easy to slip into sex as a way of connecting with him. I knew it couldn't stay like that for long, but it worked in the short run.

I slid our cocks together with lazy fascination, again and again, almost the only place we touched. There was the press of his thighs between my legs, and his hands clutching at my hips, and the dizzying brush of our erections. Excitement made us slick, which fueled my desire, and I couldn't hold out any longer.

I eased down on top of him, and Seth's mouth fell open in a low moan. His body felt incredible beneath mine, warm and eager, and I moaned too.

He wrapped his arms around me, and I lined up our cocks, trapped in the crush of our bodies as we moved.

"Jesus," Seth groaned as he thrust against me. "You are amazing. I could put up with a lot of mothering for this."

"You might have to." I shifted so we lay side by side, and I could pull him closer, hooking my leg over his. We settled into a comfortable tangle, pressed tight, with just enough room for the hot friction of our cocks. I rested my forehead against his.

"I can live with that," he said, panting lightly.

We were too tired to be overly energetic and it took a long time, building slowly as we rocked our hips in a steady grind. That was fine with me, plenty of time for kissing and caressing. He opened his mouth to me and moaned when I flicked my tongue over his. I lost track of everything but Seth and my own pleasure.

When I finally came, the intensity of it caught me by surprise. I rolled Seth to his back, holding him down with the weight of my body while I shoved my cock hard against him, moaning inarticulate words I couldn't finish for lack of breath. Seth groaned and met me thrust for thrust, clinging to my waist and fucking forcefully until he was spent. The wet heat of his climax spread over my stomach and sent a shiver down my spine.

He was flushed and breathing heavy, eyes half closed. I kissed him, first on the neck, and then on the lips, passionate and slow. I didn't speak for fear of what kind of sappy drivel might come out of my mouth.

When I finally went to find a towel to clean up with, Seth barely moved. He looked over at me and smiled when I dropped down next to him. He said, "Man, I cannot wait to teach you to suck cock. You're gonna rule."

"What makes you think I can't now?"

Seth snorted and laughed so hard he turned pink. When he was finally able to breathe properly, he sniffed and put a hand on my stomach. "Sorry 'bout that. Seriously, though."

I rolled my eyes at him and pulled a pillow under my head. Truthfully, I was looking forward to it myself, but I sure as hell wasn't going to tell him at the moment.

He leaned over and kissed my shoulder before curling up and falling asleep, and it felt good to rest my arm over his back and drift off next to him.

Chapter 33

We slept for a few hours, but eventually had to get up and face the world. I reached for my jacket to check my cellphone messages, but was met with an odd jingling from the pocket. Inside, I found the set of keys and business card Seth's customer had given me the morning before.

"Uh, oh," I said, holding them out for Seth to see. "You're gonna have one really pissed off guy on your hands. He wasn't too happy yesterday. Sorry."

Seth looked at the card. "Ah, yeah, this guy. His wife's the bitch, he's not too bad. I should be able to smooth things over. The fix is an easy one. I could have it done in a couple of hours. You willing to drop me off?"

"Sure, no problem."

It was odd to be back to life as usual. Good, of course, but odd. I didn't have any idea how things were supposed to be now that we were officially dating, or whatever we were calling it. All I knew for sure was Seth definitely wanted more than just sex, and I had finally gotten used to the idea of wanting him at all. Where we were headed from there, I had no clue.

I was mulling it over when I pulled up in front of Ed's. Seth climbed out of the car and grinned at me. "See you later?" he asked.

"Yeah," I told him, smiling back. "All right."

He clapped his hands together and gave me a thumbs up before taking off at a trot. I watched him go, and drove away thinking about what we'd do that evening.

In the meantime, I had errands to run, and a cop to kiss up to. I couldn't tell Teresa the whole story, because that would cause trouble for both of us, and I didn't want to lie to her any more than strictly necessary. I thought with some creative editing I could get back in her good graces. I'd done it before, and I could do it again. I turned in the direction of the station and started practicing what I'd say.

* * * *

I am, at heart, a very traditional guy. A very romantic one too, if I do say so myself. I knew seeing Seth wasn't going to be the same as dating women, and I was going to have to learn a few new tricks. But you don't just toss away forty-one years of teaching and experience, and frankly, some of my old tricks were damn good ones.

So, when dusk rolled around, I showed up at the garage. The air was still warm and salty, and the bugs were getting louder, doing whatever it is bugs do when the sun goes down. Seth was inside, working on some dismantled engine part he had spread out on the workbench.

I got out of the car with a bag of Chinese food and a bottle of wine. It was time to work a few of the old tricks on him.

When I went in, Seth greeted me with a smile and wiped his hands off on a rag. He also took the time to unzip his coveralls and kick out of them before coming over to give me a racy kiss that was part hello and part innuendo.

"Fuck, I'm starving," he said as he broke away and dug through the bag of food.

I grabbed a couple of plastic cups and opened the wine, pouring us each a glass. We sat at the workbench and ate in comfortable companionship, talking about the day and our adventure, but mostly just hanging out. I was waiting to put my plan into action.

When we'd had our fill and were on our second glass of wine, I made my move. I switched off Seth's radio and took a CD out of my suit pocket, dropping it into the player.

"What's that?" Seth asked when I turned it on. He looked mildly amused.

Peggy Lee's *I'm Beginning to See the Light* started to play as I slipped off my jacket and hung it on a rack of belt clamps. I rolled up my sleeves while he watched, and met his gaze, holding out my hand.

"You're not serious," he said, folding his arms over his chest.

"I am. Get your ass over here."

"Aw, man..." He made a big show of dragging his feet, but he did come forward. "I don't even know *how* to dance to this stuff."

"I can teach you."

I taught him a very basic move, which he mangled for a while before we finally started to fall into step. The next song was Elvis, singing *One Night* which had the kind of rhythm I was looking for.

"This is so sappy," Seth said, shaking his head. In spite of that, he was becoming remarkably cooperative.

I grinned. "Well, if you think this is sappy, just wait until you hear the next song."

I slipped my arm around his waist and pulled him closer, still leading him through the dance step, but pressing up to him so our bodies touched from chest to knees. With a little work, I was able to rub against his groin with each step. It didn't take long to get him hard, which made it easier. It also got me hard, which made it more fun.

Seth's cheeks were flushed, and he was breathing heavy. "Yeah, okay," he said, following my lead as best he could. "This isn't so bad."

The song switched to *Unchained Melody*, which fit the steps much better, and I put some style into it, managing to be suave as well as incredibly sexy, and just a little dirty for Seth's sake. He faltered and tromped on my toes, clutching my shoulder to steady himself.

"Keeping watching your feet," I said. "It takes a while to get really comfortable with it."

"My feet are not my primary interest right now," he said in a rough voice.

Yeah, they weren't mine either.

He toughed it out until the end of the song, then grabbed my hand and started dragging me to the side door. "Playtime's over, now we get busy."

"What are you, eighteen? Have a little patience," I said with a chuckle.

"Shut up and walk, Dino," he said, giving me a heated look. "And bring that disc with you."

He let go of me and disappeared through the door, heading up to his apartment and forcing me to follow if I wanted any more of him. I grinned and took the CD out of the player. We could worry about the lights later.

I grabbed the bottle of wine too, and went after him, thinking maybe I was going to be able to keep up with him after all.

Meet the Author

Elle Parker likes her heroes snarky and human, and she writes with a realism that incorporates humor and everyday detail into steamy and exciting stories. Although she writes a few forms of erotica, her first love and primary focus is M/M Erotic Romance. She works hard to create characters you can't help but fall in love with.

Most of the time, Elle can be found in her home in the north woods of Wisconsin, working on her latest novel, or spending time with her husband and teenaged kids. When not writing, she likes reading, brewing beer and swimming with the loons. Unless it's winter. In that case she grabs a book and drinks the beer.

Elle's Website:
http://www.elleparker.com/
Reader eMail:
elle.parker@ymail.com

Don't miss the continuing saga of Dino Martini

Like Pizza and Beer

Dino is caught off guard when his ex shows up out of the blue asking for help. His current lover, Seth, is pushing him to find dirt on his sister's boyfriend. Juggling between two cases – and his boyfriend and ex – isn't easy, but what choice does he have?Working with his ex takes Dino on a trip down memory lane, raising a few doubts and stirring up Seth's jealousy. Now he must save his ex's restaurant and his relationship with Seth before it's too late.

Read on for a special excerpt!

A Lyrical e-book on sale now.
http://www.kensingtonbooks.com/book.aspx/30206

Chapter 1

It wasn't the first time I'd found myself standing alone outside Ed's Garage wondering what to do next. I was supposed to meet Seth here for dinner, but he was nowhere to be found. Seth Donnelly is my best friend and my mechanic. He also happens to be my boyfriend. If that's what we're calling it now. I still don't know for sure. I'd already tried to call him once, but it went to voicemail. None of this would be especially unusual, except he was the one who'd suggested the date.

I got out of the car and went to peer through the office windows. I already knew the doors were locked up tight from the first time I'd been here. On the off chance I had the details wrong, I'd gone back to my place to see if Seth was there. He wasn't.

My cellphone rang, and I pulled it from my pants pocket, answering without looking. "Dino Martini."

"Hiya, sexy," came Seth's voice.

"Where in the hell are you?" I snapped. "I'm at the garage, and you're not. The last time I got a call from you when you were supposed to be here, but weren't, it didn't go down well for us."

That time, the call had led to the two of us chasing illegal drugs all over Miami while gun-toting thugs chased us. Just to make it interesting, one of Miami's big baddies expected us to do it all in record time or suffer the consequences. He'd given Seth a taste of what those might be so everyone was clear, and the whole thing still made me a little edgy.

"Relax. This is going to go down just fine for both of us. In fact, if you play your cards right, I might go down for you."

"That would be easier for you to do if we were in the same place."

"Which is why you need to come to me, because where I am is better than where you are."

"So, where are you?" This was starting to sound like a vaudeville act.

"Not telling," Seth said with a smug voice.

I sighed. "Then how am I supposed to come to you?"

"You're the detective, you have to figure it out."

"Seth, what the hell are you talking about?" I walked out into the parking lot and looked around to see if I could spot him hiding or watching me from an upstairs window.

"If you want me, you have to find me. It's like a scavenger hunt, and I'm your prize." He sounded exceedingly pleased with himself.

"You're not serious."

"Oh, yes I am. I'll even give you a hint. I'm *not* at Mama Gets anymore." He hung up on me before I could fish for more information.

That was fine. Mama Gets is a great sandwich shop within walking distance of Seth's place. It's also about halfway to the beach, and since I heard the surf pounding in the background during our phone call, I had a pretty good idea where he was. It made sense. With Seth's patience level, he wasn't going to make it too hard to get to him.

I pulled Matilda into a proper parking space and locked my briefcase in the trunk. Matilda is my burgundy 1966 Mustang convertible, named after the old ladies she resembles when her white rag-top is up.

The weather was gorgeous, so the walk to the beach was pleasant, and only took me fifteen minutes. When I got to the end of the sidewalk at the public access, I kicked off my shoes and socks and rolled up the cuffs of my slacks before heading off over the sand to find Seth. The sun hung low over the Gulf, and it was hard to spot him in the fading light, even with his telltale red hair. I finally found him camped out on one of the wide rental beach chairs scattered along the coast. He had the shell up, but given the hour, I gathered that was more for privacy than shade.

"You pay for this?" I asked, dropping my shoes in the sand and sitting on a corner of the chair.

"Sort of," Seth said, grinning at me. "I do work for the guy who owns these, and he told me to feel free to use them anytime. You got here pretty quick. I'm impressed."

"Well, you didn't make it real difficult to narrow down your general location. But, how were you expecting me to find you out here in the dark?"

He held up a lighter and snapped on the flame, waving it around in front of me. I rolled my eyes. He said, "Not only would you have found me just fine, but since you don't consider it a real date without symbolic fire involved, I'm covered on that score too."

"Lots of people put candles on the dinner table. My ma lit candles for dinner every night of my life. You don't get to make me out to be some kind of romantic sap until I light candles in the bathroom and shove you into a bubble bath."

Seth shook his head and opened the large bag sitting on my side of the chair. He produced two wrapped sandwiches, two bottles of beer and a bag of chips. "You like Mama's seafood salad, right?"

"Yep. Thanks." I moved the bag so I could sit next to him and look out across the water. Orange and pink streaks filled the sky, and two pelicans flew past.

"Listen, I need to ask you a favor." Seth licked a gob of mayonnaise off his wrist.

"Oh? What kind of favor?"

"A professional one. I intend to pay you in blow jobs."

"Are you serious? You mean like hire me for a case?"

"Yeah."

I could tell by his demeanor we weren't talking about strong-arming someone who'd welshed on a bet, or doing collections. I did those kinds of things for him all the time.

"So, spill it," I said. I took a sip of beer and shifted to face him.

"All right. You know that jackass my sister's been living with for the better half of forever?"

Seth's sister, Molly, was about four years older than him chronologically, and at least forty in terms of maturity. There was no mistaking the family resemblance. She had the same blue eyes and the same red hair, which she wore chin length and usually as out of control as Seth's. She worked as a lab tech for a hospital in Tampa, and Seth often referred to her as the white sheep of the family.

"You mean Frank? What's he done this time?"

Molly and Frank had been shacking up for about three years, in spite of Molly's wish to be a regular middle-aged wife.

"Same old shit, only I think he's doing it worse than ever." He took a swig of beer. "Molly's been complaining because money is tight, and the other night she let it slip that he's been more secretive than usual. She usually tries to hide that stuff."

"What are you thinkin'?"

"I don't really know. I mean, he's a sleazy guy and he's always onto some kind of get-rich-quick scheme or making shady deals. I don't want him getting Molly in trouble."

"So, what do you want me to do?" I asked.

He shrugged and drank more beer. "Poke around, get some dirt on him. Do what you *do*, Dino."

"The goal being?"

"To nail the bastard, what do you think?" He eyed me sharply. Then he sighed. "Maybe if we can dig up enough shit on this guy, Molly will finally see him for what he really is. She keeps hanging on, thinking he'll settle down, but she deserves better. She sure as fuck is smarter than that. I don't know what the hell her problem is."

"You're a good brother. I'll see what I can find." I wadded up the wrapper from my sandwich. "Does she know you're asking me to do this?"

Seth shuddered and widened his eyes. "No way, man. She'd kill me if she knew."

"I didn't think she was the killing type."

"Big sisters are always the killing type, you know that."

I thought of home and nodded. "True enough."

The breeze was warm and humid, and we talked about our day, comparing notes and discussing plans. It was dark when we finished. The only light came from the glow of the condos behind us, and the flicker of moon on the surf.

Seth took the empty beer bottle from my hand and dropped it in the bag with the rest of the garbage. He pushed me to my back and settled next to me, slipping a hand under my shirt. His fingers were cool, but his lips were warm against my neck, and his breath was heavy. I turned to kiss him and he pulled me closer, pressing his groin against my hip with a soft groan. Within minutes, he was all over me.

I caught him by the shoulders and held him back. "You're not gonna try to have sex with me out here, are you?"

"No," he said, shaking his head. "I'm going to make out with you until you can't see straight, and then I'm gonna try to have sex with you in your apartment."

"Yeah, all right, I can live with that." I let go of him, and he stretched out on top of me with his usual brand of easy sensuality. He's everything I'm not—wild, easy and free, completely uninhibited. It's been a big adjustment for both of us.

I slid my arms around him and held tight, opening my mouth as he kissed me. He flicked the tip of his tongue along my lower lip and moaned quietly when I ran my hands over his ass. I loved the weight of his body and the smell of him. A unique blend of spicy deodorant, warm male, and auto shop. Who knew there would be a time in my life when the scent of motor oil could get me hard.

The pounding of the surf blocked out every noise but his hot breath in my ear, and it gave me a sense of timeless isolation. I reached up to thread my fingers in his hair, angling his head to run my tongue over the skin of his neck. He moaned and pressed into me, arching his back so he could grind his hips on mine. The hard line of his erection dug into my hip and he moaned again, louder and more desperate.

"God, Dino, you are hot," he panted. He thrust in a lazy rhythm, rubbing against me through his jeans. The heat of his cock soaked through our clothing. It made me shiver, and I thought about getting him home.

I pulled him tighter to me and butted my hips, meeting him thrust for thrust. He swore and his breath grew ragged. He had his hands hooked under my shoulders, and his fingers clutched at my shirt. He tried to kiss me but was panting too hard and had to break away for air after only a few seconds. I smirked and licked the edge of his ear, biting softly.

"Oh, shit, I lied," he gasped.

"About what?"

"About trying to have sex with you here." He began to thrust in earnest, rubbing off against me like a horny teenager.

"There is no way in hell I'm getting naked with you on a public beach. I don't care how dark it is."

"You don't have to. I can do it just like this." He ground his dick into me and moaned loudly for effect.

"With all your clothes on." I narrowed my eyes at him.

"Just takes a little imagination to make up for the direct contact."

"Seriously."

"Dino, shut up and work with me here."

"Mmmm..." I held him by the waist and rocked my hips against his. "And what are you imagining while you rub off on me at the beach in the dark?"

"All kinds of stuff. You fucking me in my bed, jerking you off in a crowded club in Miami, my cock in your mouth..."

My skin flushed hot, and I moaned. Hearing that kind of stuff in Seth's voice was still something of a novel experience, and it never failed to turn me on. "You have a very active imagination," I said.

"You have no idea."

I could see his face in the dim light and his eyes were shut tight, intense concentration etched on his forehead and in the lines around his mouth. He only remembered to inhale about every third breath, and his body was taut with effort. He was gorgeous.

"Come on," I said, "I wanna see you. I want to watch you lose it right here, like a high school virgin."

"Oh my God," he groaned, pumping harder and burying his face against my shoulder.

"That's it, Seth, come for me." I slipped my hand under his shirt and ran it up his bare back, still matching pace with him. I didn't think there was any way I'd get off like that, but helping him do it was hotter than hell.

He gritted his teeth, and a hint of frustration crept into his moans. I tugged on his hair and whispered in his ear, "The next time I fuck you, I want to do it in the backseat of my car."

He cried out and clutched me with a death grip, bucking his hips wildly while he muttered a string of curse words. The relief was plain in his voice, and the tension eased from his body when he finally slowed. He was nearly laughing as he fought to catch his breath.

"Oh, man," he said, after a couple of minutes. He rolled off to the side and gave me a huge grin. "I don't think I've done that since I was fifteen."

"I don't think I've ever done that."

"Dino, I'm amazed you're willing to do it doggie style. How old were you when you finally got laid? Thirty?"

"You know what? Screw you. I'll have you know I did *just fine* with my sex life before you came along."

The argument was one we had often and it had turned into a kind of pillow talk, but there was a time when I nearly let that difference split us up. Fortunately, the chemistry we had was more than I could resist, and Seth isn't nearly the tomcat he likes to make himself out to be.

"Yeah, I'll bet that was a hell of a weekend too," he said with a grin. He grabbed some napkins from dinner and sat up on his knees, reaching down the front of his jeans to clean up what he could. When he was done, he tossed them in the bag and straddled my hips, looking down at me with smug glee. "I think you should put your money where your mouth is."

"What do you mean?" I was still hard as hell, and the warmth of him sitting squarely on my dick made it difficult to think.

He slid back a couple inches and popped open the button of my slacks.

"Hey!" I made a grab for his hand, but he yanked it out of my reach. "I thought we had an agreement here."

"I didn't agree to a damn thing. And if you're claiming not to be uptight, then you won't mind a little public display of perversion."

"No way. I am not getting naked out here, someone will see."

"Dino." He leveled a gaze at me. "I just wanna give you a hand job, and no offense, but your dick isn't that big. No one is going to see anything." As he spoke, he wormed his hands into my pants and pushed my shorts out of the way. Being the horny pushover I am, I let him. "Besides," he said, caressing my cock, "you don't really want to walk home like this, do you?"

I licked my lips and swallowed hard, shaking my head. "No, not really."

The air was cool on my skin and his fingers were warm. He wrapped them loosely around me and stroked lightly, teasing me. I was already halfway there. In spite of my protests, watching him get off like that had me wildly turned on, and I wanted to come so bad I could taste it.

"Come on, don't be a jerk," I said, thrusting up into his hand.

He raised an eyebrow, but closed his hand tight and picked up the pace. I hummed with pleasure and sat up enough to kiss him, bracing myself on my hands. All I could think about was his hot mouth on my neck and the grip of his hand, working me steadily. The crashing of the waves drowned out everything else.

Seth grinned and licked my ear. "Look at you, all wild and exposed on the beach."

"Don't remind me," I panted. It didn't actually matter anymore, though. Being lightheaded and on the verge of orgasm goes a long way toward lowering my inhibitions.

I rocked my hips and pushed up into Seth's hand, moaning with pleasure. It felt so good I was shaking. The salt breeze and the surf heightened every sensation to a fever pitch, and I bit my lip as Seth sped up. The outdoor thing definitely tripped a few triggers for me, but unlike most people, I did not enjoy the ever present threat of getting caught.

"More," I said. "Come on, please." I reached to plant a kiss on the side of his neck.

He squeezed tighter and I was there, coming hard and trying to keep my voice down as I groaned with relief. I damn near knocked him off the chair. When the last of it was over, I slid down to my back and lay there panting, staring up at the stars. It was a beautiful night.

Seth cleaned us up and buttoned my pants for me, then dropped onto my stomach, peering close enough to see my face in the dark. "I told you no one would see."

"You don't actually know that," I pointed out.

He shook his head and kissed me long and slow.

* * * *

The walk back to the garage was nice, and I had to admit I was glad not to be doing it horny and hard. Once I was no longer half naked on the beach, I would also say I'd probably remember that dinner fondly in my old age.

"I still get to come home with you, right?" Seth asked.

I cast a sideways glance at him. "There's no way I'm sleeping in your bed."

To say Seth's apartment was generally a mess was seriously underestimating the situation, and while I was trying to influence his habits, safe sleeping there usually required a Hazmat suit. My place, on the other hand, is clean, and usually smells like pot roast or cinnamon buns due to the old ladies who live in the other two apartments in my building.

We climbed into Matilda and headed for my apartment. It's only a short way, but I'd rather move the car at night than have to make that walk in the morning.

I live in the upstairs front apartment over an old hardware store, which shares the street with a plumbing outfit, a mini-golf course, and the CVS. The hardware store's been closed for years, and I had recently gotten the go ahead to renovate it into an office for myself. Finding the time to do it was another story.

When I pulled up to the building, there was an unfamiliar black Mazda parked in my usual spot. I didn't recognize the car, but I sure as hell knew the woman who climbed out of it. Ten years ago, she'd been the love of my life.